CARMEN

Carmen Marcus lives in the Victorian spa town
of Saltburn-by-the-Sea. She writes poetry for page
and performance. She has been commissioned by
and performed at both the Royal Festival Hall and
BBC Radio 3's The Verb. *How Saints Die*, which
won a New Writing North 'Northern Promise'
Award, is her first novel.

CARMEN MARCUS

How Saints Die

VINTAGE

1 3 5 7 9 10 8 6 4 2

Vintage
20 Vauxhall Bridge Road,
London SW1V 2SA

Vintage is part of the Penguin Random House group of companies
whose addresses can be found at global.penguinrandomhouse.com

Penguin
Random House
UK

Copyright © Carmen Marcus 2017
Inside illustrations © Owen Gent 2017

First published in Vintage in 2018
First published in hardback by Harvill Secker in 2017

penguin.co.uk/vintage

A CIP catalogue record for this book is available from the British Library

ISBN 9781784705510

Printed and bound in Great Britain by Clays Ltd, Elcograf S.p.A.

Penguin Random House is committed to a sustainable future
for our business, our readers and our planet. This book is
made from Forest Stewardship Council® certified paper.

MIX
Paper from
responsible sources
FSC® C018179

For my dad
Marcus Carman Thompson

I often hear voices. I realise that drops me in the crazy category but I don't much care. If you believe, as I do, that the mind wants to heal itself, and that the psyche seeks coherence not disintegration, then it isn't hard to conclude that the mind will manifest whatever is necessary to work on the job.

Jeanette Winterson, *Why Be Happy When You Could Be Normal?*

Come then all of you, come closer, form a circle,
Join hands and make believe that joined
Hands will keep away the wolves of water
Who howl along our coast. And be it assumed
That no one hears them among the talk and laughter.

Louis MacNeice, 'Wolves'

I.

Its eye – clear and reflective not dead and dull as you might expect – was willing her to touch it. Would it be hard like a marble? She pressed her fingertip into the jelly of the pupil and nothingness pushed back. Her father's warm rough hand enclosed her own.

– Bad luck to touch a fish's eye.

Ellie knew that. She retreated to her special stool, yellow paint crackling off onto her bare legs. It had been around as long as she could remember. This thought made her stomach jerk like being pushed too high on a swing. Down here Ellie could not see her father's quick hand or the blade as he cut along the seam of the fish, but she heard the familiar wet thud of the knife, knowing without looking that the head was now cut off. And then the metallic tickticktick of the knife's tip along the backbone. Gutting has a rhythm to it, like the old hymns at school that you just knew the words to – 'Fastened to the Rock which cannot move.'

Ellie holds on to these sounds and counts them off on her fingers with her prayers at bedtimes; these are hard sounds, not like the sounds on the other side of sleep which come in through the cracks and start with a shushshush like water. She keeps her prayers precise; they are not wishes. She prays for her and her mother and father to go back to the Before. When she sleeps she hears the sound of breaking glass. When she wakes to a new day in the Now she knows that prayer is not enough.

Shushshush, Ellie hears the sound now, louder than the thudtickticktick. Her dad is watching her, but the knife doesn't stop.

- Ellie.

She is off, legs too long for the smallness of the house, to the front window in the living room. She presses her hands to the pane – padpadpad. Her fingers follow the outline of the still-soft putty, looking for the tiny blue veins of cracks, looking and not looking for the break her mum went through. Padpadpad – but there are no cracks today.

Her dad watches her through the kitchen hatch and she circles back to him. It's not like Carol's kitchen, with lino and fitted matching cupboards and 'all mod cons', with hum of electric knife and ping of microwave. Carol's mum doesn't want Ellie round to play any more, not since Ellie's mum was taken away and Ellie went wild. No, Ellie's kitchen goes thudtickticktick and it rocks with the gentle muffled taptaptap that comes from the strange tin tub in the corner right next to where she always puts her stool. A small

2

tin bath holding dark water. When she hears the taptaptap, Ellie, gently, with one crooked finger, taps back. Peering in she sees her own face staring – her eyes grey-blue-green, her face pale with dark moons. 'Can you see your own people in your face?' her mother would ask, but she was too frightened to look. A large brick-red claw breaks her reflection with its black nipping tips, clickclick – it is one of her father's edible crabs. Ellie smiles and waves back.

- Dad.

He lays down another fish to gut.

- Dad? Are they sick?
- No, they're drowning.
- In water?
- Fresh water, it's like seawater so they don't know. Some would just boil them alive. Kinder this way.

She cannot take in the vastness of this thought. There they are, in their water, and they are drowning and they don't know their water is wrong. Ellie reaches up to the table salt on the shelf and tips it into the tub, the soft sloughing like sand.

- Ey, ey . . . not that salt.

Her father's hand once more encloses her own and his calluses grind into her skin as she struggles against his tightening grip.

- Why d'you tie up their claws?

Ellie is shaking because he won't answer.

- Why?
- For when their instinct takes over.
- What's that?
- It tells them summat's wrong.
- And then?
- They panic and break each other to bits.

She is silent now because she is ten and she learns five new words a day and puts them in a sentence, but she has not yet reached the words for this.

Taptaptap.

Ellie curls up on her stool, perches her whole body upon it, big then small, like Granny Lil before she died. Her father offers her the net needle, smooth and brown like the back of his hand.

- What will you make me?
- Nothing.

He thinks it is their joke.

The first time he showed her how to make a net he was mending a creel. Ellie watched his penknife as he cut anew the eye where the crab would crawl in for the bait and burned the ends of the twine. Then he gave her the needle, his hand steering hers in a gentle wave, throwing a loop and catching it. He told her that the trick was to make holes, 'all day making nothing', and he would laugh dry and loud, the cigarettes echoing back from deep within his chest. As he showed her how to make the knots he told her how her great-grandfather James had pulled a sea-god up in the nets and cut it free and that was good luck. He told her how he had pulled her up in the nets like a porpoise.

- Am I good luck?
- We'll see.

Taptaptap.

*

No knock, just a voice breaking in through the kitchen door.

- Pete, Pete I have the paper for you.

Ellie hates Mrs Forster. Hates the way she talks as if Ellie's not there. Hates the way she totters on her bunions across her pristine lawn and sniffs at the air around the stacked lobster pots in Ellie's garden. It did stink though. At dusk Ellie would sneak onto Mrs Forster's neat green grass to hide stones in her flower beds. Cold grey stones that looked like skulls.

- Look at her there, Lady Muck.

Mrs Forster has a special sing-song voice just for Ellie, like a TV voice. Ellie and her dad don't have a TV any more.

She misses *Dogtanian and the Three Muskehounds*, but not *Grange Hill*. She likes her dad's crackly radio and the pips and Terry Wogan because they are part of the kitchen sounds, the marble hard sounds that guard her sleep – peeeep . . . peeeep . . . peeeep.

Mrs Forster waves the paper at her dad through the window, and Ellie sticks out her tongue.

- You sit down for a break with me Pete, what with everything-and-all right now.

Pete is not her dad's proper name. Her dad said they needed to keep Mrs Forster 'on side', which means no more sticking her tongue out at her through the window and maybe no more leaving death stones in her flower beds.

- I've brought us a snifter.

Mrs Forster always smells faintly sweet and acidic like old Christmas cake. Ellie follows her dad and Mrs Forster into the sitting room, knowing that Mrs Forster meant them to have a 'nice chat, just ourselves'. Mrs Forster peers at Ellie through her old-fashioned spectacles, clear and sparkling, cocking her head to one side like a bird, a starling though, not a gull.

- You helping your daddy?

Ellie looks down at the net needle in her hand and the slowly forming net.

- I'm busy making nothing.

Mrs Forster spurted her snifter.

- Go and do that in the kitchen Ellie, there's a good girl.

Traitor. Ellie left the net in the sitting room and stood listening for Mrs Forster's special voice for her dad.

- . . . Got you wrapped around her finger that one . . . The hospital rang, yesterday I think . . . The nurse said she's settling in . . . Oh I can't remember, some clean smalls, that sort of thing. Something sweet, marshmallows she said.

Ellie knew they were talking about her mum and she knew Mrs Forster was lying because her mum would never want marshmallows, she always wanted Fry's Chocolate Cream.

- Now about my lawn, you said Tuesday . . . Full of stones . . . No they didn't need to speak to you directly . . . Oooh crabs I couldn't.

The crabs beat out a weak signal, and Ellie finally taps back, 'She couldn't, but she will.'

2.

- Ow.

Her dad brushes her hair roughly; he tries to be gentle but his hands are too big and too worn for the job. He is good at plaiting rope that isn't attached to little heads. The mornings are coming in darker. She does not like this big chair but if she goes to sit on her stool it's 'too much for me now to be bending down like that'. Ellie looks at the clock – half past eight. Her dad taught her to tell the time, with a little book that had a clock on the front. She had to move its hands herself, but the hands on her dad's clock move on their own.

- Come on now, it's late.

The street is abandoned, everyone else has gone to work or school already. Ellie's tummy gives a little flip as her dad hoists her up onto the croggy-bar; the well-oiled bike, silent, Ellie's hands on the handlebars under his. Sometimes he would let her steer and she tightens her grip on the bar beneath his hands to keep them steady.

The school gates are open but the playground is empty. Ellie only started at this school last term. The other kids were all together already, a wall of warm brown heads bent over wet paint making games for their summer fayre. Now it's October and the playground is yellow with the wide hands of sycamore leaves. She slides off the croggy-bar too fast and skids on mulch. She hates this moment, when she stops being herself and it feels like turning the lights off before bed.

In the corridor, every day is the same only she is different. They all have their hedgehog haircuts and trainers and ski-jackets and sports bags. She does not know what she wants from the Argos catalogue for Christmas or what a bidet is. They ask her these things knowing she does not know, and their laughter is mechanical, precision timed like the ping on a microwave.

She holds her breath as she enters their cloakroom, all a-bustle, taking off new coats and hanging up new bags. There is that warm cloud smell – fancy washing powder, pink Cameo soap and underneath, sweet farts.

- Is that your dad?

Ellie knows not to answer that one.

- He's too old to be your dad?
- He's like my *granddad*.

They find it hard to see beyond her father's wrinkled skin. They ache for sameness; she feels the same ache, not quite hunger, because it has nothing to do with survival. So full of questions to catch her out, little Rumpelstiltskins.

- What's your number?
- 2,4,6,8.

Even numbers are her favourite, round and whole.

- That's not even a phone number, don't you have a phone?
- You asked me for my number.

Laughter.

- Do you have a video?
- No.
- Do you have a car?
- No.
- A computer?
- No.

Laughter.

- No.

Laughter.

- No.

They eat her alive with their questions.

- Do you have central heating?

She curls up with a hot-water bottle and her favourite blue blanket that was Granny Lil's and she is told that she was a quiet baby.

- A dead woman's blanket? Eeurrrrrrr . . .

The smell of paraffin from the heater reminds her of dreams. At night she likes to kneel up and tuck her head under the curtain to look out at the new moon, for luck. Luck is a big thing in her house. So many things – good or bad luck. So much responsibility when you turn the bright silver coin round once in your hand and choose the right wish to make it all better. If you get the wording wrong all the luck will wriggle away between the gaps in your fingers.

She tries to make up stories for them to make them stop.

- Why is your dad so old?

Stephen asks this. His favourite question.

- He isn't old.
- He looks old.

A hook.

- No he isn't, you see he only looks old, but he is a fisherman and one day when he was hauling up the nets, they were so heavy he pulled the nets on top of himself. It was a stupid thing to do because a giant red lion jelly-fish stuck itself to his face, stinging and stinging, it was a terrible accident, he was lucky not to go blind, but you see his face . . .

And they might, just a little, let themselves get pulled in and each time Ellie drops longer lines.

- No you see, one day there was a storm. It took the little coble . . .
- What's a coble?
- A boat – it took the coble far far out to sea further than ever before. My dad and his three brothers. Drift-ing. No water, no food, no shelter. They had no flares to signal for help, no radio.
- No TV?
- You don't need a TV on a boat. They drifted, the sun burning down on their faces for days and days. They were thirsty too, the seawater looked so tasty but just one drop and they would go mad, and that's worse than drowning. They drifted for three more days in the sun, their faces red raw and their mouths like sand. They made a pact – they would all jump out of the boat together because drowning was better than this. So they held hands.
- Yuck.
- They died?

- No, just before they jumped they saw a dolphin, then another. They lashed them to the boat, like horses to a cart and they said sorry because dolphins are wild and the ropes hurt them but the brothers needed to get home to their wives and children. The dolphins took them as close as they could to shore and the little boat drifted in. The wives were so happy to see their husbands after thinking they were dead that they did not care that the sun had burned their faces old.

Ellie got the idea for that story from a Clint Eastwood film she stayed up and watched with her dad, where the baddies buried Clint in the sand and the sun baked his face wrinkled and raw. That was before the TV went.

- What's that in your bag?
- Eeeurgh?
- It's moving?
- Are they . . .

She uses her stories to fill the spaces after the questions, but there are always more questions expanding in between. So today Ellie just pushes Stephen to the floor and he lands with a wet shocked thud. The others stand statue still, red mouths silent; Stephen sprawls, his new trainers squeaking on the old polished wood as he scrambles to get up. Ellie grabs her bag and bolts.

★

She runs, too fast for her best shoes, taptaptap, patent-leather lights going out in a pile of leaves, beyond the school gate – out-of-bounds. She's breaking every rule and yet it all stays the same. The morning's low sun does not all fall down though she's supposed to be at her desk saying yes to her name.

- Ellie Fleck?

She hears the yes in her head so loudly she is there.

- Yes.

But she is running through the iron-speckled gate and straight to the dunes and then her shoes stop tapping. Snap-snap. The crabs nipping in her bag. They know the rhythm of their water and will not wait.

Out-of-bounds, that's what they call the places you're not allowed to go – by the bins or the teacher's car park, or here. Then she hears it again, 'Yes,' from the Ellie in the classroom next to an empty chair, the good Ellie, quiet and good and sitting. Let her stay there on the hard wooden seat if she wants to be good.

Ellie-out-of-bounds had pushed Stephen with the red hair and liver-coloured freckles, Stephen, who smells sharp and plastic like a toyshop. Stephen – who's good at football and running and maths. Stephen – who's followed by all the long-haired girls, a pack of flicking ponytails. And they would crush her, Ellie who had pushed him down.

She had felled one of their gods and showed them he had lost his light. That's why they ate Captain Cook in the end.

Those strange goblin people in the picture had thought he was a god with his brass buttons and tailed-coat. Poor Captain Cook, Ellie thought. 'Your relation, on the Fleck side,' her dad told her. 'Seawater in the blood.'

Ellie walks to the water's edge, pushing her feet down into the hard wet sand. She holds the image still in her mind, Ellie at the water's edge. The pressure of where she ought to be pushes against her back. She holds up her hand, the butterfly-wing skin stretches between her fingers, low sun-shining through, she is red and white, thin as paper like a kite. If it was a dark grey day she would be less see-through. She can hear them again, the voices at the edge of sleep, like glass breaking, like paper tearing. Shush.

Ellie tips the crabs out near the rocks. Their black-needled legs are still ticking, clickclacking to one another. The lady crab opens her fan, waving. Gulls shriek and twirl above, watching the juices leaking from cracked shells on to the sand. They've pulled one another apart, just like her dad said. Here is their water, the waves cupping their shells and legs and claws, cleaning them away like her dad's hand swiping the crumbs off the table.

She needs to look down, to see her feet on the ground. She sees black. Sea-coal, buckets of it. A winter-full. She should scrape it up for her dad and then he wouldn't be angry about school, about the crabs. She could say she ran away to get the sea-coal, to keep them warm. She scoops her hands around the glistening powder, stuffing it into her pockets and her school bag. But it keeps mixing with sand, and then she cuts herself on a razor shell. Sand and salt in the cut, stinging. Her dad would know what to do. She

15

wants him here, now, to show her. Without him the beach takes her up entirely, the shushshush of the sea and the coarse cackle of the waders at the waters-edge, creakcrack-creakcrackyawyaw; the wind tugging at the shell of her ear. All of it pulling, nipping, cutting at her – snipsnipsnip – and now blood, her edges ragged and wet. She sucks the sand out of the cut and looks for somewhere to sit, to be still, but the rocks are busy and awake with the shifting tide leaving itself behind in pools. She could walk in any direction, but she cannot choose.

She picks up a washed-up stick, white as bone and warm to the touch. She begins to draw a neat circle around herself and the big wolf-rock at the shore-tip of Jenny Leigh's Scaur. Ellie runs, the stick trailing behind her on the wet sand, until she's caught up in the loop of her own line. She steps inside, walking the perimeter. The big rock reflected in the pool looks like a wolf lying down, its nose tucked under its tail, sleeping, its fur the black wet of seaweed. Ellie parts the cool pelt, pressing to find the stone beneath, her fingers damp and curious. The rock is pocked with limpets, grey crusts of barnacles, rag-tag loops of mussels. Ellie kneels by the pool to get a closer look at the dark square head. She flicks open her penknife to slice a limpet off the rock, suck and pop and she will see its jelly like her dad showed her. But the limpet splits itself and opens before her knife can cut it, a warm fire-amber eye stares back at her. Blinks. Its pupil is black, clear, reflective. Bad luck to touch a fish's eye but it is not a fish. Her ears fill with the shushshush of the rock breathing.

The wash came then, right up over Ellie's kneeling

knees. She was exactly where she had promised not to be, could see the swell growing, like her dad had shown her when he told her off for walking too close to the tideline last Easter. He had caught her up in his hands.

– You see it far out, it starts like a belly rising with a breath. Promise me you'll not go to the water's edge.

She had nodded, she knew it was hard for him to hold on to her. It was getting harder for him to hold most things – like when he lost his grip plaiting her hair and his hand had cramped and he had to clench and open it, just like the dying crabs.

There he is now, her dad, she sees him before he sees her, he looks small, just like when he was putting her mum into the ambulance. Ellie saw it, heard him stutter when the man asked her mother's name and her dad couldn't tell him because for a moment he didn't know it yet.

She runs round the circle she has made, she wants him to call and take her up in his giant's hands and take her home.

Everyone isn't where they are supposed to be. Her mum taken away, her dad not in his kitchen but here watching her, out-of-bounds.

She sees him rub at his calluses, flexing his fingers.

– Ellie.

Feet pit-padding over the circle's ragged line, she runs up the beach, up on to the larger stones gathered at the bottom of the Prom, and up the steps to him, waiting with his bike leaning against his thigh. The wind has made his eyes watery and deep. He rubs her head. This is enough. She could hop up onto the croggy-bar now.

- Can I see the tide times?

He digs in his pocket for the little grey book and hands it to her. She can't really read the numbers. But that doesn't matter; they both know that no one can say for certain when the sea will run singing over the Prom and into the houses. Once every hundred years or so it will come, drawing a new line out-of-bounds in red, blue, orange, the broken bellies of wrecked boats, strewn across the road.

- Dad?

The bike lurches forward as he pushes off.

- How did you know I was lost at the beach?
- The crabs were gone.

She jumps off the croggy-bar.

- Ellie.

She was running again, feeling only run and the earth under her, into the dunes, where his bike could not follow and she couldn't hear that other Ellie who said, 'Yes.' She was gone.

3.

Peter flew along the Prom after his daughter, the wind behind him, his hands cramping on the handlebars. He stretched his fingers and could feel the weight and colour of all they had held – a child, a trigger, a bird's nest, a net, a hook, his wife Kate. Kate, holding her back from the broken glass, her blood making her wrists slippery so that he could not be gentle. He saw Ellie run, crest the dune and disappear into the dip of it. He'd lost her.

Peter felt wrung out, he felt like the sea pulled by the stubborn moon from the shore. Everything just left exposed, bare wet sand and starfish slowly drying out. He feels it, how the years don't neatly stack on top of one another but fill you up, a dense fluid with their own unpredictable tides, so that your ten-year-old self can wash over you just as you are putting your wife into the ambulance and you can't tell them her maiden name. It washes over you at once, breaking against you.

He pulls on the brakes going round the blind curve of the Prom, too hard, so that the bike gives a little skid in the blown sand and the slick ebb of vertigo rises in him. He doesn't have time for its tricks today. Go careful he tells himself. He watches for the dark brown bob of Ellie's head as the dunes flatten out into stray clumps of grass but there's no sign of her. Ellie, named for his mother and the boat, the *Eleanor*. The bike lurches over driftwood thrown up on the Prom. He wobbles again, shouts to himself to go steady but his voice and the shush of the sea are drowned out by cars on the wet road.

If he let go of all the worry he could let himself slip away. How tempting, to close his eyes and be held on the surface for a moment, floating with the sun on his face, knowing that if he didn't struggle, he would go under, out of reach. He thought of the first time his father had taken him out on the little coble. The sea's surface was rose-gold with the dawn, rolling like blown silk, and it was everything he could do just to hold still in the boat and not jump into the water. His dad had told him about the promise all fisherman make.

– If you take life from the sea you offer your own life in exchange. She can take you. Any time she wants. She'll call you to her and you'll go like it's home and not struggle.

And his dad dipped his thumb into the water and pressed the salt wet to Peter's little head.

No, he could not let that thought in because then he would be gone.

Again that sickening stillness as everything around him swerved. Kate and the hospital, Ellie and the school – Ellie. She was so light. Was she like Kate? The thought came round again with the wheel of the bike and he pushed it round and round and away.

It was dangerous to think this way. What could he give her? What was he going to do? Routine, that's what he can give her, like in the navy. Routine holds your legs so they forget they can run. Gutting fish? Old stories? Making nets? Making nothings. Everything from his world was gone already, just crap washed up at the tideline; no one knew what it was for. His world, going, gone. Again it came, the wash. He can see the swell growing. He had shown Ellie the danger. Would she double-back on him to get to the sea? Ellie, who always walks too close to the tideline. He had caught her up in these hands, a little feather, only this Easter gone. The swell could have pulled her in.

- You see it far out, it starts like a belly rising with a breath.

He'd told her. Her wool-capped head nodding and look-ing far out, beyond the lace edge of the tide.

- When that comes in it will come like a cat's paw and your wellies will be full of water before you know it.

Nodding.

- And it will pull you back with it and that'll be the end of you.

Still.

Ellie could read the tide, he could see she could, but she trusted something in it, like petting a stray cat before it turns on you. There it was, that lurch, that fear of losing her to a swell, and she would let it take her. That was the Fleck in her, as though she too had made the bargain with the sea, to go when it called her home, though he'd never let her.

4.

Ellie knew how to get home from running away in her head, not from practising writing her address at school. They want you to know your address for competitions and emergencies. Ellie writes FISHERMAN'S SQUARE and Woodsy, her teacher, always shouts, 'That's not the name of the road,' but it's what everyone calls it. Like Woodsy, who's really Mr Lockwood but only to his face. Fisherman's Square is a terrace of twelve houses all in a row. Terrace is bad and poor. Semi-detached is good and mod cons. On rainy days when they draw houses at break-time, Ellie's doesn't look like the other children's with two bottom windows and two top windows and a front garden and a garage. Ellie's house is tall and thin like her dad. One window and one door at the bottom, two windows at the top. Ellie has a real chimney that smokes. Chuff chuff. Ellie needs the yellow crayon for the sandy stone, the blue crayon for the wet slate roof and the black crayon for the smoke whilst the others nip each other for the boring brown crayon. The lifeboat used to be outside her front door, her dad said. A big white boat on two big wheels made with cork stuffed inside so it could self-right and not sink. Ellie never saw it, only in pictures and her head. Now, there's a car park. The cars are red and brown and sticky with measly sand. The salt eats their mirrors off and people shout, 'Bloody salt.' It's all council now – the council came and put in upstairs loos and plastic windows so you can't hear the sea shushshush, apart from at Ellie's house and Chicken Sam's, with his chickens out the back. Sam's as bald and brown as a boiled egg. And, 'Crack your shell,' is what Ellie's dad says to let the wind out or it will wreck the boats.

The other people who live here, like her-next-door-who-doesn't-speak – they don't remember the lifeboat, and everything they do and don't know is bad luck. From the rabbits in their gardens to their dyed red hair. 'Long ears, tuff tails,' her dad says, but he never says rabbits out loud. They're afraid of the sea, the redheads and tuff tails, won't go near it even though they live so close. They say their houses are 'not fit' because they're too close to the water. They shout, 'It's not safe 'ere,' at the council when they come to paint the doors or put in plastic windows. It's not. There's nothing to stop the sea coming in to rat-tat-tat right on your front door. The Prom won't hold it back: it's all cracked red flagstones where the water has got under and turned them. The sea doesn't like stone, wants to eat it up and make it sand.

The sea has come in right over the dunes and up to the houses before. Not since the lifeboat was there though. And Ellie can hear its shushshush through her bedroom window as she crunches sand grit in her teeth.

Now Ellie runs the way the sea would run, over the dunes, over the Prom, look left-right over the Coast Road and then the car park shiny with mirror glitter, and home. The window at the front is all latched up, so she nips around the back where she can get in through the kitchen door. Her dad might have left it unlocked – 'Nothing to take,' not since her mum got rid of the TV. Ellie used to watch the News clock ticktock around the screen whilst she dipped her chips in her runny egg. One day it was Bloody-bloodybloody on the news, bombs and dust and IRA and their milk bottles smashed in the morning. And then her mother pulled the plug and braced the TV on her hip, the pair of them singing, 'Dublin's on the Liffey, Cork is on the Lee,' Ellie following her out into the back garden, where she could hear her-next-door-who-doesn't-speak laughing.

– LookawhatthatmadPaddysdoinoweh?

Out the back of Fisherman's Square are the Baithouses, the alleyway, the gardens and then Ellie's kitchen door; she checks the handle to see if it is open.

– You should be in school.

Ellie keeps doing what she is doing.

– It's locked, your dad's gone out to look for you.

Ellie can see Mrs Forster's reflection in the clean glass.

- Your poor father, worried sick, where is he now? He could have come off his bike, he could have had a heart attack running off like that after you.

She heard it then, a faint creakcrack.

- You'll be the death of him. Eh? Don't you keep your back turned to me.

Ellie turns.

- Just look at you? Hair everywhere, mud on your feet. Wild you are, wild.

Ellie shows her teeth in a smile. Mrs Forster raises her hand but Ellie's head whips forward, her mouth opening towards the bird-foot fingers.

- Now then Ellie.

Mrs Forster snaps back her hand at the sound of Peter's voice.

- Take her back to school where she belongs Pete.
- She's not well.
- Is-she-sick-is-she? The school won't put up with this Pete, they'll have Social Services on to you.

Ellie knew these words from her pocket dictionary. Social – living in a community; services – a helpful act. Mrs Forster isn't helpful, she is just like the kids at school. She needs to find someone bad and wrong so she can prove she is good and right.

Ellie looks at her father; she wants him to draw a strong black circle around them both with Mrs Forster on the outside looking in. Her bird-eyes and hooked little feet, scraping, squawking, screeching.

– Sick-is-she-is-she-sick? She's not that sick if she can have you chasing her up and down the streets. What kind of sickness is that? Pete, someone has to tell her she can't get away with it.

Her father had hands that could pull a great black-backed gull out of a chimney. She watched him do it, smoothing down the angle of its wings, whilst it stabbed him with its beak. Instead he unlocks the kitchen door and starts to crack Chicken Sam's big brown eggs into the pan.

– Hungry?
– Pete?

He slices tomatoes into the bacon fat, which spits. He had hands that could wring the life out of something, but he won't put this old cow out. Ellie hates his useless hands. Traitor.

– Well, I can't stand here all day talking.

But she does, she stands there blocking the kitchen door, keeping it open with her big waddle bottom, letting in the cold.

- It's ready now.
- Shouldn't she wash her hands?

Ellie was going to wash her hands. She reaches up to the sink and rubs the big block of Fairy soap in her palms. She can see the blackbirds in the garden eating the fatty cakes her dad put out. Ellie cannot eat at school. Her fork is stumped by the square orange certainty of a fish finger. She thinks about all the trapdoor mouths, open-shut-open-shut around the sloppy mash. She thinks about bringing a crab claw into the dinner hall, its black tips snip-snapping at the red tips of their fat tongues.

Her dad makes hot sweet tea, full of sugar and worry, and she sips it carefully so as not to burn her tongue. Now with the morning and being home she feels something like hunger, and the fresh air mingles with the smell of tomatoes, eggs and bacon frying, heady and salty. They do not talk. They get ready to eat. But Mrs Forster is still there. Her dad puts out two plates only and carefully makes the wave pattern on the buttered bread with his special knife, and this means he will not take her back to school. He lifts out the egg, bacon and tomatoes, crisp and blackened and glistening.

- You have her spoilt. She shouldn't be eating that if she's poorly.
- Ellie, take this in the front room to eat.

The front room faces front and back, it should be called the front-back room but her dad always says front. The street

28

window looks out all the way to the dunes and the fat grey line of the sea, but also right onto the street. This is the window Ellie hides from sometimes because people look in. The postman looked in before breakfast to see if they were up. The gas-man looked in to see if they were hiding. The neighbours looked in when her mum broke the window but they couldn't see in for the rain. It is dry today so Ellie crawls right under the sill on her hands and knees, thinks, 'Ha, you can't see me now,' and pokes the fire sending spits and sparks up the chimney. She's not really allowed because the sparks jump out onto the fire rug or her dad's rocking chair and whoosh – 'up in smoke'. But she likes the woody smell that is their smell and the way everything around the fireplace is smudged and sooty like a good night's sleep; even her lucky rope that hangs by the fire is flecked black. She knows her dad likes it too because he always takes a big breath in 'hello' when he gets home.

The back of the front room, where the big table is, looks out into the garden. There are glass-panelled French doors with wooden frames that are swollen and sticky with gloss paint, so when you open them you have to give them a shove. But they don't get opened. No one can see in from here and everything good happens just outside – blue tits and hedgehogs and clear-night-stars – all the things you have to get out of bed to see. Douglas likes to lie in the yellow puddles of light and chatterjack at the birds.

Ellie sits on the fire rug, her breakfast on her knee. One bite and creakcrack. She can feel the loose tooth inside her mouth. She runs into the kitchen to show her dad and spits out blood and a white pearl tooth into her hands and smiles. Pearls are bad luck.

– Don't you spit your food, dirty girl.
– Go on now Ellie, get yourself cleaned up.

She will get a silver coin for her tooth, she will get a wish. But now someone else is peering through the front window and tapping on the glass and it's too late to hide.

★

– I know of Katherine's troubles. I'd like to help.

Katherine, he said, as though he was her mum's friend, his sluggy tongue licking over her name like that. Why had her dad let him in? Father Doorley, black storm crow. What did he know?

– This is Father Doorley, Mrs Forster.

She soon shifted then. Ha. 'Devilry and poppery,' she tooted and she tottered off out of the kitchen door.

– Ellie, get yourself up them stairs.

Ellie's dad steered the priest into the front room with a full tea tray. Ellie clomped her feet sixteen times for sixteen stairs then settled on the bottom step, just out of sight, watching Doorley sip his tea, his eyes bulging. He had a flat wide frog's mouth and grown-up words, mumbling over the KitKat Ellie had been saving for Sunday.

- They have their treatments these people . . .
- She's fine where she is.
- Dr Milligan is very . . . ambitious, but he can't give Katherine what she needs.
- He knows what he's doing.

Ellie shuffles closer to the door, open just a touch; she can see that her dad isn't drinking his own tea.

- Dr Milligan wants to use ECT, Mr Fleck . . . Peter . . . Do you know what that means?

Ellie knew – big words for devils, little words for gods, her dad said. The priest dipped another finger of her biscuit into his tea. He said,

- I've seen what it does.

Then his mouth went dark red with chocolate goop like old ladies' lipstick. Her dad put on his 'had enough now' voice.

- It's the last thing they've got to try.
- That is their Last Rite, I'm offering mine. Before . . .
- Before what?

Suddenly her dad got hold of the priest by his shoulders pulling him to his feet and his nose wrinkled – the priest must smell. Ellie wanted her dad to get him the way she wanted to get Stephen. Go on! She pushed her thought hard into her dad's fists.

– Is she dying? Is she? Do you think that's what's happening to her?

The men look like they're dancing.

– I am only saying . . . it's an illness, of the spirit as well as the body. Let me help her.

Her dad dropped him back down into the chair.

– Let me pray for her then.
– Don't, it's that shite that got her locked away in the first place.

Ellie jumps when her father swears and the priest smiles, his eyes flicking across the room. He'd seen her.

– Now then little miss what prayers have you been saying for your mammy?
– I say the Mass.

She did, she ran the cold tap in the bathroom so her dad couldn't hear – choughchoughstooosh, whispering 'Amen's over the water.

– Little girls can't say the Mass.

Ellie looks at him, laughing at her prayers, her chocolate on his lips, her mother at his feet, and she sticks out her rude pink tongue.

- Sweet Jesus, she's wild.

The priest slams the front door goodbye. Ellie stands firm, her eyes hard questions pushing into Peter.

- Ellie. It will be all right.

She goes to the front window and watches the black back of the priest get smudged away by her own breath. 'Bog off,' she writes in window steam and presses her hands up hard against the cool glass, which means, 'Is it breaking?'

- Come to the kitchen Ellie.

Her dad goes into the pantry under the stairs and pulls out a fish from the ice-water – slippery in his hands, like her mum had been.

- What's ECT?
- Ellie leave it, come here and help your dad?

She watches him, smells the cool salt-water smell of the fish.

- Watch. It's time you learned to gut a fish for yourself.
- Will ECT bring her back?

He fans out the dorsal and pectoral fins. Which means he doesn't know.

- This is how they steer in the water.
- If I say my prayers like Father Doorley will it bring her back?

He slices off the fins. Which means no. He opens up the gills.

- This is how they breathe underwater.

He puts the heavy knife in Ellie's hand, keeping her steady with his own hand, which means no more questions.

- Keep your wrist straight.

Together they bring down the knife in an arc of silver light, cutting the head off just below the gills.

- Good girl.

Her hand is steady and sure. She does not hesitate. This is good. She takes the head and carefully wraps it up in newspaper for the bin.

★

That evening Ellie empties her school bag on to her blue blanket. She dare not open *Modern Mathematics for Schools*. Instead she pulls her English book towards her.

'Thurrrrrrrrrrrthurrrrrrrr,' thrums Mrs Forster's cat. Douglas likes it here best of course – it's a fisherman's house.

Topic 1: Write a story about your family.

Her dad says it's not the end of the world not to do your homework, but he doesn't know Woodsy. 'Ellie Fleck, how difficult is it to simply write a story about your family?' Ha!

There was once a mother . . .

Her dad comes into her bedroom, smelling of smoke, and looks at her one line.

- Just make something up pet.

Making it up is like making a net, you don't know what will get through the holes and what will get stuck. She touches her granny's blanket – soft, it even feels like blue, the satin edge, colder than the wool, like the different currents in water.

Before sleep she must count off her prayers on her fingers because God can see inside her head and will know if she doesn't. She prays for her mother to come home but it hurts to pray for things she knows her dad does not believe.

Prayers are not enough to bring her mother back; she knows this the way she knows that six and seven don't make fifteen. She saw her father shake the priest and he cannot make her come back either. Ellie finds the tooth coin under her pillow and turns it once.

- I wish . . .
- School in the morning.

Her dad shouts up from the kitchen. Trying to stick his wish to hers. She spits on her coin and starts again but he comes upstairs wiping his hands and gets out the spiral notebook.

- Now then, what do I say was wrong with you this time? Flu? . . . Ellie, don't go quiet on me.

Ellie looks up different words for sickness in her little pocket dictionary, trying to find a word she and her father have not used before. They have gone through poorly, ill, unwell, ailment and even nauseous, which was her favourite.

- Well then?

Ellie stares at the word she has chosen. She can't pronounce it, as though it knows she will use it for a lie. She closes the dictionary.

- I have homework.
- Finish it in the morning.

But he does not go, he stays where the smile ends so he might let her ask —

- Dad?
- What?
- What time is it?

Which means – where did they take Mum?

- Bedtime.

A bristled kiss and lights out.

5.

Mrs Forster was thinking about rituals; reading the *Daily Mail* was a ritual, not for herself, but marking the articles that might interest Pete. A ritual, Mrs Forster thought, must be deeper than a wish and ground-in like the grooves on the breadboard. She lives inside grooves now but she remembers a time she could choose which way, right or left. There's a twinge of pain as her half-moon spectacles pinch at her nose, always some pain. Awake since seven this morning, she heard Pete waking Ellie at eight, too late to get to school on time, what was Pete thinking? Children take time, they grasp it and hold it, she knew. Mrs Forster aims to be washed and dressed by eight-thirty in time for the News headlines, although it is taking her longer and longer to get ready. There is the temptation, silly really, to one day bank left and wear her dressing gown till after breakfast, but it is unthinkable that she should do it. Those support stockings, what a struggle? Now she must sit on the bed and roll them into little doughnuts, looking down at her legs, speckled and bruised, a maze of swollen veins.

Arthur was a leg man, she thinks, but she will not touch that thought, more painful than her resistant knees. Clarks' sandals, thank God for Clarks; she gets them on whilst still perched on the hard bed before her feet start to swell. She steps into a silk-slip, she likes the swush sound it makes as it slides up her stockings. A sound from long ago. Pure silk, a devil to handwash in cold water, now that the cold grips her hands and tries to pull her down.

Mrs Forster hates the way clothes don't have linings any more and everything clings and sticks to legs and other bulges. A heavy skirt, to deal with the uncertainty of autumn, and a good jumper. A heavy skirt, which Douglas can't get her practised claws through. All this will take at least forty-five minutes. Then make-up, so many don't bother, but not Mrs Forster. Moisturise first, she makes the sign of the cross in pink dabs of Ulay then works it in, in sweeping circles. The cream has not kept its promises but she obeys the rite nonetheless. Her eyes are flecked, hazel with little marmalade pieces, so she works green cream shadow into the creases to bring out the colour. She finishes off with powder; she used to use the cream foundation but after an hour or so it would migrate to all her deep lines – useless. The fine white powder clings to the tiny hairs on her face, but it will do. No blusher, she never needed it, her colour always high, an easily embarrassed girl. 'Alice has gone red,' the older girls would shout; she was always saying the wrong thing. Just her hair now and it's eight-twenty-four already. Rollers out, tease out the curls with the sharp end of the comb and lacquer as protection against that wind-straight-in-off-the-sea. This town is no lover of hairstyles. Nearly, nearly done in time to wave at Pete as he sets off to school with Ellie, she makes it to the front window just to see him turn the corner, Ellie on the cross-bar, his back to her. Damn and damn it she will have to set the alarm earlier tomorrow.

And all the time the Black Douglas yowling for her breakfast – well, she can wait. That damned cat had pushed its way in between the grooves. 'You've got a cat,' Maisie had said, shocked that something came to Alice for love. She called it Douglas, for the rebel, for her father. Stubborn brumous cloud of a man. Turned out to be a Queen not a Tom after all that. Alice, she thought to herself, you should have known.

'Poor Pete,' that's how she described him to Maisie on the phone,

– Poor Pete, a child at his age, and the wife where she was.

– You're hard Alice, hard as nails, a child is a blessing.

Mrs Forster was not a natural mother. She had gone through the motions, but she had not felt the necessary twinge of, well what would it be? Fierceness perhaps? Then Gareth was gone. She felt it after, somewhere in the mix-up of the grief and the shock – a fierceness, yes. Her hands hurt with the emptiness and twitched as though she wanted to tear into something, or they just wanted to hold something. She had only ever held his hand to cross the road, her little man. But Pete, he held Ellie's hand as though she was a kite, like a boy with something too precious. Pete, Peter the rock, she thought, and he was, yes, he was brittle, made brittle by all that love. Stupid, stupid old woman to be frightened for him.

She would bake something, something to take round for elevenses, nothing too fancy. She had never enjoyed baking and her hands, she was always dreadful with her hands, little lumpy scones still soggy on the inside. She nudged Douglas out of the way with her toe. Pete would eat them, he was a gentleman that way; she felt her cheeks go hot – scones, stupid Alice.

Eight-forty-five, Pete would not be back yet. She had put last night's dinner in tinfoil ready for the birds this morning. Douglas had already tried to have a go at it. Eating was a ritual too; eat when you're supposed to. Feeding the birds was new to her routine, she hated birds, that's why she let Douglas stay, the black rag-tail. All that noise and the mess they made of her washing, but Pete had made her a birdhouse when she first moved in and put up coconut shells full of lard. 'For the birds,' he had said, standing at her front door, holding the gift out to her before his name. He loved the birds, he made sure things like that were looked after. So she had to feed them. Then the cats came, watched the birds and shat in her proud pink roses and bloody Douglas watched them do it.

The garden got the most of her love. She would cut all the best flowers and take them to Gareth's grave. Arthur had taught her the sanctuary of routine after Gareth had died; get up, eat at the proper times, walks and fresh air and straight to sleep and no time to think or speak. You

41

could hide in it, sliding along those well-worn grooves, and if you weren't looking you would never meet yourself coming.

Here he is now, she must take something, quick, what? She had been holding her empty beaker from this morning's tea. She knocked the handle firmly against the kitchen top.

- Pete, Pete. So silly, I've broken it, my favourite, would you be so kind . . .

She shouted as she tottered towards him, quicker over the lawn than the path, stubbing her toe on a big grey stone.

- Bugger. My foot.
- You all right Alice? I've got some glue in the Baithouse, let's take a look, clean break eh, be a while before it sets.
- Oh well, I was going to the post office but I can wait.

The phone, she could hear it, she had left the back door open, they could both hear it. Damn it, damn that phone, she knew it would be for him, the hospital, the school, the doctors, they all had her number down for his emergencies. He did not have a phone. Who doesn't have a phone nowadays? Still. She can feel him trying to edge around to overtake her, in step with the quick little ring-rings, but his politeness won't let him.

\- Ooh, my toe.

She stops for effect. The phone is still ringing. Only at the last moment does he break and reach for it but she's already got there, slowly lifting it to her smile.

\- No his neighbour, yes I can take a message . . . Oh, she did . . . yes, I'll tell him right away.

She could hear Pete pacing and his breath quicken, but she could not pass over the phone. 'Cruel,' Maisie had said, 'you've got selfish and cruel.' She put down the receiver, his full attention on her and she glowed, lit up by news that did not belong to her.

\- It's Ellie . . .

She held it, she knew she shouldn't, she knew that as soon as she opened out the news and shook it he would run, straight to Ellie that stupid stupid kite of a child who did not deserve him.

\- Pete, she pushed a boy down and ran, you need to get her back to that school quick sharp and face the consequences, you need to take her in hand . . . Peter?

He was gone.
She pulled the vegetables out of the banana box, they were starting to rot already, nothing lasted. 'Old Mrs

Foster,' she heard him say once. Old? Who's he to say who's old? She went to the linen cupboard and got out the thread-bare towels, the blue one and the peach one, soft and worn. She patted them into the box and carried it out to her shed. There, she thought, if I don't wake up one morning and she won't come in, she'll still have a bed to come home to, bloody cat. She'll be all right.

6.

- Hough.

Or a sound like that, she had never made a sound like that before.

- Hough.

As his fist sank itself into her empty stomach, Ellie thought something far off, something about boys not hitting girls, but it doesn't matter any more. He was waiting at the blind corner for her, behind the prefab hut, just as she came into the school. He must have known that she would be late. She cannot get a breath into her body, suddenly gone rigid and not thinking and she bends over. From here she can't protect herself and he pushes her on her knees; she feels the weakness of her position register and then a hard slap, stinging her face. She did not know boys slapped. All wrapped up in her red coat, her hood up, she can only hear her stomach saying, 'Lie down,' so she does. Then she feels his hand on her shoulder and everything slows with the tenderness of the gesture, and she thinks he is going to help her up. But both of his hands are pushing her face into the dirt, not as hard as he could, she can feel him holding back – as though he is somehow disgusted – but still he cannot stop, not now his hands are on her. She tastes the dirt and a little blood, grainy and salty. She expects him to say something but he just gets up and brushes himself down. Ellie lies still, waiting for her breath to come back and it does, slowly rising in her tender stomach. She had thought she would be safe sneaking in late, trying to stay unnoticed. She had been certain that Stephen would've wanted witnesses. She had pushed him, the others had seen, this was not the same back on her.

The girls' toilets are quite dark, they smell of old wood and damp coats, and the lights are dim and fizzy so she can only just make out the dirt on her face. She turns the grey streaked soap over and over in her hands trying to make a foam. She rubs the foam into her sore skin, working it into her hairline where she feels tiny flecks of gravel. Then rinses, then does it all again. She does not want them to see the dirt, not any trace.

– Err look at the dirt, smellyElliesmellyElliesmellyEllie.

Her hair is all wet and unravelling from her plaits. Her cheeks pink, she smiles, a practice. Was it a fight if she didn't fight back? She looks again into the mirror, and she isn't the same: something had been rubbed out. But she is more real.

Her breath is still tender as she walks up the corridor through the library to her classroom. They are still only partway through the register, how could so little time have passed? Mr Lockwood smiles wide, his teeth flat and stained.

- Well Miss Fleck, late but at least with us. What affliction kept you from us yesterday?

Mr Lockwood took the note written in Ellie's best Dad's handwriting.

- A malaise, Miss Fleck? A malaise?

So that's how it's pronounced, like mayonnaise. And immediately Ellie sees it as a sticky yellow sickness.

- It means . . .
- I know what it means. Did I say you could sit? Stay where you are, Ellie, until I say you can go.

He continues down through the register, barking out each name, whilst Ellie tries to stand still. From here she can see the neat plaited pattern, rows of yes lines next to names; next to hers a shock of bubbling zeros. Her face stings. When he gets to Stephen, he calls the boy to the front.

- Ellie, hopefully you are sufficiently recovered from your malaise, as I believe you have something to say to Stephen?

Ellie could see the dirt on his hands. He had not gone to wash. She could still feel the weight of his fist in her stomach. She knew what to do: the grey order of Mr Lockwood's desk, their lines and her zeros, Mr Lockwood's smile, all told her what to do, so that she was doing it already. She was reaching out to take his hand and he was reaching out to take hers. She was holding him, his skin, soft and dry, and their hands were moving up and down and she was saying she was, 'Very, very sorry'. And she is, because there is the desk and the register with zeros where she should have been.

As she presses his hand he watches her stomach rise and fall. Her mouth, too small for the breath wanting to come out, fits only around the sorry. She will not cry. Stephen knew he could put his dirty hand in hers and she would have to take it, that was the rule. Even after he balled his fist into her, which no one saw and she will not tell, that is the rule, and the shock of this rule makes her shake with heat.

- You can sit down now Ellie.

She will have an invisible day now, which will be good, but the chair next to hers is no longer empty.

- We have one more announcement. I'd like us to welcome Robin Fletcher to our class.

They all chorus, 'Hello Ro-bin Flet-cher,' stretching out his name into ups and downs. This Robin Fletcher, the new boy, is at Ellie's desk. When she was new no one had wanted to share. Now she is not new and she does not want to share. Fletcher – he even shares the same part of her name. 'Fle' like run away, leg-it, bolt. Now he is so close, he can touch her by accident, like he does just shuffling his chair – yuck. Her head starts to thump, thump thump, the way it does just before sleep.

It happens again as she slides off her chair to open her big duffel bag. The rope, which binds the top, is from her dad's Baithouse. She reaches deep inside and pulls out her maths book, the biggest, and slides it on to the desk without looking at the boy.

- What are you doing?

She can see him through the criss-cross legs of the desk. Then she pulls out her English exercise book and her reading book and her comprehension book and slides them into a pile above her head. The boy passes a book back down again, holding it in his brown hands.

- We haven't got reading today.

How does he know?

- It's written on the board, look.

The boy flicks through the book, frrraappp, all bicycles and adventures and jam and no dead people.

- I've read it, it's stupid.

49

Ellie's mouth creases up at the corners; how did he know?

- What's next?

Ellie passes him a ragged folder; she had drawn a light-house on the front cover and everyone else had done a telephone. And Mr Lockwood had said, 'Typical Miss Fleck,' and laughed and everyone had laughed. But Ellie was only being truthful because she did not have a phone but had been to the lighthouse with her dad. The light-house said in its winking words, 'Stay away from the rocks or you'll die,' and on the phone people only said stuff like, 'We're having micro-chips for tea.' So lighthouses were better at 'communications' weren't they?

- That's cool.

Ellie raises her eyebrow at him. Her dad taught her how. The boy wriggles his eyebrow trying to copy.

Right now it's maths and Mr Lockwood draws the ques-tions on the blackboard, which is really green, and Ellie gets a good look at the boy. He looks strange, smells strange, like soap powder and something else, tangy like leather or shoe polish. He's got thick blond hair and eyes like a . . . well . . . they are definitely a bit doggy, an Alsatian or more Labrador, not a Yorkshire terrier and definitely not a Jack Russell. She will check this boy's eyes again to be certain though, Alsatian or Labrador – it's a big difference.

- Ellie Fleck, what's your answer to number three?

Ellie looks down at her book, where she's copied question one out so neatly, focusing on the dual curve of number eight. Eight was one of her favourite numbers, the way it flows back in on itself like a wave. She has swirled her pencil around the numbers carefully but still they will not reveal their mystery to her.

- Ellie, number three?

She stares at the emptiness after the equals sign. Mr Lockwood twitches happily.

- One and three-thirty-two-ths.

The boy is speaking to Mr Lockwood, without being asked; he does not know the rules.

- I am not interested in whether you know the answer, I want to know if Miss Fleck knows the answer. Miss Fleck did you perhaps in one of your mysterious absences stumble upon the answer to number three?

He likes to make small incisions into Ellie, little papercut questions, 'Why were you absent? Why don't you look ill? What are those shadows under your eyes?' Ellie winces, he smiles. This is his game and then he moves on. Snipsnip.

- Wiggins, number four?

The boy stares at Ellie, she has failed him. He will move soon. She passes him the brown maths book silently, he nods.

- I finished that one at my old school, I'm on the green one, where are they?

Ellie points to the shelf next to Woodsy's desk. This is surely one of the longest conversations she has had this term that has not involved someone punching someone else. Fletcher stands up but she catches his arm gently just as Woodsy's radar turns on them.

- Sir, he needs a new . . .
- Ellie, did I ask you to speak?
- I finished this one in the holidays, sir.
- That may well be but finished does not mean correct. Sitting next to Dolly Daydream I would expect errors – you may even disappear altogether as Miss Fleck frequently does.

The children laugh on cue, sharp rat teeth.

- I think it's right.

Ellie prays hard inside her head for the boy she does not know and Woodsy hits the boil.

- Right! How do you know what's right? I tell you what's right. You could tell me one and one is two, you could tell me the decimal fraction of one-seventh for all I care . . . you don't *know* what's right until *I* tell you what *I know* is right.

- Noughtpointonefourtwoeightfivesevenrecurring, sir.

Ellie's eyes are wide: this boy speaks the mysterious language of maths and he is clearly much more weird than she is. This worries her. Woodsy swivels his rodent head at the boy.

Silence as he takes him in.

- I know your mother. I know what she is.

Ellie feels the boy flinch. Whether Woodsy really knows anything you can never tell, he just presses his ratty nose deep into you until he gets the scent of something odd. That's enough to give the whole lot of them the scent. They do the rest, scritscratscatter at your strangeness until the light of you goes out.

What's the boy doing now? He's trying to get her attention. Whispering.

They must stay invisible now and he's whispering.

- They can't be pounds and pence at the same time.
- Shush.
- What? You've done it wrong.

She has always written it like this, like her mum, and Mr Lockwood has always put a question mark next to it in green, so she has just kept doing it, thinking that it's one of Mr Lockwood's succinct yet unhelpful expressions of hatred.

- It can't be one pound and one pence at the same time can it? Look.

He writes in her book to show her, in *her* book, his elbow pressing up against hers, urgh – yuck. But ah, it sort of makes sense now. She might miss him when he moves onto the boys' table, but he had written in her book so she ignores him for the rest of the lesson.

The bell sounds and she doesn't have a page covered in jumbled guesses neatly written out for Mr Lockwood to scrawl question marks and red crosses all over. She knows that this time they're right, that there is a right instead of the spongy mystery of not knowing.

The boy keeps pace with her quick step to the school gates. She tries to outrun him but his warm blond head bobs alongside her like a float. It's too late. Her father's there, turning the corner into the school road, and he's just an old man on his old green bike, which is not BMX or Raleigh – just Bike. And the boy would see and she couldn't explain the numbers between them. She wants it to be summer and just her and her dad, helping him scrape off the rust with steel wool and paint the bike green again. But her dad's ragged blue coat is weighed down by October damp, his cap pulled far over his face and over the tiny bald moon on the back of his head. The boy is following her out to the gate, he will see it all – the end. Her dad pulls to a stop next to them. Two worlds crushing her between them.

- We can't play together.
- Who's this then Ellie?
- It's er?

Robin she said in her head but a name like that made the white featheryness of him breakable – hough.

- It's Fletcher. Fletch.

The boy took his new name the way he would take a toffee.

- Now then, Fletch.

Ellie begins to see that they don't fit together. He is so healthy, so open, so light. If she were Stephen she would want to push that lightness into the cold mud. It's blinding. She reaches up in sharp black lines like a winter tree; he is the solid hard fruit of summer, full of light and juices. He couldn't split the way she can, even if he had two names. She needs to give him something, something heavy and dark to protect him. She has a good skull stone in her pocket. She was saving it for Mrs Forster. She folds it up into his hand. He looks confused. She has not shared her magic with anyone else before. She jumps up on the croggy-bar, leaving the boy still standing there, then he sticks his thumbs up at her.

- See-ya.

He stood waving goodbye on the edge of out-of-bounds. She waved back. Labrador eyes, yes definitely Labrador.

7.

Today is not a school day, but Ellie doesn't have that not-a-school-day feeling. She had woken late and her sea-coaling clothes – old grey trousers and checked shirt – were not on her chair. Instead, her father had set out her church clothes – blue corduroy skirt and red jumper – even though she did not have to go to the smoky old church any more, not since her mum was taken away. The people at church looked down at Ellie from underneath their big hats. Ellie liked the way the candles made the air wavy but she did not like the crumple-faced demons carved in the pillars whispering through their stone lips, to people like poor Padre Pio. Her mother carried a small black-and-white card in her purse of Padre Pio, like a playing card, only Padre Pio was the two of bleeding palms. The holes in his palms were big enough to poke your finger through. Ellie's mum prayed to him because like him, she heard voices. Ellie hears voices too, not the sound of breath over stone, but the shushshush of water on wet pebbles. They can't be the same as her mother's voices but she rubs her whole soft palms sometimes just in case.

Today is Saturday, and it is Halloween, when the dead come to visit. Last year her mother showed her how to light a candle and leave milk on the table and the window off the latch, and in the morning the milk was gone and the candle was out. There were Ringtons' caramel wafers on the table too. It was bad luck for Ellie to eat them. Ellie's mum was much more excited about these dead visitors than living people. The neighbours visited one another with carrier bags full of beer-cans and Tupperware on all different days but Ellie's mum wouldn't ever invite them in, not after what happened with the sheets. The sheets had had to go in the bin because there was dog-poo on them, and the dog-poo said, 'IRA'. Ellie asked her mum what it meant and her mum just said, 'Stupid, dirty scum,' stuffing them in the rubbish. Her mum cried then because they were her mother's sheets and she said that you could not buy sheets like that now. Ellie had chucked many skull stones over fences into their gardens.

Ellie might like to be a ghost, she thinks, to slip in through windows, and not have to worry about breaking or school. She wonders if her mother would visit like this now. But she knows her mum is not dead.

Her dad takes her past the pencil-spired church, past the library, and all the way to the bus stop. Just then the bus swings around the corner, wheezing to a halt. The morning is still dark and the pensioners form a slow and creaking line on to the bottom deck. They all greet Ellie's dad and he gets loud and puffed up like a strange bird she does not know the span of.

- Who's this, your granddaughter?
- My daughter.
- Yerauldbugger (laughter).

So her father gets the questions too, and Ellie can feel his shame, an upside-down version of hers. They do not fit one another in other people's eyes, too many numbers in between. Letting her hand slip out of his she counts the distance on her fingers, she one times ten, he five times ten. Then she slips her five fingers back into his hand to make them ten together. He fumbles with their return ticket. Usually Ellie likes to hold on to the tickets but her dad does not give her this one to keep safe. They jump two steps at a time to get the best seat – front on the top deck – and here Ellie is eye level with the trees and she can see ragged nests left behind in fingery branches. Her dad had woken her up just before school started again to watch the summer birds fly away over the sea. When all the black flecks in the purple light had finally gone neither one of them could take their eyes off the sky.

The snake of crooked pensioners gets off at the clock in town. They shout, 'Bye Petey.' They do not ask where he is going. Ellie's reflection shows her eyes bright in the mucky window. The bus moves past all the stops she knows, huddled together on the High Street: the butcher's, that smells of cat's breath; the stop for Hinton's where her mother used to get the yeast for the bread. This is as far as she has ever been on the bus. The shops turn into thin straw houses and the faces getting on are like squeaky leather window rags.

- Don't stare Ellie.

Ellie flinches and tries to focus on the windows, their grey veil blurring the sharp edges of winter beginning outside. On the wide-open road it starts to rain, and the raindrops bulge into swift rivers writing strange words across the pane. Steam forms on the glass inside and her dad takes her wrist, holding it steady, the way he did with the knife for the mackerel. Together they draw on the window: the first half-circle for a head, then the breast and a low sweeping arc for the wing and then a little stub tail. His blunt thumb blots out the breast so she can see it's a robin. Ellie copies her own, a delicate smaller version, which blurs in places with the shaking of the bus.

Strangers get on and off, bright and loud in the rain. Two girls with blue neon eyes and Hubba Bubba lips push buggies on board. They are not dressed for church. They share a cigarette, puffing out clouds as big as their hair, whilst their kids flick red tongues out of devil masks. Little witches run up and down the helter-skelter stairs, pushing out their jackdaw calls. Ellie draws another robin, then another, perfecting the circles, learning how to keep her wrist steady. Her fingertip ice cold now, she makes the arc of the wing so perfect she can feel it beat. Her dad taps her shoulder and he is already crouching low to climb down the stairs. She stumbles after him, forgetting to get dizzy. They are here.

There are big glass swishy doors, the kind that used to frighten her mum, but they don't go through these. Her dad leads her along a narrow path to a building that looks like a school. There are lots of steps up and another door that says 'PUSH' and so they push. There is also a brass bell that says 'RING', and Ellie wants to press it when a woman appears behind the criss-crossed glass and speaks to her father. The stone sign says St Luke's but this woman can't be a priest. Girls can't say Mass. The woman looks down at Ellie, then quickly back up at her dad. The doors open by themselves making a hard buzzing sound, like a wasp hitting a window.

- Are you an angel?

The woman laughs, not unkindly.

- Is this a church?
- We're going to see your mum, Ellie.

Ellie can hear the sea and because she knows the sea is very far away she also knows that her voices must have followed her here. Her dad tries to take her hand, but she pulls away. Is this the way back to the Before? She had wished it. It's happening now.

- Wait here.

Says the not-angel.

Ellie and her father wait at an octagonal table by a wall of windows; Fletch taught her this shape from his new maths book – octagonal, October, oct, eight. Ellie counts the sides, and it is like having Fletch there, but in her mind's eye eight is always the swooping of a wave, not lines.

This is not a church: church rules are you wear your best gear and a hat. In here the people wear pyjamas with dressing gowns over the top. The rules here are 'ready for bed'. Ellie's dad would get angry if she kept her pyjamas on after breakfast. Here, it is bedtime, always. Her mum must not like it here. She doesn't wear pyjamas.

The pyjama people walk funny, with delicate slow movements, like walking on quicksand. Ellie has played quicksand by herself on the beach – slideslideslide then sink. There is a scrag-tag bird-man with berry-black eyes. There is a young woman holding her hands like squirrel paws; if she fell she would not be able to stop herself. She is not going anywhere, she just walks into the corners then turns and turns. There is a man as fat as a baby sitting cross-legged on the floor, and when the squirrel woman gets too close to him he throws his head back and shouts, 'Nahnahnah.' It sounds like a baby noise, but from a man's mouth it is hard, a stone of sound thrown in warning. Ellie sees his yellow-and-black teeth and thinks he might bite someone, 'Nahnahnah.' No one tells him to get off the floor.

There are other people in everyday clothes who hold teacups, and sit with the pyjama people and do not speak.

They lift the dirty grey cups, they put out their lips but do not drink. They put down full, steaming cups to grow cold. Just like with the mud-coffee Ellie made in Carol's back garden. Ellie and Carol whipped the muddy water into a thick foam with a spade.

- Do you want a cap-poo-chino Miss Carol?
- My mam says you've to go home.
- Why?
- Cos of your mam 'n' that.

There are people, the not-angels, in off-white uniforms who watch Ellie, and her voices get louder, shush. A young pyjama woman rocks gently then faster, faster, next to an older woman wearing a hat with a pheasant feather in it. The feather shakes gently, afraid. The pyjama woman's head is about to smash into the hat woman's head when the not-angel man jumps in. The hat woman starts to cry and leaves the pyjama woman struggling with the not-angel, not looking back at her, forgetting to say goodbye. The rules here seem to stretch around this forgetting. Her mum would not like that. She always says her 'hello's, 'thank you's and 'goodbye's in the right places, except for the last time.

Ellie's father edges in front of her; he lights a cigarette and the smoke puffs out around them, like a spell hiding them in a fairy tale. A not-angel calls, 'Peter Fleck,' and the nahnah man stops shouting. Ellie and her dad follow the not-angel through a different set of glass doors into a yellow-windowed corridor, the light straining and barely touching them. They walk so far in that Ellie knows she could not find her way out again; she holds her father's hand, they are lost together.

The last door they push opens into an empty room with a little bed and a big window, and it is not the shape of any wish Ellie made. This is the wrong place. Her mother cannot be here. They must go. Ellie tugs at her dad's hand. But the door opens and a man with a thick black beard like a hedgehog comes in. His beard shuffles when he sees Ellie.

   - This must be Kate's daughter. Hello.
   - Who sleeps in here?

The man smiles, the smile is for Ellie, she doesn't smile back. He has a long white coat, like doctors on telly. There is someone behind him, holding his arm.

   - It's my bed.

It is Ellie's mum but she does not even lift her feet, which is strange because this is what she has always told Ellie to do.

   - Lift your feet Ellie, they are not made of clay.

And Ellie would lift her feet high off the ground and they would both high-leg it along the beach leaving strange toe prints behind in the sand.

That was Before. Her mother's feet scrape the floor. This is not the Before.

The hedgehog man makes the bed clink and clunk until it's low enough for her mum to sit down on. She moves like clockwork, like the other pyjama people, but she has a long white tail which trails out from under her dressing gown. The hedgehog man holds his hand out to Ellie.

- It's nice to meet you Miss Fleck. You're very like your mother.
- I had a mother once.

That's Ellie's mum, she talks as though she's very far away. The man asks her –

- What was she like Kate?
- She sent me away from home.
- Where's home?
- Over the water. The water's coming in.

Kate reaches up to the window trying to touch the rain.

- The rain? Is there a leak?
- No, the water, it's coming to take me home.
- Why?
- I wished it. I wish the world would open up and swallow me.

Ellie stays at the far end of the bed. Her mother smells of the wild things Ellie isn't supposed to touch.

She turns her head.

- Come here where I can see you?

Ellie doesn't move. In her mother's voice she can hear the hunched black oak tree outside the window, the sucking and the pinching snippety snap of insects' bites along her own spine – the sound of being eaten, tooth on bone.

- I don't know what you are, or where you come from, I'm sick to look at you.
- Katherine, that's your daughter.
- Mother?
- I want you to take these.

The hedgehog doctor leaves little blue pills, like beetles.

★

Ellie is a traitor, even now she's frightened to get too close to her mother's sharp white fingers. Then she feels her dad's hands under her shoulders lifting her up onto the bed right next to her. Now Ellie sees the short dark fur where her mother's hair has been shaved, velvet like a fox's ear. She wants to touch it.

- Who are you like?

The cracked red lips ask.

- I don't know.
- I can't see . . . Now.

Flick. Warm too warm. The light burning into Ellie's eyes.

- Who are you?
- Put that out Kate.

Her dad shakes the struck match out of her mother's hand. It falls to the floor. Flame spills onto her white dressing-gown tail, lighting it up and then her dad stomp-stomping it out. All dark again. Rain butting the glass, the smudged street lights winking in. Her mother makes a deep underwater sound and lunges for the window. Ellie feels the creak-crack inside her of splintering glass but the windows hold like a net, run through with little squares of steel thread. Her dad tries to hold her mother's hands.

Her mother's trying to go home, not home-home but breaking her own door back to somewhere Ellie can't follow. The Before? Ellie had wished it.

Ellie bolts.

Traitor.

She runs through the yellow corridor, her dad throwing her name after and it sinking. She runs past all of them, floating slowly in their pyjamas – like rescue-badge day at the swimming pool. Ellie wasn't to learn to swim. She had a note. It said bad –

- Hough.

Ellie runs straight into the solid cloud of one of the not-angel nurses.

- Eh now, you must be Kate's little 'un?

The nurse cradles Ellie's face in her hands — her thumb cool and clean tracing her jaw.

- Yes, ah can see it now. Come on.

Ellie feels for what the nurse felt that links her to the bone woman on the bed and the dead people her mother looks for in her face. The nurse pushes the trolley, herding Ellie back to the room. Her dad is standing at the window.

- Lost something?

Her dad takes only a half-step towards her.

- Now then Kate, you've not taken your sweeties.

The nurse taps the table and the little pills shake and Ellie's mother picks them up in her beaked fist. The nurse holds a flowered cup, full of tea the colour of tights, up to Kate's cracked lips. Kate steadies it with her own hands, like a baby. The nurse's quick eyes see the brown scorched dressing-gown tail.

- What's happened here then?
- She just dropped a match.
- Oh dear, Katie, no more ciggies.

Ellie stares hard at her mum sucking the cup, and the tea running in tendrils down her chin.

– She's doin' so well isn't she?

Ellie nods, like with maths, not understanding the question, not looking at her dad.

– Mum. Mummy?

Ellie tests the sound. Her mother turns and puts her lips to the soft shell of Ellie's ear.

– What day is it today?
– Halloween.

Kate smiles and lifts her yellow blanket for Ellie to follow her underneath.

– And what happens on Halloween?
– The dead come back.
– You know what to do don't you? Say it back to me?
– I light the light, I put out the treats, I open the window.
– Break it if you have to. Bring my mother back so as I can get home.

The nurse looks at her father.

– Get that child home.
– You will help me Ellie, help me get my mother back?

Ellie sees her father from very far away, his suit on under his blue quilted coat, his cap still on.

- Say goodbye to your mum.
- Yes.
- Be good for your daddy.

The nurse pats Kate down into the bed until she is just dunes of yellow wool and a red mouth setting. She tucks Kate's hands deep into folds where she can't reach out. This is what you did with broken things, Ellie knew. You wrapped them up tight so they couldn't break more.

Ellie followed her dad out, to the ends of the corridors where there were trees and roads and buses and school. 'Write a story about your family,' Woodsy had written on the board. She wanted to laugh out loud in his ratty face. *There was once a mother,* she thought in pen blue enough for him to believe. *Minus a gazillion house points*, he'd write back in red, *xxx* for incorrect, for wrong, for liar. She almost wished he was here, but she pulled back the thought; she couldn't afford to waste a good wish on Woodsy, not in here, not with all she had to do.

Outside at the bus stop it was growing fully dark, the strange lights of traffic floating past like stars falling, the sky broken up by bare trees. Birds scrit-scratting in the leaf mulch. Scrit-snaff-charp-scatter then a low thurrrrr sends them shooting up in one criss-cross cloud of wings. A black ragged thing paces, its reflection weaving across the glass of the bus shelter.

- Ellie. Spit it out. You don't want to hold that in.

The hospital stink of chemicals, wee and burned matches was still on her clothes. Her dad said you should spit to get the muck out of your system. He taught her how, hawking deep down to scrape the bottom of her lungs. They stood at the bus stop in the half-light, not speaking, spitting with the wind so it didn't blow back at their faces.

- Muck – this whole place, inland muck.

He spat again.

- Come here. Let me look at you.

She goes to him with her hands in her pockets though he has told her always to walk with her hands free. Her hair is a little singed at the fringe.

- No harm done.

The tiny burned ends crumbling in his fingers. No harm done.

- What a daft game eh?

He watches, looking for her smile.

- Now don't you think that she'd try to hurt you because . . .

- She wasn't going to hurt me.
- Good because she wouldn't. What did she say to you?
- It was about you.

Something was breaking between them. Her mum had struck the match, he had seen her.

- What did she say?
- She told me to be good for you.
- Right then. She'll be home for Christmas, good as new.
- Right then Dad.

Ellie looks down at the bad words written on the shelter in thick black marker; there was no red pen to tell them they were wrong.

- What's up pet? You sick? Do you need to spit again?
- No.
- What?
- Tell me my story.

He catches her up and swings her onto his shoulders, like a fallen leaf.

- Where am I from?
- Under the sea.
- Who caught me?
- I did.

- How?
- I cut you free from my nets.
- Why?
- For luck.

He holds her tighter.

8.

As soon as she gets home Ellie tidies up for the visitor who will come in through the window. She pulls the sheets off her bed and gets clean ones from the ottoman in her dad's room, careful not to look in her mum's mirror. She snaps the under-sheet and folds the corners square, smoothing down the blankets the way her dad showed her, pulling the blue counterpane tight like a drum. Now that the bed looks so cleanly angled and smells of outside, everything else looks wrong. She pulls her clothes out from the pile in the bottom of her wardrobe. Too-big dresses sent from Ireland in brown-paper packages, from girls she'd never met. One day she was supposed to grow into the wide full-skirted hips. She loops them onto hangers, where they float like people so she closes them in. She runs downstairs to get the dustpan and brush.

– What's that for?

She does not answer her dad. On her knees she sweeps the floor and buckles up her back to get under the bed. She empties the little sparks out onto the wind – fly away. She breathes on her own small mirror, and makes circles and circles and circles – smeeksmeeksmeek – with a bit of tissue until the glass shows all the pieces of her back to herself, her mother, her father and the people she has never seen from under the Green Hill. She is blue in the light of the paraffin lamp with dark moons under her eyes. She is here in the dark blue and her mother there, in the in-between with the pyjama people. There is still such a long way to go.

Standing on her chest of drawers she pulls down her little brown suitcase from the top of the wardrobe, her box of broken things. It was her dad's first, he took it away with him when he joined the navy; it came back home with him, empty. It is the place for her broken things and precious things, wrapped in old blankets and put away safe. Snapsnap she takes them out now – her teacups for the feast, one broken. Headless Barbie, the Red Queen. Her dad pulled her head off the day her mum was taken; it was an accident – he needed her long white train for her mum's wrists. Later he squished the head back on, good as new, he said, but she wasn't. She is dead and so invited too. Ellie's Communion candle. The tooth-wish coin. She spreads them out on the clean blue sea of her bed. There are treats too – KitKats and Tunnock's caramel wafers that Ellie took from the pantry for later.

Snapsnap – she closes the lid.

– Bath's ready.

Ellie needs to get this stink out of her hair. The bathroom is all steam and warmth. She takes the bottle of No More

Tears and sinks into the too-hot bath, submerging her head to get rid of the medicine, wee and burning smell. Pouring the honey-coloured shampoo into her hands, she scrubs till her fingers tingle and her scalp is sore and she sinks under the water, opening her eyes beneath the white lace of the bubbles and looking up at the light. It is beautiful. The pressure of the water makes her whole and she is sad for the first time that her father cut her out of the net and brought her here.

- Ellie, are you all right pet?
- I'm OK Dad.

★

She can hear him snoring, little putputput sounds like a baby. It is late but not yet midnight. It is still Halloween. She slides down the stairs with her suitcase on her knee, keeping to the side so she doesn't creak the second step.

She spreads the Red Queen's white lace train over the big table and sets out the cups. There are four cups so she sets out four places, including the broken cup she fixed with Sellotape. She pours in green American cream soda, which is her favourite. She does not know what her granny's favourite was. It fizzes through the Sellotape onto her hand and she licks it clean, her lips sticky with vanilla. She badly wants another sip but it is not for her. Next she sets out the KitKats and caramel wafers. She leaves the wrappers on. She lights her Communion candle from the dying fire, drips wax on a saucer and balances it in the warm pool. She pours milk into a jug and puts that on the table too. Nearly done. She climbs up onto the chair, and uses the broom to knock open the front window latch that she can't quite reach, so that they can get in.

This is what her mum used to do. Then she would hold Ellie's face in her hands by the fire and say, 'Can you see your own people in your face,' and Ellie would be frightened to look in the mirror. She cannot stay in the room, that's bad luck, but she knows she cannot sleep. So Ellie waits on the stairs and pictures her mum at one corner of the table smiling and sipping cream soda with pink-painted lips and her best green dress on.

Scritchscratch.

Ellie wakes up, her neck cricked from leaning on the stair wall.

Grrrooowww.

Ellie jumps out of her skin. But it's Douglas skitting up the stairs past her. The black cat scowls down from the top step, caroowing at Ellie's door. She lets the cat into her bedroom and Douglas scuttles under the bed. The cat does not want to meet the dead. It knows the rules.

There is a shudder and a shaking and a crunching of glass breaking but it does not wake Ellie's dad.

Scritchscratchslurpcrack.

They are here. They have come through the window. Broken through, too many for the little crack she left open. She mustn't look. Ellie mustn't look. Her granny has come like her mother said from under the Green Hill, where all the kings and queens of Ireland are buried. She loved her even though she was not yet born and left her the blue blanket. Ellie feels the emptiness where her mother should be. She puts her hand on the door and before she thinks she shouldn't open it, it's open.

The room shifts in the candlelight, flickering on broken glass. It's from the back door. That's wrong. She looks at the front window, it's fine, still open just a little. Something is moving on the table.

It is not Granny Lil.

It stands on the table, its back legs curled and crouched to fit its whole body on the wooden square, its head down snaffling and licking at the feast. Licking its black lips. The great grey head rises up slowly, nose-tip to the air; it sniffs and turns its amber eyes to Ellie and her head fills up with the gruffle of a coal-black growl. Its ears are huge, tilted towards her. It shakes from nose to tail, covering Ellie in rock slime. The jaw opens with a wet ticking of white teeth, all lined up together.

The wolf stretches out its front paws, then stretches back, pushing its bottom into the air. It creaks and cracks with mussel shells popping as it moves. Ellie can smell it, salt and grease. Then it rocks back and lunges straight for her, its tongue a wet ribbon, its paws pressing heavy on her shoulders. Hough – its breath pushing hers out, hough – filling her up with deep-water, salt-broth smell. Ellie sends herself up and out of herself, slipping out on a white breath, leaving her body behind. From here she can see the wolf on her shoulders, hooded over her. Shush. Ellie doesn't scream.

Teeth nip gently at the part where her shoulder meets her neck dragging her over the table, knocking over the cups – the fizz of cream soda and the hiss of a candle flame falling – and smash, it leaps out straight through the back door, the way it had come, with Ellie in its mouth. She jerks and shudders until it drops her on the cold flag-stones with a yelp, as though it was Ellie's teeth in its neck. She watches it lope away, head down into the deep dark of the back garden, its warm fire eyes going out, gone and then only the smell of burning.

9.

- Tell me my story.

Kate asks the doctor. Because she can't find it, the line she crossed, the break, to trace her finger along and say there – that's when she stopped being Kate. There was no line.

- Tell me my story.

But Milligan doesn't know, he's not interested in stories, he opens her eye with his thumb and forefinger and is trying to make a bright nothing inside her. He shines the light, clickclick for each eye. He says her brain is a broken machine. He says the things it remembers and replays aren't true. It just wants to fill up the dark. She's not to trust it. Clickclick.

In the dark she can smell herself, her growing-back-hair, an animal smell. She cannot wash her hair by herself because she is not to get the bandages on her wrists wet.

- Nothing in here is clean, it's driving me mad.

Ha.

But Milligan doesn't laugh. There are crumbs everywhere; they get under your fingernails, from that white foamy bread. She won't eat it. It's not been risen. In her kitchen at work she'd turn the warm loaves out of the tin onto her floured hand and knock on the bottom. Tocktock, she'd tell the young chef, that's how you know it's done. If you tried to knock the bread in here your knuckles would sink in like a punch. Breathing in the air was like drinking cheap packet soup.

- Could you open a window?

Milligan smears something on the electrodes that smells like gin. Her mind pulls at the darkness, it is hard to put words around the shapes – the sheets flap out on the washing line at her mother's; the blue window; her mother inside; the white tiles; the kettle boiling. Kate feels the nip of the IV tube, soon she will feel the cool running water, running over her head, cool and quietening. She closes her eyes and feels the rain streaming down the back of her borrowed coat, finding the line of her spine, her mouth open – something cold and solid and tasting of rubber.

- Can you keep your mouth open wide for me Kate?

He stoppers her up with her stories still inside.

★

The man was watching Kate take great pouncing strides, two steps at a time up to the pier ballroom.

- And who are you looking at?

She said with her fierce eyes on him, taking him apart and putting him back together. He was very English looking. Tall, fair hair, blue eyes, wide shoulders. He had one of those pale ganseys belted above his trousers, and he stood like a film star.

- I don't know. Who are you?

He said, bold as you like.

- I'm the chef.
- That's handy. I'm Peter, the fisherman.
- Sure you are, and I'm the Holy Virgin.

He was shy then. Strange to see it in a man so handsome and so much older than her. She was twenty-three and he would be almost twice that, but when he dove down deep inside himself she saw the boy in him.

The next time she saw him was late after her shift at the Swan Hotel. He was watching the sky to see if it was worth taking the boat out in the morning. She was walking at the tideline in her bare feet, swinging her sandals. The tide was right out and the last of the light dazzled on the wet sands. She left her shoes on a sandbell and walked in and kept walking, the sea tangling her skirts, the salt spray cooling.

Something sent the night waders flying up, she could hear a clumsy crashing behind her that didn't fit the night sounds, making the oyster catchers teep teep their annoyance. He'd gone in after her. Only he couldn't swim.

She heard him then, it could have been her name but his words were sputtered shut by the fierce water. She saw him go under, once, twice. She grabbed him beneath his shoulders and got him ashore. She pounded his back until he spat water. When he opened his eyes she was still there, her dark hair sticking to her face. He told her that she looked to him as though she was walking on the water and then the next minute she was under. He did not ask her if she was trying to end it. She came back. That was all he needed to know. He just wanted her to stay, here, with him. He lent her his coat, it was wet, heavy on her shoulders; he smelled like sweet conkers, thumbed shiny. The nights were coming in. The dark made him more solid and she leaned into him for warmth; beyond him the air was cooling, the wind shaking everything. She shone, moving into his darkness, she shone, the last of the summer light in that first touch of the autumn, his coat around her, certain and warm. His lips, though, were cold. Creakcrack – her heart opened. The hurt that had made her walk into the sea, she could feel it tilting. If she could just be here now, nothing behind her but the water, with him.

- Shall I teach you to swim?
- Bad luck.

Swimming was for tourists he said, the Flecks, they never learned, kinder not to. Kinder to give in than to struggle if the sea took you. He had stories to keep him afloat, stories which made the grey sea's surface seem solid as iron, certain as his rippled brow. Always, Peter was frightened to let her swim.

- Do you think I'll swim all the way home?

Her eyes sparked, flecks of gold and green, like her green dress.

- I can see your home in your eyes.

It hurt him, her white church and her people and always the saints. 'I want to go home,' she said. 'You're my home,' he said. As though that were the end of it.

★

Her mother would not let her bury the child she lost. Not in the church at Lagg where all the other family were. And so he wouldn't be safe under the Green Hill in the good soft earth. He wouldn't know to come when she lit the light, he wouldn't know or be known by his own people. But he was there, tucked in tight in the blanket of earth by the Malin House.

- You're never to tell it. You'll go to England with Mary's cousin like nothing happened. But I won't have you back, I won't see you here again.

She couldn't tell Peter out loud. She tried to say it in other ways. Slammed doors. Burned toast. It stuck in her throat like a bone. That was maybe why when the new child was coming Kate just stopped breathing with all the not telling. Peter had covered her lips with his own and pushed his breath into her but she would not take it. He pushed his breath inside her to the child, so that she would take her first breath from him and love him and live. But it was bad. The child wouldn't come. He had to cut her out. He slid one of his fish knives along the seam of Kate's belly. Kate wouldn't touch the child. She didn't look like anything she had made. She looked like a porpoise, all purple and blue, something stolen from the sea.

Peter sewed a pouch in one of his smocks and carried the baby round to keep her warm. Kate told him, 'I don't know who she's like.' He held the child up to the light and said she was like herself. Kate wrote for her mother but she wouldn't come, she wouldn't come and see this baby and tell her who she was like. She just sent an old blanket in a parcel with no letter. It was a shit thing to do but the blanket was blue like the sky above the church at Lagg. Peter wrapped the child in the blanket and Kate held her and smelled her mother and home.

He wouldn't see she was broken, like anything you get used to; like a window latch, you just keep using it, you work around its little ways. You hold your wrist just so, then you don't put pressure on the handle. It takes a shock one day, a letter from home. You're there just making the bread and your own little girl is watching you flour the table. You open the letter and there's a picture of a place you know, where your people are from. You've butter on your fingers from making the bread and it smears the writing. So you have to read it over and over.

- Mammy's dead.

And you drink your tea and pull on your cigarette and your throat burns and out of the blue smoke it comes again. Dead. Swallowing up the whole kitchen and your mother with it. And you're too hot, but it's raining outside so you get up to open the window to get to the rain and you forget the knack and you break it. And there is no denying it any more, it is broken. And your head is splitting and you wish, you wish the world would open up and swallow you. And it does.

★

- Hold your head still Katie.

The water was too hot and tasted strange, rubbery. It was the wrong water. She felt her head give in to the sure kneading pressure of the nurse's fingers rubbing the mean lather into her scalp.

- Not long now and you'll be doing this yourself at home.

Knead, knead, knead, the pressure at the centre of her skull – her head was splitting.

IO.

Ellie's dad dabs at the burned tuft of her hair with his Bryl-creem but it's no good, it won't stay down. He pulls out her school plait and musses her hair so that it is all wild and sticky-uppy. Ellie likes it.

- No school today. Sea-coaling.

Sometimes her dad said the best thing. This was the best thing he could have said today. There'd be no note. What could it say?

Fisherman's Square
2nd November
Dear Mr Lockwood,

Ellie must go sea-coaling today because it's sea-coal time and it doesn't wait. Sea-coal time is the tide lapping no-clock of out or in, no hands, no face, just swell and sand. When it's there you get it and when it's gone it's

gone and we'll have nothing to burn and keep us warm.
So stuff your register and your absences up your bum!

Yours sincerely,
Ellie and Dad

Ellie leaves the empty page behind

There was once a mother . . .

and goes to the Baithouse to get her sea-coal rake, the little
one her dad made for her from a toy spade. Her dad straps
the little rake and his own to the croggy-bar of the bike
with twine and away they go ticking down to the sea. No
one else is up yet. It is all theirs.

Her dad always wants to get to the beach early in case
someone else sees the sea-coal, but no one else needs it;
they all have gas fires with blue flames or electric fires with
bright red liquorice tubes. The beach is dark, but the fingernails of mussel shells glint in the sands. A crescent moon
is setting. Waders treeptreep their pretty little song and
punch into the air as Ellie gets close to the tideline where
they feed. The wind picks them up and shakes them in its
teeth. Her dad pulls her hat down tightly.

- Don't want a head cold. What's this?

His finger grazes the fresh scab on her neck.

- Nowt, I scratched myself.

She pulls her hat further down but the wind gets right inside her through her ears, makes the sound of the sea out of her like a shell. The wind tugs her towards the water's edge. She has to think into her feet just to pick the coal clean, pulling out the shells, stones, scraps of seaweed and slag from the smooth black drift. If you didn't clean the scraps from the coal it would sizzle and spit and pop when you burned it, sending flaming skites onto the rug. Her dad says it's bad luck to hear the fire talking to you. It's hard in the dark though, she can't see what she's picking. The little stints have written their feet round and round in circles in the shiny black grains. Ellie likes to see the stints run, tracing the edge of the water with their quick march. Sometimes when she picks she finds little treasures – tiny triangles of broken pottery worn to a jewelled nub of blue so that they aren't even broken or sharp, they are their own thing again. These things she keeps. Today – whole razor shells. Real treasures if she can get them home without breaking. If not, they'll go in the box of broken things.

The sea-coal's so deep Ellie can push her whole finger into its dark grains and not touch sand. It's freezing. The light is creeping up and the sea pulls right back so it's just her, her dad and the shiny black coat of coal on the shoreline. It's hard to grip the rake for the cold.

- Tell me our story.
- Which one?
- Great-grandfather James and the sea-god. The Fleck story.

- Great-grandfather James was out on the boat –

- *Eleanor*, same as me.

- That's right, and he pulled up the drift nets just like he had done every day – but that day, there was something wrapped up and tearing itself up in the nets. It looked like a –

- Pup.

- Yes, a seal pup, or a porpoise, but with human eyes like a new baby. 'Kill it,' shouted one of the Hoods.

- Stupid man.

- He didn't know what it was. But your great-grandfather James was held fast in the little thing's dark eyes. He took his knife from his belt. 'Kill it,' Hood said again.

- But great-grandfather James wouldn't would he?

- No pet, he wouldn't, he'd sooner kill his own blood. It could've been such a catch though, it would've made a good story.

- Not as good as our story.

- A newspaper story – a picture in the *Gazette*. But your great-grandfather could see in its eyes – it wanted to go back down to the deep water. 'Cut me out,' it said.

- And he did.

- He did. He cut the net and the catch and the creature fell back to the sea. And before it swam back down into the depths it bobbed back up once and said, 'I am a sea-god and the Flecks will always be safe at sea.' But there was no catch to take home. No happy wives that night. No full bellies.

- What would've happened if great-grandfather James had taken it home with him?
- What?
- Like that tame seal the Hoods had.
- That was sad, that was. Lived in the yard. They'd tek it down to the breakwater in a barrow. And d'you know what, it would swim out and then it would come back. Bloody come back eh? To go back in the yard. You could hear it barking at night. Relp relp.

Her dad barked out loud to her, she didn't want to laugh. He always made her laugh when she didn't want to.

- No Dad, the sea-god, what would've happened if James took it home?
- Well then, the wolves of the sea would 'a come for it. They always come for their own. Arooo.

Ellie scratches at her neck, the wool of her hat itching the bite. Her dad doesn't see, he arches his back and harools into the dark, his mouth so wide that Ellie can see the gaps between his teeth. She feels it too, the tickle in the place where the laugh was, the harool growing in her belly and she joins him.

- Arooo.

They work hard together singing their arooos, Ellie scraping the sea-coal into little black hills as the lights of the ships lining into port wink out. Her dad works behind her, scooping her hills into the big sacks and packing them tight. The shore is getting lively with tide coming in, shush, shush, talking over the night waders and their arooos. The waves are high and grey-flecked in the half-dark, furred and tumbling right at them, roaring behind them then whispering out in tiny reaches of white feathers. Shush.

- Look Ellie, do you see them, the wolves of water running.

She can only see the black pips of seals, turning, rolling, playing in the hips of the sea. She sinks her rake into a thick seam of sea-coal and there in the wet belly of the sand is a huge footprint. She kneels down and presses her fingers into the delve – it's much bigger than her hand.

- Ellie where you going?

There are more prints, they lead to –

- Wolf Rock.
- It's a story pet, there's no wolves. There's no time for that today.

She knows the way. In the half-light the clouds scurry in and tumble down onto the wet sand, so up is down and down is up.

- Ellie come back here.

All that remains in the pool now is a hollowed-out rock, the water clouded over with sand. It's gone, the wolf in the rock is gone.

- Must have been a storm rolled the stone out.

Her dad sees it too. He looks around for where the stone is now.

- Leave it Ellie.

And he goes picking up nice wide pieces of driftwood. But Ellie can see where the wolf must have pushed itself free of the sand, sucking and dripping out of the pool. It came from here, from the water. It hadn't come for the light or the feast. What had it come for?

*

- We'll fix that back door now.

Her dad likes to work slow when he's mending, he likes to set all his tools out in front of him. He lays out his jar of oiled nails, a rag, a hammer and a toothy saw. Then he picks up the driftwood.

- Look at this Ellie, it's got a bend in it see.

He smooths his palm along the broken wood following the curve.

- The wind bent this tree, it's larch, strong, it would have been a boat once. A beauty. Look at the sweep on that plank, she could 'a taken a breaker or two, it must 'a took summat to wreck her. Imagine that eh? This bit o' wood holding you safe above the water? Shame.

He says as he cuts into the wood, sawing it down into slats to fit the hole in the broken-toothed door where the wolf came through. He hands a sawn piece to Ellie, it's heavy, sand locked in its grain and flecks of blue paint still holding on to what it was. Ellie struggles to hold it up.

- It's swollen with water pet, that's what holds a boat together, the planks swell, plug the gaps, keep her water-tight. This'll dry out o' the water and shrink and the wind'll get in and shake the whole house. Then we'll know about it.

He pops a nail in his mouth still not asking who burned the table or who broke the door.

Bangbabangbang.

But it's not her dad hammering, there is someone at the front door. A thin man in a long grey coat. He huffs and puffs, he has no fur or teeth, only a flat brown folder that he carries tucked under his arm like an axe. Her dad lets him in and once he's inside he's staring at the blackened table where Ellie's Communion candle burned it. The thin man wants to know, 'Just what is going on here?' and he throws out questions like stones.

- Why hasn't she been in school today? Has there been a fire? Who started it? Is she hurt? What are those marks on her neck?

And her dad says, 'Not in front of the child.' They go in the kitchen and Ellie can still hear words she knows like 'absence' and 'social services' and words she doesn't know like 'report' and 'at risk'. These words cut her father down, and he falls, creakcrackcraake like a tree in the woods.

Now Ellie has to be good and be the Ellie who says yes and go to school tomorrow, 'Or else they will take you away.'

II.

Mr Lockwood rolls the green-blackboard round and writes *3rd November* in his loopy writing and underlines it with a wavy line. There are five new *Spellings*. Ellie quickly writes them down in her grey narrow *Spellings Book*. Mr Lockwood wants them to look up the meanings and then put them into a sentence.

<u>Today's Spellings</u>
  i)   The <u>bough</u> of cherry blossom swayed in the wind.
  ii) The <u>trough</u> was made of ancient stone.
  iii) The snake <u>sloughed</u> off its old skin.
  iv) The <u>arrows</u> pierced him again and again but he did not die.
  v)   The boy's <u>shadow</u> was stolen.

Ellie wants to follow the path of these beginnings. But Fletch pulls her book towards him.

- What sentences have you got?
- Write your own.
- I have, I just want to see yours.

She could hurt him and make him go away and she would be less tired but empty in a different kind of way.

- ELLIEFLECK . . .Your sentence for 'shadow'?

Ellie stares at her answer and knows it is blue and bad and wrong. When Ellie first arrived at the school Mr Lockwood had said she had such beautiful handwriting that she could be the first in class to get a pen. He gave her the Berol with its perfect blue nib. The other children watched the blue ink swirl across the page whilst their blunt pencils scratted grey dust. Now she thinks Woodsy did it to make sure they would hate her.

- Stand so we can all hear clearly.

Her voice creakcracks at the back of her throat.

- Theboysshadowwasstolen.
- Again, slowly.
- Boysshadowwasstolen.
- His shadow was what?
- Stolen?
- What could steal a shadow? Where do you get these nonsense ideas from?
- From my dad's book on Norse . . .

- Thank you, Miss Fleck, we don't need to or want to know about your dad's book.

Laughter.

- Thank you for this . . . contribution. Minus one house point.

Laughter.

She is boiling inside now, she shouldn't have said 'Dad', it set them off.

She takes her pen and crosses out her sentence; she will lose another house point for crossing out but as she does not have a pencil she can't erase it. Fletch is breathing hard, as though he wants to run.

- That's not fair. Why did he take a house point?
- Shush.
- Why does he hate you? Ellie, Ellie don't cross it out. It's right.

Fletch lays his arm across her book to stop her. She tries to keep writing, budging his strong brown wrist, but he holds and her pen snags his arm. He makes a noise – it must have hurt.

v) ~~The boy's shadow was stolen.~~
v) The lamp post cast a shadow.

Or not a shadow at all, but a swarm of black beetles, tacketytacktacketytack, marching off her page and up Woodsy's arm to burrow themselves into his ratty eyes.

She takes out her Highland Toffee bar from her bag and puts it on Fletch's side of the desk, this means sorry. In his own book Fletch had written:

~~v) Shadows move in the opposite direction to the sun.~~

v) The boy's shadow was stolen.

Ellie does not know what this means.

★

At break-time Ellie finally stops walking when she reaches the shelter by the bins, it is within-bounds, only just. He won't follow her this far out, it's too close to the edge of the rules. She burrows in against the bitter wind and he's still there watching her. She takes out her book but he won't go.

  - You should play on the field where the boys play. Stephen's there.

  - Stephen's a wazzock.

Wazzock she said it again inside her head. He had said wazzock, and now he's nearly out-of-bounds.

  - What are you reading?

  - Robert Westall.

  - I like *The Machine Gunners*.

Fletch holds his arms out as if he were cradling a machine gun, pointing it straight at her.

  - Ackackaackack.

His whole body begins to shake; she looks around hoping none of them will hear or see.

- You're supposed to die.

She keeps staring.

- Like this . . .

He judders forward until he hits the floor then begins to jerk in fitful starts and stops, from his shoulders to his feet, moaning the whole time. Is this boy an actual loony? Finally his feet still, no, one final judder followed by –

- Eeuuurghhhgggg – hough! Now I'm dead, see?
- You're not very quiet for a dead person.
- Now it's your turn.

He stands there expectantly with a clear line of fire. Ackackack. She shakes her body around as convincingly as she can, flinging out her arms. For the second time she tastes the rough grit of playground dirt. She jerks her knees towards herself and into the foetal position with one last judder.

- Eerghghhough.

She wasn't certain what would happen next. She lay there with her eyes closed, hardly breathing, waiting.

- Yeah, that was really good, you're Best Man Dead.
- Um?
- What?
- Can I get up and come back – dead?
- No, that's stupid, you're dead.
- Saints come back. They appear to people.
- That's cool. You a saint?
- No.
- Well you can't come back.
- Is that the rule?

Fletch doesn't answer; he's found something on the ground. It's the Highland Toffee bar Ellie gave to him in class. It must have fallen out of his pocket when he was dying. She picks it up and gives it back to him.

- Ace, thanks.

He chews messily, talking out loud all the different ways to die: 'guns', 'swords', 'electrocution'. Ellie knows better ways from saints.

- You could shoot me with an arrow?
- Excellent! How?

Ellie pulls back her elbow as though drawing a bow and the boy copies and looses his arrow at her.

- Missed.

He tries again.

Ffffffhhhhhh.

- Hough.

Ellie arches backwards as the second arrow catches her just below the rib cage, a soft knock which lifts her up into the air, leaning into the wind and then down, down. She claws weakly at the shaft deep in her heart. You cannot pull an arrow out, you must break off the fletched part and push it through. She knew this from watching *Robin of Sherwood* before her mum dumped the TV in the garden. In the Before on Saturday nights Ellie's mum would put her hair in ringlets for church the next morning. She would have to hold one end of the long rag and her mother would pull and wrap the cloth around a length of hair. Each turn of the cloth would tugtugtug. She opens up a river of blood as she pulls out the arrow. Ellie's heart slows. She balls her fist under her body and beats a slowing rhythm against the frozen ground.

Thudthud ... thud-thud ... thud ... thud ... ... thud.

She looks up to the splayed fingers of the bare trees, the clouds opening behind. Fixing her eyes on the moving clouds helps her to be still. This is already Ellie's favourite part of Best Man Dead, the stillness after the death, waiting for the sparkles. Fletch approaches slowly and dips his ear to Ellie's lips, while Ellie holds fast onto the breath bursting inside her.

- Epic, now you kill me.

Does this mean they are two-together? She picks up a fallen stick and swings it deftly in an arc.

- Hanging?
- Too difficult.
- Catherine wheel?
- What?
- Crucifixion then, but with your arms like this? Like St Andrew?

Ellie jumps so that she lands in a cross shape.

- Go on then.

Fletch leans up against the kitchen wall and splays his arms into a star-cross shape and Ellie hammers the nails into his outstretched palms.

- In the Stations of the Cross the nails go into the palms like this, but really the nails had to go through the wrists here.

She pulls back the grey sleeve of Fletch's parka and touches the thin skin of his wrist with a cold finger, where his blue veins criss-cross.

- Otherwise the weight of the body would have just pulled the nails right through the palms.
- Well put the nails in my wrists then.
- OK.

Ellie diligently hammers the long nails through Fletch's wrists whilst he shatters the icy air with barks of pain.

- Who died like this again?
- St Andrew, but he might not have died from the nails.
- How then?
- They might have just tied him to the cross and left him there to hang. He didn't want to die like Jesus.
- Why?
- Because Jesus is too important to copy.
- How long does it take to die just hanging here then?
- Too long.

So she kept hammering in the nails. In her old school Mrs O'Dowd had made them all stand up in assembly at Easter. She told them to stand with their arms held out in a cross, like Jesus. They all obeyed. She said, 'Do you feel that? How difficult it is to breathe?' They did. 'Now you know what Jesus felt as he suffocated on the cross for your sins.' After that they would have competitions in the playground to see who could hold out their arms for the longest without dying. Mrs O'Dowd watched them from her window, proud.

- Ellie?
- Yeah?
- How come you know so many different ways to die?

Ellie just knew about the saints and their stories, she had drawn pictures of them in her red book at her old school, using all the crayons – blue for the Dead Sea, yellow for the deserts. She had won a tube of Smarties for her story about St Catherine.

  – It's all the saints – you have to know how they died. Are you ready for the spear?

  – Why is their death always really –

Ellie drove the spear slowly into Fletch's right-hand side above his hip.

  – It's what makes them saints. You can't just get a cold and die, that's not enough for God. You're not making the noise.

  – Eeeuuurghhh.

  – So what happens then?

  – People keep their bodies and bones and their stuff and they are magic and cure people.

  – So are they dead or what?

  – They're saints.

  – That's mad.

  – As mad as this?

Ellie jigs her whole body again as though bullets were passing through it.

  – All right then what do you want to play?

  – Mass, bagsy I'm the priest.

  – Aw.

She pulls him within the big clouds of steam choughing out from the kitchens.

- This is incense, it's like holy smoke.

- It smells like cabbage.

- Shush. Say after me – In the name of the Father, and of the Son, and of the Holy Spirit.

- Cool.

- Say it.

She puts her hands on his shoulders.

- Now you have to kneel down.

And he bends down before her and she thinks that old Froggy Doorley the priest must feel like this when all the people kneel in front of him, like the sun in the sky, real and magic all at once. That's why he didn't want little girls saying Mass. Haha. Amen, Froggy Doorley!

- Eat the Host and it will clean out your sins.

- What are sins?

- They're like germs but in your thoughts. So like when you think – I want Ellie's Highland Toffee, that's a sin cos it's not yours.

- What?

- Just open your mouth.

Ellie puts a white chocolate button on Fletch's tongue.

- Don't chew it.

Her mum had shown her how, kneeling at church and by her bed. At church they stood at the back and did not talk to the ladies with hats and bright red slashes of lipstick the same shade and shape as the gash on Christ's side.

– Close your eyes and say after me . . . *We believe in one God, the Father Almighty.* Go on, you say it out loud and at the same time picture your soul clean.

God flapped white, inside the darkness of her head, just out of sight – God who burned and God who healed – suddenly it's not a game. Ellie prays for her mum to come home, words breaking off into specks of light, swarming out to her mother in the nowhere place with the pyjama people. She wants her mother to see these dancing lights and know the way home, to know that Ellie wants her to come back.

– What do we say now?
– *Hail Holy Queen.*

Ellie tugs at the net full of half-remembered words, feeling just the rhythm if not the exact sounds.

– *Mother of mercy, hail, rain and hope. To thee do we cry, poor burnished children of Eve.*
– Are you sure it's burnished? Burnished is like burned.
– Yep – burnished. The fires of hell.

- They burn children?

- Yep if they're bad – *To thee do we send up our sighs –* ow ayaz *– from the fires and the burning.* You're not saying it.

- *Ow.*

- *Weeping in this vale of tears. Turn then, most gracious adder-cat, thine eyes of mercy toward us.*

- Adder-cat?

- Yeah – it's like a snake, you know, in the Garden of Eden, but also a cat. Cats and snakes have the same eyes with a slit you know? It looks at you and sees inside your soul with its eyes.

Ellie holds up her hand, fingers pursed like a snake's head staring into Fletch's face.

- Ellie that's from that book on Egypt we read, that's a different god.

- Say it or you'll get burned.

- *Turn then, most gracious adder-cat, thine eyes of mercy toward us.*

- *And after this our exile . . .*

Ellie had done what she was told. She set out the feast and lit the Halloween light but Granny Lil didn't come back. It was a ragged wolf that came out of the dark and ate the feast and burned it all up.

- What's next?

What if the wolf hadn't come to help her at all?

- Don't say any more out loud.
- What happens now?
- Don't pray, it makes things happen inside your head and they can get out.

What had it come for? Then she sees them – wolf hairs on her winter coat. She breathes in their salt-water smell.

- Ellie don't be daft. *Holy Queen* . . .

Fletch says kneeling, his eyes closed, his mouth open.

- What's he doing?
- Spaz boy!
- He's a Queen.

She knew they would come for him. She knew it was her fault.

- Spaz boy, what's six times seven?
- Forty-two.
- Queer.

No don't, don't, don't. That's not the answer.

It's Stephen and Ed and David. The cold has driven a pack of them, the most vicious, to the warmth of the vegetable cloud. The cold makes them hungry; their empty bellies rumble but they don't know what for.

- It's her. The mad Paddy's kid.
- The Fenian kid.
- Where's your mummy madPaddy?
- What's up with her?
- She lives with her granddad cos her mum's mad.
- He's not my granddad.
- But he's way old.
- How old's her dad number-spaz?

Ellie slumps down below the dirty glass of her shelter, paint flaking like snow, her hands holding her head. She could make it to the gate but that would be Ellie-out-of-bounds and the thin grey man again.

- Where's yer mam now Ellie? Locked up in the loony bin?

There it is now – ragged and pacing where Ellie wants to run, its long body making quick shadows behind the school gate. Thurrrr it says and Ellie hears it in her belly. Its eyes are shiny with smite and burn. The group huddle in and the wolf throws itself against the blue bars. Ellie feels it below her lungs, red leaves flying.

Smash and cold then burn. Not running and the earth under her, but hough, and stop and hold her still, like a net, like a mother. Now there was blood.

- She's mental.
- She's bleeding.
- Leg it.

The pack drift back behind Stephen, the blood worries them and only he holds his ground.

- Where is she? Where's your mam?

There is crying, a low deep song beneath Fletch's crying, 'Thurrr,' Ellie feels it in her teeth and bites down hard:

- She's dead.

Ellie and Fletch sit at a table by themselves; their plates are full of the cooling grease of sausages and beans and the gritty glasses of scalding cocoa grow a skin. There is a blackberry clot on Ellie's head. The silence pulses in her hot turning stomach.

- Why did you hit your head?

Ellie does not answer.

- Is your mum really dead?
- I don't know. Not really.
- Where is she then?
- An in-between place with pyjama people and not-angels.
- Why d'you always lie?
- It's real, I've been there. There were nurses and bandages and . . .

These words huff and puff out of her chest, they are scare words and not for children but she can't not tell him now.

   – Please Fletch it's not lies. What's ECT?
   – What?
   – Electro Seeee Teeee something. It's what they're doing my mum, Father Doorley said.
   – Electro is electricity. Electricity kills human beings. Like electrocution or lightning. Why are you making this up? Why did you say she was dead?

Dead. She had said it out loud, which was just as good as wishing, it splintered out of her mouth and swallowed everything. She shook a little; he stayed until it was time to throw away his dinner, not watching her.

★

Mrs Hill, headmistress, has a big brown mole on her chin, Mrs Hill's mole, Mrs Mole Hill. Her office smells of cigarettes, coffee and the sharp tang of saddle soap. She is mostly brown, earth piled up into a solid woman. Next door, Mrs Clarkson bangs on the typewriter – snick . . . snick . . . snicksnick . . . ping. These sounds are very close.

Ellie tries to sit still holding wet paper towels to her head. Mrs Hill is wearing her headscarf from parading the grounds at lunchtime. It's got golden horseshoes on it. Ellie counts the tiny horseshoes so that she doesn't have to look at the mole, it's like melted chocolate. Mrs Hill opens her big green box for accidents, she kneels down so the mole is very close to Ellie.

112

- Close your eyes.

She squirts something very cold onto Ellie's hot head, it smells like Christmas cake.

- What have you done to yourself?

Ellie cannot speak, she is making tiny clucking noises, scraping the roof of her dry mouth with her dry tongue. She feels dizzy and thirsty. She must stay here inside her own head and listen and not drift off. She anchors herself to Mrs Hill's voice.

- You're getting quite an egg on that head.
- Will it split?

Like her mother's head?

- No, but we'll have to write this in the accident book, now what am I going to put?

Just like her dad and sick notes. Adults always want to write on paper when children are ill or not, but they only ever want a story.

- I hurt my head.

Ellie touches her head, it feels bigger.

- Mr Lockwood has spoken to the boys. They said you banged your own head.

Ellie closes her eyes. If she keeps them open they will cry. Not sad crying but the crying that won't stop and shakes your chest and pulls you about the sky like birds too small for a fast wind.

- Is it true?

Ellie keeps her mouth tight closed around the creature flapping inside her and Mrs Hill tries to tempt it out. Maybe she wants to see Ellie cry.

- Why Ellie, why would you bang your own head? Is this because of your mum?

Sometimes when Ellie wouldn't let herself cry she could laugh. She opens her mouth to laugh now, but it doesn't come out like that, the sound she makes is like a howl. She cannot say any more words. She had made the words to protect Fletch, 'She's dead,' she had said, and now something would die. The creature inside her shook then. Mrs Hill pulled Ellie onto her knee, her skirt riding up, and Ellie could see a pale pink slip beneath the layers of brown. Mrs Hill rocks her, her head feels light but the creature flaps its wings against her lungs, along her ribs, pushing against her heart. Mrs Hill keeps rocking until it can fly out of her mouth without tearing her apart. Hough.

- There now Ellie let it out.

Mrs Hill's voice is circling Ellie, coming in close low swoops, too close.

- Do you know what you can do to help your mum?

Ellie does not know. She had put out the feast of KitKats and cream soda for her granny and the wolf had come. She didn't know what for, to take her away, to bring her mum back?

- You need to be good, come to school and stay away from trouble and your mum will get better in her own time. Yes?
- I said dead . . . I wished . . .
- No, wishes are just for fairy tales, come to school and don't get into trouble.

Ellie knows enough to nod. Mrs Hill stands up quickly and she slides down the pink slip to the floor.

- That's enough of that now or we'll make you soft.
- Yes.
- And how is everything else at home. How's your dad? How's he managing with all of this?
- My dad?
- Yes, is he . . . well?
- He is . . .

Ellie thinks of all the words she knows, trying to find one that means that he is frightened but he is still a grown-up.

- He's OK.
- Good, good. Give him my regards.

Mrs Clarkson came in then with some hot orange and a shortbread biscuit and put them down in front of Ellie. Ellie dips the biscuit into the hot orange and bites, scalding her tongue.

12.

May Fletcher was early, the car steamed up from her coffee and waiting. She was trying to use this scrap of time to think about Christmas. It was only the beginning of November for God's sake, but the women in her team had it all worked out already: presents, decorations, dinner – the lot. May hadn't even booked time off yet. So far she'd only thought about taking the crappy decorations from the old house out of the garage. That awful white tinsel tree. Robin wanted a real one this year: 'Ellie always has a real one.' And he was not Robin any more, Fletch, something harder and older than the name she gave him. How was she going to find the time to sort out a real tree between work and school? Her mind was too tired, it just wanted to sit pooled under the street light in the warm car, and drift. She turned off the radio to listen to the rain slapping down on the bonnet. She sucked down the coffee, the borrowed heat runnelling through her.

Usually she loved this time of year. It reminded her of

when Robin was born and she lived in that teeny flat in York with the Narnia street light outside. It was so small, his breathing filled every room. She cupped the tiny shell of him and they listened to the swish of traffic in the slush and she told him that Mr Tumnus would come and take them to Narnia. Midwinter, she even loved the word, because it was the waiting in the darkness, the part before. That's what she wanted from Christmas, for her and Robin, that magic, not a white plastic tree with a fire-hazard warning.

She could taste Tom, in her coffee, Robin's not-dad. The grit at the bottom of the cup, rough on her tongue – strange what the mind threw out in the dark. She had thought the waiting was love, when really it was the beginning of what he was too much of a coward to say. By the time he arrived, four hours late, she already knew they were not going to be a family. What a shit-boring story? She looked out at the street lamp for a better one.

When Robin jumped in the car, he didn't talk, he just made angry slicing shapes in the condensation. He hadn't been this angry since they first arrived, before Ellie.

- Where's Ellie today Robin?
- My name's Fletch.
- Have you fallen out?

Silence.

At home he stayed curled like a fist around his bear at the other end of the couch watching TV, only looking up now and again at the cartoon snow falling. He was stubborn and held fast on to things that hurt him. But today she only had to say bed and he broke open.

- They were picking on us. She did it to herself and they stopped. They wanted to hurt her but she hurt herself first. She hit her head against the glass. I don't get it. They said her mum was mad and then she smashed her own head. She said her mum's dead but she isn't, she isn't dead. She's a liar.

The heating had gone off so she pulled him close to her, opening her soft big cardigan around him, he bulged out of the grey wool, a little pup, his knees tucked up under his chest. His hair was almost white. His head was hot. It was the time of year for colds and she stroked his hair, reading him, feeling for a change in temperature, listening to his breathing. Then she stroked for comfort, her own and his. She had kept him too close, too innocent maybe. Those cruel little shits at his last school. Kids just don't think up that sickness by themselves, they learn it at home.

May had looked into their families. She took her report to her supervisor. They were at risk, May said. 'Only from you,' she was told. 'You can't abuse your power like that even for your own kid.'

So she had made a fresh start, here. She had let him settle in. Then he came home from school, full of Ellies. He packed his bag with sweets Ellie would like – white chocolate buttons and Highland Toffee and didn't eat them if she didn't turn up that day. Ellie would never come close to the car, she would just wave. She was wild, but you wanted her to come close, you wanted to learn to be still enough to reach out to her and for her not to run away. She knew that Robin felt it. Was it healthy? It was the first time he did not share. Ellie and Robin, Ellie and Fletch. She had given him a new name, just for her.

   - She doesn't understand pounds and pence, but knows words and spellings and is best at Best Man Dead, she died really well Mum, held her breath and everything.

His Ellie was perfect, but on paper Ellie was 'damaged', a word May knew well; she used it daily in her assessments. That's how they would describe Ellie when she got older, if she followed the pattern. The Fleck case was still open; it hadn't been flagged up but it was flammable, the signs were there. The fax had come through on the Monday morning, her first day in the post and everyone slow in the heat, baking in their council prefab. They always put social workers right on the edge in the slapped-up temporary buildings, as though they were just a temporary fix too. She was the first to see it chug out of the fax machine whilst she was waiting for her own paperwork to come through.

Crisis. Main care-giver. Attempted suicide. Sectioned. Child. 10. Father present.

She went running to get Maggie.

   - Hold your horses, I'll pop out and see Dad, you find your feet and I'll keep you posted.

Maggie went round there on the Monday afternoon. Met with Mr Fleck. All was fine. No – he didn't want school informed. No need to meet the child. No risk. No further action needed. Father's wishes respected. Then Maggie had come back to her this morning in the team meeting.

– Missing school, Dad says she was sick but the education social worker went round. He said the little girl didn't look sick, looked like she had set fire to something but Dad said it was an accident. She had scratch marks on her neck. Could be nothing. We can't rush in without real evidence.

Now the little girl was banging her own head off brick walls and saying her mother was dead.
She made the call.

– If you think you're ready for this one, May, I'll back you. It's up to you how to handle these first steps.

★

A few days later May Fletcher knocked on the front door of the fisherman's house, too heavily – she was nervous. She couldn't believe it, nervous, when she had done this a million times. He opened the door. Robin had said he was ancient but he could not be more than what, forty-five, and even then he didn't look it. He was blond, receding a little, but still very handsome. He stood well, gracefully, a touch of the Jimmy Stewart about him. She had thought she knew what she wanted to say – who she was, what she did, something about mothers and girls needing them at this age, something about support – she had got her lines ready in the car, she was going to speak slowly, simply – but she could not speak.

– Are you from the school?

There was a very old woman behind him, her voice high, forcing her vowels.

– No I'm . . . who are . . .
– Are you from the hospital? Are you here about Mrs Fleck? Do you have some form of identification?

May tried to talk over the top of her, to explain who she was, but the old woman was advancing with more questions. May felt herself being sized up, in her good boots and camel coat; she knew she looked official. The old woman had sussed her quickly as a threat.

– Sorry, I am Robin's mum.

She wasn't going to say what she was in front of the old woman. Mr Fleck was still a wall, not angry, not welcoming – inscrutable – yes that was it, she could not read him.

– Fletch's mum.

A smile, thank God.

- That scrawny boy?

The old woman again.

- Sorry. Who are you?

She'd said sorry again: women like this still threw her. You should never start with sorry, they've got you then. The questions – sharp as a beak, the eye cocked, ready to peck the answers out of you.

She was also the type to ask, 'Where's your husband then?' May had to train herself not to be startled into giving answers.

- I'm just the one who takes all the phone calls.
- I am really here to speak with you Mr Fleck, it's about the children.

May tried to stare the old woman down but this only seemed to encourage her.

- Ellie's wild, I've told him, she runs wild. Missing school, knocking other kiddies down, she's a lost cause.
- That's not what Robin thinks. He would be lost without her.

That smile again.

- Would you like to come in Mrs Fletcher? I'll see you later then, Alice.

The old woman, Alice, took her time, each step resistant, registering the slight. May waited out the awkward silence of her going, but she could imagine the old dear racing round to press a glass against a wall as soon as she was out of sight.

She should tell him now who she really was, but the kitchen held that sweet clean smell of Fairy household soap, like her grandmother's house. There it was, the brick of green marble by the sink. Peter filled the kettle and placed it on the hob. He slowly took out the tea things, proper tea things – pot, loose tea, china cups and saucers. May felt like a child.

– It's not bad, what I want to say. Ellie is Robin's first friend since we got here.

He swirled hot water to warm the pot, then put in three heaped teaspoons of loose leaves. One for the pot, she smiled. He put it all onto the tray and led her into the living room, where the open fire was stacked ready to be lit. No fireguard. There were no toys left out. There were books, some with old heavy spines worn rough – myths, stars, animals – stacked in rows along the dresser, the smaller ones within reach of a child. There was no carpet, only a large rug, bare in places, the roses still recognisable though fading to white. Only one photograph, not recent. Mr Fleck with his wife – she looking stunned and pale, Mr Fleck holding the small pink baby. May could not stop her mind from doing this – looking for the cracks. The chair he pointed her to had once been covered with fat cabbage roses, and she could see the weave exposed and that the solid wooden arms had been rounded by many hands, or by the same hands for many years. An oak table stood sentinel before the glazed back door, reflecting the weak winter sunlight. The table had a dark charred stain at the centre, polished over. One of the glass panels in the door had recently been broken and was boarded over with rough wood. Everything was so clean now, no traces of what could have happened, all bleached out and scrubbed away, except for the breeze getting in.

He watched her watching the door; she turned too quickly and had to steady herself. While he concentrated on the ritual of the cups, she kept scanning the room. There was something missing, May could feel it – no TV. She let Robin watch too much TV, what was it this year, *The Box of Delights*? This house was like a museum. Could they really live like this? She stopped herself. She was losing the thread of what she was, why she was here, it was the quiet, she felt herself opening – anaesthetised by the clear sweet smell of the soap. It was up to her, Maggie said, how she would handle it. She was Robin's mum and Robin needed Ellie. That's who she was here.

– Ellie, she told the other children her mother was dead. It frightened Robin.

He paused, a small shake in his large hands as he held the sugar spoon; a few granules fell. That's all.

– She isn't.
– No, no, I know – I . . .

125

May couldn't stop herself, she turned to look at the front window – the report said that his wife had tried to break through it – all perfectly fixed now, then she made herself look down into her tea. Did he see her? He could hold on to silence though there was a storm in the room; she had shaken him loose, but he could hold on to this silence and still stand. She saw Robin, shaking, and saying nothing, just like this man.

- I thought . . . Sorry, I'll start again . . . I'd like to take Ellie with us, with Robin and me, shopping on Saturday, to York, get her out of herself a bit.

Christ, what would he think, was this too much? She reached for her tea, and slurped loudly, and the leaves churning and swirling to the surface sank down again, hiding the future.

- Her mother, she . . .

Oh God, she doesn't want him to tell her, she doesn't want him to think she would ask. She can't do it, not with him, cross-checking his version with the locked-up file. This was stupid.

- No it's all right, I just want Ellie to come.

She knew what was private. The things people would ask still shocked her.

- Where's your husband?
- Does he work away?
- Can you manage on your own?

Questions like incisors. Who the hell were they to ask and think they deserved answers? She had a son and bills and a home and a job. Robin did not have a father, that's all there was to it, but still he learned his silence from somewhere.

- I didn't come with questions Mr Fleck.

That is what she is choosing, to work with the damage and try to contain it.

- Peter.
- Peter. Can Ellie come?
- Come for her at ten, she'll be ready.
- OK, brilliant, thank you.

What was she thanking him for? For Robin. He finally stopped shaking when she told him she would find a way to bring Ellie back for him, and now she had.

Now that it was agreed, May didn't want to leave, and not because she needed to tell him the truth. It was – the house, the tea, the smell of Fairy soap – it was beautiful. She stood on the step not going, waiting in the time he gave to her; then Peter enclosed her hands in his, such an intimate thing to do that she stumbled on the step, her low heel turning over. He caught her elbow and she realised he was pressing something into her hands. A tinfoil boat?

- A dressed crab.

At home she unfurled the parcel, precisely wrapped to keep its shape. The brick-red shell scooped out and refilled with the white meat and the whole legs of the crab, with their spear hairs intact, the two fleshy claws as centrepiece on top. It was arcane, like those medieval organs made from sinners' bones, and yet she could smell the sweet salty meat too. She was hungry and pulled out one of the claws and sucked at the meat like a lollipop. She thought of the crude tins of tinted crabmeat on shelves in M&S, sour and mean and of a different creature entirely. This gift was not meant for her, but for Fletch's mum – a friend. She ate it anyway, just to feel clean. It had made her so hungry, the house, the smell of Fairy soap, his love. 'She'll be ready,' he said. It was beautiful, this man, his daughter – 'Come for her' – his love circling around her.

13.

- You can have anything you like, Ellie.

Ellie did not think that she would be able to eat, there were so many people. Old ladies with false teeth and powdered faces mashing scones and smudging lipstick and tinkling teacups and hmmnning and oohing and didsheing. There's so much noise, not like the noise inside her head of shushing and sorry sorry sorry and dead. Ellie stares at the swirling writing on the menu, looped in solid rows, too neat for a story. Her menu says *Betty's* and *Darjeeling* and *Croque Monsieur* and she does not know what they mean. She has her own menu because Fletch didn't want to share.

- Robin? Do you want your usual egg and chips and a banana float?
- Can I have that too, please Mrs Fletcher?
- Yes certainly Ellie.
- I don't like egg any more, I want sausage and chips.

Mrs-Fletcher-Call-Me-May talks about the shops they will go to – C&A and M&S and the Christmas shop. Ellie feels her feet warming and drying under the table whilst they wait. When the food comes the hot vinegar smell wakes up her stomach and she dips the fat yellow chips in her runny egg. She remembers to eat with her mouth closed and it burns a bit but it means she doesn't have to not talk back to Fletch because he's definitely not talking to her. She wants all the chips now but does not know when they'll eat next, so when Mrs Fletcher goes to the 'ladies' Ellie rolls them up into the napkin for being hungry later and puts them in her pocket.

Ellie rubs her head where there is now a crescent-moon scab, a sharp pain between her and Fletch.

- How's your head now Ellie?
- Good as new Mrs Fletcher.

That's what Ellie's dad says about broken things that he can't fix.

- How's your mum?

Ellie's angry with Fletch now. If he was talking to her then his mum wouldn't think she had to talk to her and ask Ellie questions she didn't know the answer to.

- Sorry Ellie, I know it must be hard. But you can talk to me you know if you want to.
- Stop it Mum. You don't have to say anything Ellie.

Mrs Fletcher's jaw goes tight but she doesn't tell Fletch off. Fletch is on Ellie's side again. She watches his pale head, his back turned to her, the blue veins, the pink skin shining through his feather hair. Something so delicate, so perfect as this made the kids' teeth itch, they did not know why they wanted to break him. Ellie knew. But she wouldn't let them.

After Betty's they 'hit the shops' and there are lots of people walking at a jagged tumble pace, slowly slowly juddering past one another.

- Hold hands – we don't want to lose anyone.

Fletch takes Ellie's empty sleeve loosely in his hand. It's still there. Dead. The word fills her head, opens up and swallows everything. York is old and dead is everywhere. It's nothing like the sea that rolls its dead up and softens them to sand, or the Green Hill which keeps the dead safely knotted in its roots. York wears its dead on the outside. All the houses are stacked on top of one another, fat squares of whitewashed stone risen up from the ground only to be squashed by bigger buildings. Black lines criss-cross and stitch the stacks together, shining with winking-eye windows. Here the dead don't need windows to come through: they are clickclacking on the cobbles and crouching in the hooded roofs that lean towards one another, whispering between themselves, narrowing the darkening sky.

Mrs Fletcher is wearing red leather boots like the lady version of Ellie's own red wellies and Ellie stares hard remembering their exact shade. Red is an alive colour and she follows it through the crowds, as though Mrs Fletcher is an upside-down lighthouse. Ellie can't see above the people jostling into her, surrounding her with a damp wool smell, she sees only the boots.

- Shall we go take a look in the Monster?
- She means the Minster. We're not five Mum.

At the end of the street a huge building rises up and up, peaked spires for ears and raised haunches like a sleek stone cat. It is Church, the biggest church Ellie has ever seen.

Its insides smell like Ellie's church and its noises sound like Ellie's church, the scuff taptap of shoes on tiles. But this church is full of stone people. Grey kings standing up, fat men lying down, cut-out woody husbands and wives kneeling for prayers. None of the living people are really praying, only walking with their heads tipped up to the ceiling making themselves dizzy. Whisper whisper and oops sorry. Fletch's mum leads them past a big blue clock, the colour of summer sea. It has hands that move by them-selves and it tells time-time but it also tells the sun and the stars. Ellie looks for the stars her dad has shown her – the Big Dipper, the North Star – and they are here on this clock, their same sky tucked inside. She snaps it all inside her head to take back for her dad, who would love to see the star o'clock. This is his clock, Ellie thinks, no crash bang tick-tock just the slow blue arc of stars, where he isn't old because the days are too small to matter.

- This way.

Mrs Fletcher leads her through more passages and arches and corners and then big black wooden doors and then –

- This is the Chapter House.

The whispers are louder here. Shushshush they go, sailing up criss-cross arches that fold into a roof-star. Ellie wants to send a sound leaping all the way to the top. She licks and purses her lips, blows the way her dad showed her – a wet whistle, a skirling sound, springing up the ribs of stone. It is a shocking sound, so loud, a kiss, better than prayers and candles. Ellie felt it on the soft part of her neck.

- Stop that.

An old lady in a squished-bun hat peers down at her and wags a fat finger.

- Whistling women and crowing hens bring the Devil out of his den.

She points up and Ellie tilts her head to see hundreds of small stone faces, not statue-still, good-faced saints, no, these stones are pulling faces, fingers in noses, tugging hair and lips and cheeks and fighting, bird-faced, wild-pawed. Not saints who died; dead and back again.

- Ellie, would you like to light a candle for your mum?
- I don't like it here, can we go?
- Don't you think your mum would like a candle?

Yes, her mum would like a candle but who knows what would come in through the window if Ellie lit one in here? What if the stone-head people came rolling in, with their fingers up their noses and their tongues out? Ellie shakes her head.

- When was the last time you saw your mum Ellie?

No one had told her not to talk about her mum and the pyjama people. She knew that out loud it would sound like lies and wrong and red pen. But no one asked her any proper questions either, like, 'Where's yer mam?' which doesn't have to be answered. Mrs-Fletcher-Call-Me-May knew how to make sticky questions like treats, like banana floats that were hard to say no to. So she said –

- Pyjamas.
- Leave it Mum.
- Ellie you can tell me the truth about your mum's breakdown.

Break? Her mum's not broken. Not down. She's Mum and soft-velvet-head and light-the-candle and be-good-for-your-daddy. She's the same. What does Call-Me-May know?

- Did you say she was dead because it feels like you've lost her?
- Bog off.

Ellie pulls away from Fletch, his too-loose grip letting her fall into the crowd, out of the Monster, taptaptap her wellies sliding over the rockled cobbles. She presses into heavy coats that smell of strange houses and different ways. There are dark hollows in the city, little open mouths, and Ellie dives into a tunnel that splits two buildings – a ginnel, her dad said, they run between the Baithouses at home. She hears drip drip, frost-melt from the bricks above. Ellie can touch both sides of the wet ginnel, guiding herself in the tarry black, the cold pulsing through her gloves. If she keeps going she thinks she could walk to dead. Then the soft rocking hush of – pit pad, pit pad. There. She is not alone. Stand still, her dad had always told her. Don't run. She presses herself against the wall, trying to push her heart still against the cold stone. The pit-padding stops.

Wet meaty breath warms Ellie's hand through the thin wool of her mitten. 'Hold your hand out, let it smell you,' her dad had said. That was stray dogs though, not wolves who have come from the sea. Ellie pulls off her glove and drops it to the floor, holding out her bare hand to the darkness; nothing, then breath on her skin, feathery whiskers, a cold nudge – a nose, unmistakable – pressing itself into the cup of her palm. A rough tongue laps up and around her fingers. Ellie slides her other hand over thick coils of matted fur, exploring. This is the wild thing she is not to touch. The wolf's eyes are open, smiling coals in the dark. The wolf's growl thrums, filling up all the darkness outside and inside Ellie's head.

- Go on then. Take me away.

She shouts but the wolf doesn't move. She pushes it with both hands, digging her fingers into its ribs.

- Eat me then.

But it turns and circles back to her.

- Go on.

Ellie speaks the words into the deep fur of the wolf's neck; it dips its head. Ellie curls down, leaning into its warmth. The wolf nudges its head into Ellie's pocket – the chips.

- You're hungry.

The chips had stuck to the paper napkin but the wolf eats them, paper and all, and licks her fingers clean. The wolf gives a few exploratory bumps to her other pocket.

- All gone.

She turns her palms up, open, empty. The wolf taps under Ellie's hand with its nose; Ellie understands now that this means head rub. The wolf closes its eyes in contentment as

Ellie rubs the short velvety fur of its brows, working her way down, behind the ears, her fingers catching on something rough and bristly at the wolf's neck.

- What's this?

A fisherman's rope, the kind her dad uses to make the mouth of a net. The rope still has a little lace skirt of twine tied to it and a chewed nub of float. A ghost net, broken and drifting, you don't see it and then – too late. Ellie has found dead porpoises and gulls tangled at the tideline, drowned, wearing nets like this. She works her little curved penknife into the rope, sawing, for luck. The fibres are wet and tight and hard to cut. The wolf wriggles and pulls away and Ellie leans into it, pushing it against the wall with her knee and hip to keep it steady so she won't hurt it. The last fibre pops and she tugs the rope away, leaving an angry raw line where the rope has bitten into the wolf's skin and worn away the fur. That's all it wanted. That and chips. Ellie rolls up the short coil, exactly like the rope her dad keeps by the fireplace.

- Will you bring me luck then?

The wolf yips, a little happy sound. Ellie does what her dad did when she got hurt on the beach. She spits on her finger and dabs at the sore skin.

- Better now. Good as new in a bit.

The wolf flinches a little, opens its mouth, its tongue flickering red, drinking in a deep sniff at a new shape in the ginnel.

- Ellie.
- Fletch.
- No.

Ellie catches at the shadow moving hungrily towards Fletch, knocking him onto his back, then out of the ginnel and into the human crowd of two-legs and bags and hands, bashing and knocking. She stares into the thick mass of feet but the wolf has gone. She tries to help Fletch to his feet.

- Ow get off.
- You get off.

They stand and are quickly pulled into and along by the moving swell of people.

- Who were you talking to?
- You followed me.
- Why did you run away?
- Your mum's weird.
- Sorry.
- Why's she like that with the questions. She's worse than maths.
- I know. But you shouldn't have said bog off.
- Sorry.

- You ran.

- You let me go.

- I couldn't find you and then I heard you, talking to someone.

- Where's your mum then?

- I lost her.

- Will she be mad?

- Yeah.

Ellie takes Fletch's hand.

- Get off.

But he holds on tight as she marches through the crowd, looking down for the light of the red boots.

- We're lost.

- No we're not.

Ellie pulls up the hood of her red wool coat, head down marching on, pulling Fletch behind her, walking right through a group of older boys who are taking up the street with their big-dog laughing and rough-push tumbling. One of them pushes his big nose into Fletch's face.

- Hey blondie.

The boy trips Fletch so he tumbles behind her and she stops then. She sees what his mother sees and she brushes his damp hair out of his eyes.

- It's OK.

Ellie turns and butts her head forward into the face of the laughing boy, his well-fed smile around white perfect teeth. But she has seen sharper teeth than his today.

- Bog off.

Fletch is shocked when the boy backs off.

- You said bog off. Again.
- Yes. Bogoffbogoffbogoff. You say it.
- Bogoffbogoffbogoff.

An old lady with a floofy hat mumbles through her slack teeth.

- Where's your mummy?
- Bogoffbogoffbogoff.
- Eeh well.

Two-together, tongues tapping their swearing march, and all the while Ellie's eyes scan the ground for red boots and the wolf. Then May's hand, the smell of soft leather reaching for Fletch.

- You're OK?

She pats around him, smoothing, straightening him back to her.

- Get off Mum.

- Ellie Fleck – what the hell were you doing running off like that?

- I didn't . . . I just . . . You said broken.

- I told you to stay close.

- I . . .

- What's wrong with you? Look at me!

The red glove reaches for Ellie, open palm. Ellie knows, after Stephen, how to tense for a hit.

- Mum, what are you doing?

Fletch jumps in front of her and Ellie watches May's hand curl and retract.

- I wasn't . . . Oh God. Sorry, Ellie sorry.

It was Fletch, Ellie knows, he made you want to hurt others to save him. May kneels down, taking all of Ellie in.

- I'm sorry, both of you. We'll all hold hands like this now.

Her grip is too tight, and weighted by an adult for the first time, Ellie feels pulled down.

In the car Mrs Fletcher puts on the tape of *Fantastic Mr Fox* and Fletch falls asleep whilst Mr Fox is busy tunnelling, tunnelling, tunnelling. Out of the dark window, past her own reflection, Ellie watches the rough black shape

running between the hedgerows alongside the moving car.
It is OK. It is running with her – home. Then she too slept.

- Ellie, the house is dark, is there someone home?

But as May says it, Ellie's father opens the front door.

- Now, if ever you need me, if ever you need to talk
to me I'm here.

Ellie remembers the red hand. Fletch's head tilts up, he's
awake.

- Shut up Mum. She can look after herself. Bye Ellie.
See you at school.

Her father opens the car door.

- All fine?
- Yes Peter, a lovely day out.

Big fat liar, Ellie thinks.

- Say thank you to Mrs Fletcher.
- Thank you Mrs Fletcher for a lovely day. Nosy, stupid traitor, want to know where my mum is? I'll light a

candle and they'll come take you there and you can play slappy face with the pyjama people.

But Ellie didn't say that last bit out loud. She might have to save a skull stone for Mrs Fletcher though, if she didn't stop asking sticky questions.

Ellie holds her dad's hand, dry and warm, on the way back to the front door. The night is freezing, made colder by the snug car, and the cold pinches her face.

– Cars make you soft.

Her father said, yes they do. They stand in the porch to wave Mrs Fletcher off. This is how you say goodbye when someone leaves; this is the difference between went and taken. In the heavy part of her mind Ellie saw the ambulance, the men's grey backs bent like beetles as they held her mother down, who did not wave.

There were no lights on because Ellie had the meter money. The fire was blazing and smelled like the sea.

– Are your feet wet?

Her dad had put out thick socks to warm, so she puts them on and stretches out on the threadbare rug. Douglas is on her dad's chair, sitting in the recently vacated patch. She yawns at Ellie.

Ellie goes to the electric meter to put her coins in.

- Just wait pet and look at that moon in the dark. And there's the Evening Star.

- I nearly forgot. There was a clock, Dad, a star o'clock. I think it must be for fishermen. Why do you need to know the stars?

- So that when there's no land and nothing but water you look at the star maps in the sky to get home.

- It didn't say the way home. It only told the time in stars.

- So what star o'clock is it then?

Ellie leans against the window squinting to see before her breath rubs out the sky.

- Seven stars past the moon.
- Bedtime?
- No way, that's two hundred stars past the moon.
- Go on then put the lights on.

Ellie puts her coins in, one, click, two, click, three, click, four, click. The lights jolt on. Ellie's rope isn't on the wall by the fire. She takes out the rope that she cut from the wolf and hangs it on the nail.

- Eh, I've told you not to play with that, you'll lose it.

A sneak gust blows in from the broken back door, disturbing the fire.

- Dad? A board's come loose.

Ellie shoves it back into place – pushing the nail back in, grey fur snagged on the splinters.

- Look.

Her dad rubs the top of his head under his cap.

- Bloody cat.

Ellie knew it wasn't Douglas's fur, which was soft and downy black. This is rough and smells of salt and grease.

- Dad, I need to make a net.

14.

The best thing about no-church Sundays are Baithouse Sundays and the Baithouse is the best place in the world. It is along the path and through the gate out the back of the garden. It is squat and white like a hand-drawn house. It is not for playing – don't touch, you'll get filthy, pass me that. It smells like tallow and oil and smoke and tea and tar and salty as chips and fish skin. It smells like her dad. Ellie plays outside on the cobbles and watches his head bobbing through the open top-half of the door. Or she helps him skein mussels for the long lines with the flat little bone-handled knife. She's only allowed to touch this knife when he's there watching. Light won't go in, it's like it's scared of getting mucky. The window is only four small squares of glass. It doesn't open for visitors. The sou'westers hang from a hook by the door and her dad once told the nosy kids they were spacesuits.

- You tell your mam I'm going to the moon on Monday.

They did.

Floats bulb across the beams and nets roil like storms on the ceiling. Netting needles hang like wooden fish from the wall. The shelves, made of salt-bitten wood, hold screws and nails in oily jars and paint. They're deep so you have to reach your hand right to the back for the thing you want. Ellie's little hands are best, so it's her job. She closes her eyes and mouth so as to feel what she's looking for. Cottony webs and long-line hooks tickle her fingertips. Prick. Red dewdrop. Make a wish. Suck your finger. Packed in by the door, keeping out the drafts, are their fat-bellied sacks of sea-coal.

- Make yourself useful.

Ellie shovels the powder into newspaper packets for the fire. Seams of black grains line the moons of her fingertips. Only a long soak in the bath will get them out. Pictures she painted long ago with finger dabs curl up in the window. Mum, Dad, Ellie in blurred fingerprints, fat whorling thumb bodies. The black stove sits crookedly in the corner, chuffing smoke and eating whatever is thrown inside it, like a dog – don't touch. She chucks in a sea-coal packet and the fire spits and whispers. Shush.

- Are you watching?

She is. She watches her dad tug the bight and make a starter loop for her. She wants to do it. But he says no, it will take too long.

- Watch.

He says again. She could do it herself. But now, watching him, it looks impossible. The way he tosses a perfect loop of silk twine and threads the needle through and pinches with his thumb and finger and, magic, another mesh and another and another, drooping white in the Baithouse murk.

- Here.

The net needle's smooth, slippery in her hand. The twine wriggles. She throws her loop, pulls the needle tight – snag – wrong.

- No you've dropped your loop, the trick is to pinch here, look.

It's so awkward with her short fingers. Her knuckles and joints are bony just like his but have none of his grace. He shows her again, his hands flickering. She knows they hurt. She heard him crack his fingers, joints popping like sparks from the fire. She makes a loop, the knot holds this time but it's sloppy, looser than her dad's neat row of diamonds. She kicks her legs on the stool.

- Show me again.

This time she watches, eyes open, mouth open, she copies the loops and knots in her head, letting them sink in like wind-cuts in sand. She makes her loop, threads it. Exactly like his.

- Well done chick.

He rubs her head, the pads of his fingers warm on her scalp. Her hands are always cold.

- What's it for?
- Homework.

He laughs.
It's sort of true.

★

There was once a mother . . .

This story has no end, it can't be finished even with And then. But a net, like the one that had pulled Ellie up from who knows where? A net was exactly what Ellie needed. And a knife – but she had one already, curved for cutting the caught thing out.

Ellie makes the net pulling it tight with the wooden net needle and Douglas tries to catch the empty loops with her paw. She does not rush, using the gauge to keep the squares neat, not too small, not too big, so it will just catch what it's meant to.

15.

The sky breathes shallow breaths, its great grey belly full of a storm, heavy with the promise of snow. On Monday it was still grey boring November and now it's Tuesday and 1st December. Ellie puts a curling tail on the D. Christmas is sneaking in on all of the classes, blurring them together into a fluff of cotton wool. History and science have been replaced with window painting and paper chains, looping great fronds of crêpe into strings that are already sagging from her classroom roof. One snaps in the heat and snakes its way across their desks, making everyone jump. The sharp edges of maths are blunted as they all plot snowmen on graph paper and paste more cotton wool over the blue squares. Fletch shows her where to mark her x's, then snowmen appear where once only jagged lines crawled meaninglessly up the page.

In assembly they make Christingles – Mrs O'Dowd would have hated them. Ellie got a white letter from Mrs Hill, which said, 'You will need an orange, cocktail sticks and Dolly Mixtures.' Ellie brought hers in her bait-box. They stuck a red tape belt around the orange. All the children seemed to know that the orange meant the world and the red tape is love and blood somehow both together. The cocktail sticks with Dolly Mixtures are the sticky fruits of the earth for the four corners of the world. Her Church, where she took her Communion and drank Jesus's real blood, did not do this, did not know of this, did not know about the orange and the world and the four corners – how could the earth have corners? They, the priests and the sour-faced grey women who guarded the Communion wafers would never have let an orange – something so sweet, so fresh – be God's world. Such a gift, with no hidden bitterness, no secret test of temptation offered up in blood and love together – just itself, no catch. Even the name – Christingle, jingle – sounds like Christmas and everything forbidden. It glows with the songs she is not supposed to sing, a bright new language of 'Joy to the World'. A language which does not belong to Dead Seas, deserts and Pharisees. At her mother's church you ate God, but he was dry and stuck to the roof of your mouth and you had to kneel and beg and say Amen and the wine made your eyes sting and your stomach flinch – and maybe that's what they meant by madPaddy? Because the Troubles as far as these children could see were just angry shouting fat men on TV, loud and spitting words that they could not understand. But the mean-dirty-trick-of-it-all – to give you sour wine and dry bread and call it a miracle – that, they could understand and fear. These oranges of a gentle Jesus just gave themselves up to you. The juices run down Ellie's chin in sticky rivers, her lips tingling – Christingle – all through the snow-waiting day.

★

- *Oui*.

French Club is after school and they make Christmas cards that say '*Noël*'. In French, Ellie is good at drawing the smiling spikes of holly leaves and dusting everything with glitter and even though they are the same Christmas card cut-outs that they use in normal lessons, they are different, better. In French everyone speaks to one another in concentrated bursts of smooth '*ooohs*' and clipped '*aas*'. The surprise that these sounds can be passed across a desk and understood means that they are sacred and therefore not for nastiness. Everyone speaks to Ellie in feathered dancing syllables and wants her to speak back, to know they too have been understood. They do not know the words for mad or Paddy in French. The questions are not trick questions and the answers flow out in lilts, '*Il fait froid.*' Ellie likes French Ellie. French Ellie smiles and says, '*Oui.*'

So, when Ellie sees her father standing in the heavy darkness, glitter stuck under her fingernails and her breath hot and orangey and light – she feels she is bursting.

- Do you want to go for the tree?

She reaches out to him to give him some of this light, the starlight at her fingertips, a whole universe full.

- *Oui!*

The few remaining children wave at Ellie and dash into cars whilst she lets her dad guide her up onto the croggy-bar. He pedals into the wind, but her face is still warm from the French room.

They cycle to the bottom end of the town, to where its wide mouth narrows slowly to the town clock, brick red and dangling with Christmas lights flitting in the sea wind. Ellie likes this end best as it opens out onto the Stray. It's dark, but Yvonne's is still open, they can see the red and green lights – onoffonoff. Yvonne's fruit 'n' veg shop stretches out like a big dog between the posh shops. There are spray-snow patterns on the long windows – waving snowmen and a leaping three-legged deer. Big boxes of earthy vegetables – cabbages, potatoes, carrots and sprouts – tumble out and smell of plodding long walks.

The Christmas trees, a rootless leaning forest, have a new smell, a Christmas smell. Her dad shakes out a tree from the bunch; it is scrawny but there aren't many left to choose from. The tree is almost as tall as her father, bigger than last year's, and Ellie wants this one with its outstretched branches, even if they are a little bare and bent. She takes off her gloves to touch a bud, sticky with sap.

- How much?

Yvonne shuffles out to talk to her dad; she's a big woman who can suck down half a cigarette in one smiling breath and she's wrapped up well with thick protective gloves. Ellie follows Yvonne's gaze to the prices, in pounds on the window, sprayed out in snow. Her dad should not ask, not when the price is there, but he has to, Ellie knows that. She bites down on her embarrassment (with two r's and two s's) and it warms her from the insides. Yvonne turns her smile to her dad and winks at Ellie.

Ellie nestles in and breathes the sharp tang of pine sap. She feels it at the back of her head and in her belly at the same time, like being awake and hungry – the sharp spike of life. Evergreen, a new word. Jesus had to die, but the tree does not. Jesus died for sins but the tree does not care, it keeps on living. Yvonne puts some holly in a paper bag and hands it to her, her cigarette dancing in her mouth as she moves. Her dad shuffles deep in his pockets and hands the money – less than what it says on the window – to Yvonne. He straps the tree to his bike with the orange twine he always carries coiled in his coat.

– You walking home in this cold? Snow's comin'? It'll be bad.

Ellie's dad shrugs a little, still smiling. Yvonne shakes her head and drops two big tangerines in her dad's wide blue pockets, orange like the twine.

Ellie likes to walk, to be out in the cold with her dad, half closing her eyes and squinting at the stars stretching their light across the dark sky. She wants to hold on to this, the smell, the wink, the cold – Noël she thinks, this is

Noël. She had been waiting for the snow and now in the deep blue light it comes, a plump drift of cotton, slowly slowly, a soft tickle then a bite as it melts – ftsss. The first little falling thing lands on her bare hand, soft then sting, and the next lands on her eyelash, blurring the whole sky white. She can barely hold on to her grin. The clickclick-click of her school shoes is muffled as the air and ground grow thick with it. Her dad is grinning too.

They set off through the back streets, huddling close to the old red-brick walls, plumes of woodsmoke lifting from freshly lit fires and tempting them with someone else's warmth. Down, down through cobbled back-alleyways, stacked with lobster pots, salt and weed tang, even in this cold. These alleyways have their own rules, not street and road and lights and 'look what's coming', but hush and hide. The bike bounces unsteadily and Ellie keeps their pace quick. She breathes out and in through her red scarf that smells of home. More flakes are landing and bursting on her eyelids. Her dad turns around, his face alive – a child's. The tree, the snow, her father – the shadow of his cap over his face, and his face shining, the gift of it all. The snow lands on his dark blue coat making another sky with other stars, like the star clock.

He kneels down to Ellie, taking her pale hands into his own, his gloves wet and shining with tiny crystals. He lifts her hands to his mouth and blows a fire full of breath into the cup of her palms. From his pocket he takes out her soft yellow mittens. She wants to put this night away for safekeeping – to keep her father safe. She can see the lines framing his mouth, the tiny red cracks in the snow of his eyes. She holds tight on to his hand.

- Hey, settle down Ellie. Shall I tell you your story? I pulled up the nets and there you were, all blue and cold.

- Like a porpoise?

- Yes, like a porpoise. Like a pup. And I cut you free.

- And you took me home.

- From the sea.

- For luck.

- All right now? Come on then, quick march. Left, left, I had a good job and I left.

Ellie falls in step with her father's giant strides and whispers out into the snow hush.

- Left, left . . .

The bike ticking and the snow softly ftssing to the ground.

*

Ellie checks the boards on the broken-toothed door as soon as they get home whilst her dad puts the tree up in a bucket of sand. They leave it bare because his vertigo's 'playing up now' and it's bedtime and school in the morning. Ellie waits until her dad's sleeping and then crawls into his room, keeping low and quiet. This is when he looks most strange to her, when she can see the little boy in him under his grown man's skin.

Her dad is talking in his sleep; he does it a lot. Ellie likes to listen to the half-stories he never tells out loud, which wash over her and pull her under with him.

- Take me out with you.

He's talking to his dad, Ellie knows. He wants his dad to take him out on *Eleanor*, his coble. Ellie loves the coble because her dad does; she looks more like a sea-creature than something human hands made, with her horseshoe stern and her whale's belly rucked with barnacle tops. But *Eleanor*'s not her dad's boat any more. If they walk past the boat on the Prom her dad lifts her up to look into her orange insides, like a cut mussel. 'How's she lookin'?' he asks and Ellie says, 'Lookin' good.' But the last time Ellie looked was the summer and the paint was bubbled up and flaking, exposing the tender wood to salty teeth and there were painful gaps where the planks had started to dry out and shrink. Traitor. She knew the boat's hurts hurt him, the way it hurt him to be grounded on land because of the trick sway in his head. 'You can't keep a boat out o' the water you know.' Ellie knew.

Her dad could only make the nets and creels now, repair and bait them for other fishermen. They'd knock on the door and stand behind their barrow full of nets, the smell of the sea still on them. Sometimes, on a good day, her dad might get a spot on someone else's boat. Then he'd be out in the morning and come back steady, as though it was the sea that made him still and the land that shook him. He said it was like a rough sea – the vertigo – but inside his head. He said it was as though the sea had crept inside him one day for company, as though it had known he was lonely. Ellie frowned, 'Are you lonely dad?' He said his no-nos and shook his head. But Ellie knew from his sleeping that he would drift out on the pull of the sea inside him. Ellie crawls under his bed. From here she can see his hand over the side, clench, unclench – trying to hold on to something. She puts her hand inside his – he holds her like an oar.

16.

- Swimming today.

Ellie forgot to get a note. She always has a note because she is not to swim. Her father says he doesn't trust those life-guards – 'They're not looking, thinking about all sorts, they'll sit back and watch you drown.' But it's really because it's bad luck. Fishermen aren't supposed to learn to swim. Badluckbadluckbadluck.

- I can't.
- Do you have a note?

She can't say it's bad luck, not to Woodsy.

- I don't have a swimming costume.
- Go to Mrs Hill.

Mrs Hill does have a swimming costume. It's silver and Ellie likes it even though she doesn't want to like it. It glints and sparks like diamonds on the water on no-school days. Who did it belong to? Did they drown and die, were they taken and this is all that's left?

- I'm not to swim, Dad says.
- Why does he say that?
- I'll drown.
- You won't drown if you learn to swim will you – off you go Ellie. Don't forget this.

Mrs Hill hands her a towel.

It takes ages to get on the bus because everyone wants to skid on the frost patches on the path until Woodsy shouts. The bus smells of cigarettes and chips and bleach. Rachel is showing off. She's got a swimming badge on her costume and a certificate: 'Ten Metres' in swirly script and signed by Mr Lockwood in blunt black pen. Ellie doesn't know metres, only feet, and ten doesn't sound like much. She follows the girls into their changing rooms – turn left, turn right and another and, 'Hurry up Ellie,' a what turn? Where? So many doors.

The changing rooms are alive with racket as though noise might make them warm. Ellie's skin goes bumpy. There are only three cubicles. Magic little doors. Rachel and her sacred bra get one. Then it's a rush to see who will take the other two. Push and squabble. Amanda has a swimming cap for her long hair. She looks like an egg. Ellie doesn't want to take off her clothes here. Nononono. How could her dad forget the note? She knows beneath her clothes her skin is white, shiny as a fish's belly, not like their toffee-brown skin.

She watches Amanda wrap the towel around herself and step into her costume, making her own little private cocoon. Ellie does the same. Her skin looks translucent in the white lights, veins racing up her legs purpling. What will they see? What will they say? She wriggles the silver-skin costume up and under the towel. She is fish-skin. She is scaly-back. Fisherman's daughter – bad luck in the water. Rachel steps out from her cubicle in a bikini; it's like Hawaiian Barbie's, purple flower explosions. They all go 'ooh' like it's fireworks. Rachel's belly is white and buttoned tight just like Ellie's. A whistle blows and they push under the showers, soak hair and then have to walk-splash-walk through a little bath of stinging water to clean their feet.

It's warm and sticky inside the pool room like bath day. The pool stretches out, blue and square with perfect corners, nothing like the sea: it is tame water. Crabs would drown in here. It smells of sting and bleach, not salt. It says slap and patter and the voices screech around the tiles, no shush. This water doesn't speak to Ellie, it has no wolves hiding in it, no waves; no white claws curving in on themselves, just ripples cut with black lines.

Bad-luck shivers shake Ellie as she steps to the edge. The others push past her and jump straight in, the water catches them in their splashes. She stands well back because the edge makes her dizzy – is that vertigo?

– It will be all right Ellie. You go down the steps. Just hold the rail.

Fletch bobs up from the water then disappears under.

- Fletch is drowning.

The lifeguard doesn't hear. He's thinking all sorts whilst Fletch drowns. Then Fletch's head pops up again. He walks to the steps not drowned.

- You have to get in now.

He's right. They are all watching and she doesn't know which door would take her out even if she could run on the wet floor. Just walking is hard. The steps are all bumpy under her feet like tiny stones and she grips the handrail tightly. The water is a wet shock. Every step down takes her deeper. Over her knees. Soaking the costume, turning its light silver to storm grey. The heaviness of the water holds her hips. Bad luck.

- Come on Ellie.

They are all in, floating like the black pips of seals she sees early in the morning. Floating and splashing like it's their water. How is it so easy? Now her teeth chatter and not with the cold. The water pulls and pushes, slapslapslapslap as though it wants to crawl up and over her. It goes up to her shoulders. Wrongwrongwrong.

- Ellie you need to keep moving.

She can't.

- Look, Woodsy will see and he'll make you jump in. He makes everyone who's scared jump in. You have to listen. You have to put your face in the water, then you won't be scared.

No no no no. This is her first worst dream. The back door – rattattat – and the water coming to take her away. She's caught. There's no way forward, no way back. She can't move.

- Like this Ellie, just pinch your nose and . . .
- Ellie Fleck!

OK, OK she will. She will. She puts her lips to the water and it closes over her face. She pulls her head down, fighting the air inside her. Shush, the water over her ears. Shush and shush. She lets it push her shoulders down. The quiet is enormous. The warm weight of it. She is shining – her skin opening into a thousand eyes. She lifts her feet. No earth beneath her, no running. All Ellies are here – yes, and out-of-bounds, and the water can hold them all.

Fletch is waving. Hello. He is pointing up. No. He can't see it. Above her is her own back door, rippling, unbroken. She must not break it. She can stay here in the quiet, no breaking, no cutting. But hands close around her and pull her up, head first to the surface – creakcrack – breaking through.

- Spit it out Ellie.
- What's the madPaddy doing, trying to drown herself?

- Spit.
- Ellie – how did you hold your breath for so long?
- I don't know.
- You nearly . . . Ellie don't ever do that again.

★

At home-time, Mrs Hill says she can keep the silver-skin costume. It is wet in her bag. She will not tell her dad that she went swimming: it will scare him and she won't be allowed back to school and there will be the grey man again. But also she cannot tell him what it was like to be under, not breathing, alive in her own skin and in the hold of deep water. She cannot say that to him because he cut her out and took her home for luck.

Ellie waits till most of the others have gone. She likes the quiet emptiness of the school after the screamers have left. She is picking up her bag from the cloakroom when she hears slurping. Stephen and Rachel are huddled up, Stephen's hand on Rachel's waist. They look as though they are about to – no they were – kissing.

- Yuck.
- You're yuck. Ellie! Come back here. Don't you tell.

Ellie starts her stompy walk, as fast as she can go without running, but she trips, her bag spilling out across the floor. Rachel catches her.

- Promise you won't tell. Eeurgh. What's this?

It is Ellie's net, all rolled up, the wooden net needle still stuck in, and the wolf's rope, her rope, damp and tarry.

- Is this your clothes?
- It's none of your business.

Rachel picks up the net, stretching it, dropping loops, the needle dragging on the floor.

- Promise you won't tell about Stephen.
- I'm not going to tell anyone, it's so yuck.
- It's not yuck it's private.
- But you've got his spit in your mouth.

She rushes at Ellie and wraps the net round her, pulling it tight.

- Have not. Take it back.
- Stop it, ow, you're ruining it, ow, you're hurting.
- Just take it back.
- No. Why do you care?

Rachel stomps on the net needle, splintering it with her patent heels.

- Hey, Ellie. I was waiting for you.

Ellie turns to see Fletch; now it's Rachel who is running a stupid huffy run, pushing past Fletch.

- Hey! What did she do? What's this rope thing?
- Just get me out.

Fletch's gentle fingers work to unravel Ellie, tapping gently at the loops binding her at her neck.

- You're touching me.
- I have to.

So close, kneeling next to her, she can feel his breath on the parting between her plaits and the soft pads of his fingers. It makes her skin tighten.

- You're out. Are you OK? Let me . . .
- Bog off.
- Hey stop being a cow.
- Bog off please.

He backs off into the dark playground. Rachel and the kiss and the slobber and the net, she feels yuck and Fletch is part of the yuck. She didn't mean to do it but it is getting easier to hurt him to keep him away. She promises herself she will be better. Highland Toffee will make it better.

Ellie bundles the net into her bag and bolts out in the cold air beneath the stickle-black shadow of trees. A darker shadow purrs under the wind, making puffs of smoky air with its breath. The thurring gurroww makes Ellie feel alive just as the water did. Two moon-lamp eyes shine. Ellie holds out her hand into the darkness. She feels hot

166

breath cooling on her skin, then the wet cold nose and dripping whiskers. She smells that salt-water-sweet smell. She hunkers down, putting her two hands on the ground in front of her. The wolf shoves its huge head up under Ellie's arm, toppling her, licking her face, Ellie digging her fingers, scritscrat, into the wolf's deep rough.

The wolf noses her bag, nipping at the canvas.

- There's no chips. Look.

Ellie takes out the net, only a little damaged by stupid Rachel. The wolf paws it, curling its black lip up into a crooked grin. It tilts its head, not like when it wants to play or eat.

- It's good, look, only Rachel sort of messed it up a bit. It can't hurt you now.

Picking up the net in its mouth, the wolf runs out onto the road, weaving across the white slush.

- No, wait. Hey! It's mine, it's for her, it's to bring her back.

Ellie runs, her feet scattering out from under her on the slippery mulch. The wolf is gone. A car swooshes to a stop right next to her, kicking the day's pocked slush into her face. Cold little nips.

- You need to get in the car sweetheart. It's your mum.

Fletch's mum. Nosy Parker. But she said 'mum' so Ellie scrambles into the car whilst Mrs Fletcher talks too fast. Fletch opens and shuts the glove compartment with loud thunks that say he's not talking.

- Robin, stop that. Ellie your dad couldn't come for you, he's sorry.

Fletch's mum has been nervous with her ever since the red glove. Ellie did not think that she would ever have really hit her, but that she was angry because Fletch had followed Ellie and Mrs Fletcher loved him first.

They drive past the post office corner, where the lollipop lady stands, where her dad would wait for her, but not tonight. The warm velvety grey of the car is trying to lull her into a sleep.

- Now Ellie, if you need me for anything, you or your dad. Let me know.

'No way nosy cow,' Ellie thinks loud and red but she says —

- Thanks for the lift.

All the lights are on. No one is waiting at the white door, blue in the winter dark. Ellie presses down on the brass handle. Locked. She knocks. She waits. Things feel wrong. From outside looking in the tree lights blink cheerfully, exposing the tree's bare patch, and the walls glare white, freshly painted. Her dad had painted the room without her, even though Ellie always stirred the paint and did the skirting boards with her little brush. It should have been a no-school day but he'd done it by himself. The white spits of paint make stars on her father's skin, she can see him through the window. She can't go in – not with all the wet of the bad luck still on her. Her father is talking to someone. He sees her and the door opens.

– Ellie's home.

Ellie smells her first, sweet and wrong somehow, a new smell into the smoke-and-scrubbed-salt air of home. She's wearing a dress, tight in all the wrong places as though she had not dressed herself. Her lips are still raw and cracked, unable to smile – even though Ellie waited. Smiling still.

– Say 'hello' to your mum Ellie.

Ellie's mum, Kate, Katherine, Katie – turning Ellie's rope in her hands, twisting the frayed edge tight again. How did she get the rope? The wolf?

– Give your mum a kiss.

Ellie leans to kiss her mother but she feels like a light just switched off, still hot. The wolf had brought the rope and Ellie had made the net, nipped it and looped it with her own fingers, made the holes and then . . .

- Hello Mum.
- See good as new.

Ellie's mum opens her mouth, making a clacking sound, and turns to her dad, like a baby bird. The best way to get her dad to love you – be broken, be fallen down a chimney, or washed up with oiled feathers, be caught in a net. He dashes into the kitchen clattering tea things, his bigness making his rush more difficult.

- Ellie come and help.

Ellie realises then, running to her father and reading his slow out breath, that he won't leave her alone with her mother, he's frightened. He arranges the tea things all on the tray and jingles back into the front room.

There are biscuits – chocolate digestives – dark not milk, for her mother. Ellie half-fills her cup with milk and tops up with tea, pale, with bubbles floating on top – 'Money,' her father would say, as though it might come to them. She dips her biscuit in deep and sucks the melting chocolate layer. Her father pours her mother's tea, a deep tan colour, two sugars and a ting ting of the spoon on the side of the cup. Not looking at either of them, her mother grasps the cup with both hands and takes harsh slurps and gasps, hot brown strands of sugary tea running down the sides of her mouth, unnoticed. Ellie feels hot, the itch of the yuck feeling coming back, and she turns away. Her father looks at the round brass clock, wrapped in tinsel for Christmas, the second-hand palpitating around its tiny private circle. He takes out a brown bottle from his coat pocket. He puts a tiny pill down next to her mother's saucer. Without looking, her mother takes the pill between finger and thumb and opens her mouth wide to take it.

And then . . . Mr Lockwood had told her to stop writing 'And then' in her stories; he said she had to make the pieces link together, but she didn't know what he meant. How else were you supposed to explain the strange way time buckled in on itself and threw you off its back? A new path – a sharp fin shudder – had risen up out of the old path and carried her on it – away from the thudticktick and hard sounds of just her and her dad, to this new place. The old routine, sleep, wake, the rough gentle mangling of hair into a plait, sailing to school on the croggy-bar, or no-school and the sky smudged across the beach and sea-coal and the tide, shussshshusssh and Ellie-out-of-bounds and ftssss – all gone, all rolled into neat little pill time. And then . . . Ellie takes another biscuit, her tea barely warm enough to melt the chocolate; she looks to her dad for disapproval, but she doesn't get it.

The fire is lit and they stay like this, three around the tea tray. Ellie is on the rug watching the broken door held together with driftwood. Her father is on the couch still wearing his dark blue coat – just in case. Her mother is on her rocking chair trying to keep still. The bright lights take the heat out of the fire. There they sit and a smudged stain of a family stares back at them from the window's reflection as the night sets in. The tea goes cold and her father stands once to close the curtains.

Bedtime is kept and Ellie counts off her prayers on her fingers – not having had enough time to think up what new things she should ask for, she prays for the safety of all the animals and for her mother still to come home. She falls into a thick gooey sleep. The fire downstairs laps at the edges of Ellie's sleep, so she dreams of waves creeping crawling quietly up over the dunes. Her first worst dream.

17.

Ellie is up early, long before the lazy winter sun, to do her jobs before school. It was Ellie's job, in the Before, to bring tea and toast to her mum in bed on Mondays, the first wake-up of the week, a treat her mum used to sleep through. It is her job now, again. Ellie makes the toast, the butter melting and sliding over the edges, the marmalade glistening – it all looks so alive on the rusting tray with the pretty flowers, bright with bursts of red and peach. In the Now, her dad loops the loose knots of routine back around their lives. The Monday toast for Monday 7th December. Seven is good luck. It will be an everything-in-its-place day. There is a pill waiting on the tray, pale blue like Rachel's new shoes, even though school shoes are supposed to be black. Routine and blue pills, they make a ghost net to wrap tight around her mother and Ellie hopes she doesn't struggle or see.

- Mum.

The word feels wrong in Ellie's dry mouth. 'Muuhm' is too heavy to put into a whole sentence. 'Mum,' she tries, it sinks the line again. It's like feeding the birds, holding the food and trying to hide at the same time. Ellie sets the tray down and touches her mum's shoulder, then gently smooths her hair. She smells of sleep and old-lady toffees – too sweet, that's because of the medicine. Her mother reaches past Ellie for the pill. Ellie listens to the dry gulp as she swallows it whole and her eyes fizz out. Then a splinter of light pokes in through the window. Ellie dips her finger in the slush of marmalade and butter, tasting sun in the juice, watching for something shared like hunger. Her mum smiles and picks up a soggy slice of toast. Her lips smack hungrily around it.

- Good Mum.

Still too heavy for a whole sentence but lighter – orange and sticky.

★

Ellie packs her school bag ready but the pages in her homework book are still full of long empty grey lines.

There was once a mother . . .

She could write it now for Woodsy. **The mother was not dead. She ate her toast and drank her tea.** Not the part about pills and 'side effects'.

The mother put on her dress but Ellie did up the buttons.

Her mother's fingers were stiff and had forgotten.

The mother plaited the little girl's hair. (That was a lie, but Ellie couldn't help herself, the story always wanted more from her.)

The mother waved to the little girl before she went to school. The mother waited until the little girl got home from school and she would have a story.

Ellie could do a picture and she would only need the brown crayon. Boring and normal and good. And then what – **The End** – she couldn't just write that. Even Stephen tried to make his stories ten lines long. And then and then . . .

*

– We're in the hall today.

The great arched hall, the ribbed ceiling breathing in and out the hot breath of children, the cast-iron radiators round the walls burning comfort into reddening fingers. The floor spread out in a repeating pattern of dark wood blocks, sticky with polish. Woodsy tenderly gathers together a bunch of stapled paper booklets with a wobbly hand-drawn donkey on the front and passes them around the children.

– This is the Nativity Play. You are each going to audition for the main parts.

Hands shoot up.

- Those with no parts will make up their own religious performance for the end.

Hands drip down.

- You will have forty-five minutes to practise in your groups. I have taken pains to write the script, please stick to it.

Mr Lockwood floats off to Stephen's group where kings are already looking down on shepherds and Rachel manages to appear both trendy and serene as Mary.
Fletch looks to Ellie.

- How are we going to do all the parts?

Ellie flicks through the script quickly looking for the story she knows – Herod killing babies, swooping angels with messages of burning light – but there are only more badly drawn donkeys and the wrong story.

- It starts in the wrong place. They get straight on the donkey. Look: That's rubbish. First Mary is visited by the Angel Gabriel and then the Holy Spirit puts Jesus inside her.
- What? Ellie, he said we have to do his script.
- But it's wrong.
- Ellie stop, you have to be good or Woodsy'll kill you.
- This will be good. We'll just change this little bit here so that Mary meets the Holy Spirit and then Joseph

gets mad and then they can get on the donkey. Have you got your pocket torch?

   – Ellie.

   – Just this bit here.

   – Why can't you ever do what he says? Just be a normal kid. This is why Woodsy hates you.

No one had said it out loud before. But it was always there, like a splinter you couldn't dig out. She doesn't want him to hate her. She just wants to do things right.

   – But Woodsy's done the wrong story!

   – OK, OK, we'll do it, just this bit.

The Holy Spirit was feathered and light and God and not God. It was hard to explain so Ellie lay on the floor, flickering the torch around the arched ceiling. The hall's soft darkness allowed the Holy Spirit to appear shaking, shivering above them.

   – That's cool.

Amanda drifts from the edges of Rachel's group towards Ellie and Fletch and the light. She has taken back her rolled-up cardigan, which Rachel had stuffed up her own jumper.

   – Oi. She's taken the Baby Jesus bump.

   – Can I be in your group?

   – Yeah, do you want to be the Holy Spirit?

   – Yes please.

Ellie instructs Amanda to start the Holy Spirit on the ceiling, then fly down in holy swoops to flicker in her face.

- So that's when Mary gets Jesus inside her, good, next we need a row between Mary and Joseph.
- You said just the Holy Spirit bit.
- But Joseph wants Mary to get on the donkey and ride for miles and miles and she's worried the donkey will get tired and sick. It's ages to Bethlehem. You can only ride the Burnisons' donkeys on the beach for thirty yards and then you have to get off. I don't think Mary would get on the donkey at all, I think she'd rather walk.
- Woodsy is going to blow.

Mr Lockwood summons the children together.

- Let's see what you've got. Stephen's group first.

Stephen bellows loudly at the innkeeper, Rachel stays stuffed and silent, they follow the script perfectly. Three kings bear precious gifts of one Garfield pencil tin, one solar-powered Casio scientific calculator and one collection of scented rubber fruit. The shepherds adore with ties tied around their heads whilst the other Steven, the donkey, watches Rachel, hungrily munching prawn cocktail crisps for hay.

- Excellent. Ellie, Robin, Amanda, what have you got for us?

Ellie lies down on the floor, covering herself with Fletch's blazer, Fletch turns off the lights and Amanda's Holy Spirit dances on the ceiling, swooping down over the children's heads to rest, flickering on Ellie's eyes. The lowly shepherds let out an involuntary 'ooh'. In the darkness Ellie's eyes burn and she realises that Mary must have been afraid of letting the light inside her.

- Yes Holy Spirit, I will be the Mother of God.
- Ms Fleck you are off script. What are you supposed to be?
- I'm Mary, the Holy Virgin, being visited by the Holy Spirit and getting Jesus.
- Can I be in Ellie's group too?

Asks Steven the donkey.

- There is no Ellie's group. Well done Stephen and Rachel, your group wins. Ellie get up, saints don't lie on the floor.

The children drift, Stephen and Rachel's group pulls away and together, sucking Amanda inside. Theirs is the well-done-best-group boring group. Amanda settles for being demoted from Holy Spirit to lowly shepherd. Ellie and Fletch are left stranded on the edges of the hall. Fletch folds his arms in a huff and he looks like his mum.

- So what'll we do now? Woodsy said something religious.

- I was thinking Best Man Dead?
- Woodsy'll flip.
- Not if we do it with saints.
- Best Saints Dead?
- No – How Saints Die.
- Ace. Which saints should we kill?

The bell rings for home-time before they can decide.

Ellie says goodbye to Fletch at the gates, she doesn't want to see his mum all smiles and red boots and 'What did you two do today?' 'Kill saints,' Ellie would say, Ha. But Fletch comes hopping right back to her.

- Mum says I can come back to yours but only for half an hour. We can make the rest up by then. We'll make it really good so Woodsy'll have to stop picking on you.

The car has already driven off, Ellie can't tell him to go home.

- OK.

But there are rules at Ellie's house.

- You can't come in the house; you can't look in the windows. Or else.
- Or else what?

Ellie didn't know.

Ellie's dad meets her at the corner by the post office but she can't get on the croggy-bar to get back to her mum quick sharp today. Her dad looks at Fletch.

- Where's he going?
- With us. We need to rehearse the play Dad, for school. Just half an hour. Only in the garden.

He doesn't say no.

★

Fletch is out of breath by the time they get to Ellie's house because Ellie and her dad walked so fast to get back to her mum. Ellie's dad goes straight in and closes the door behind him. No 'Hello, come on in and have a cup of tea,' no visitors' rules.

- This way.

Ellie leads Fletch down the alley that runs to her back garden. She can hear the soft scrape of his gloves against the brick as he guides himself with his hands in the dark. She pulls him by the elbow around the sea-coal sacks so he doesn't trip.

- Watch it.
- Watch what? I can't see a thing.

She lifts the sneck on the gate open. Her dad has put the kitchen light on for them, so the garden swells with blue glow. Fletch stops by the shed.

- What's that smell?
- Lobster pots.
- This is your garden?

Stiffening sheets hang from the washing line; thick oily ropes coil in towers; driftwood for kindling is piled in wrecks; the path disappears into the bottom of the garden swallowed by snow and tangled trees.

- Yeah. Come on, we need to practise.

Quick, before pill time, lights on and left left but Ellie knows not to say that last bit.

*

The dark at the bottom of the garden pulls them in, they can barely see one another, just puffs of white breath. Ellie hangs from the washing line, she can feel her arms stretching and breaking as he spins her again on the wheel. The freezing snow soaks through her uniform, though it's nice and soft to land on when she opens her arms like wings. St Catherine would have liked the snow, especially when the wheel burned beneath her and shivered to splinters.

- Are you dead now?
- No.
- So how is she a saint if she doesn't die?
- She does die, but not on the wheel.
- I don't get it. It's your turn to kill me now. Use arrows.

All in all Ellie was not convinced death by arrows would work well on stage.

- Where're we going to get arrows from? And even if we did, we might hit the audience.
- But that's my best dead.
- It wasn't even the arrows that killed St Sebastian.
- You just said it wasn't the wheel that killed St Catherine.
- Yeah, but there aren't really a lot of fun dead lady saints to choose from, they're all, 'I don't want to marry you, I love God,' and then the men were all, 'Squish, you're dead then.'
- I want to die in a cool way too.
- We're good at stoning and crucifixion, and you get to die twice that way.
- I like arrows.
- I know ... but even without arrows it'll still be better than Stephen and Rachel, 'Ooh look at my hair I'm Mary.'
- Is that your mum?

The light in her parents' bedroom is on. Lights on for pill time. Kate stands at the window in just her nightie but it isn't bedtime. Statue still, her hair wet and shining, like Our Lady Star of the Sea.

- Don't look.
- She looks like you.
- Hough.

Ellie knocks Fletch down and the snow goes spuff around them like the flour when her mum used to make bread. Spuff.

- Ow.
- You have to go home now.

She needs him to go before he takes it all in – the garden, the nightie, her mother, the boarded-up door – and starts to add up all the broken pieces. Ellie drags Fletch back out to the street, where he belongs all bright and safe with the milk bottles and long-limbed lamps.

- Go home.

He sets off wrong, over the car park.

- That's towards the beach.
- I don't know the way.

They sit on Ellie's front step to wait for his mum. Ellie can feel the sulk rising in Fletch, not because she knocked him down but because he broke the rule and she made them stop.

- You were pretty good tonight, maybe you can get arrowed dead.
- But we need stuff to make it real, you know, like the kings had their gifts.
- I can make stuff. I promise. I'll show you tomorrow.

And she means it even though she doesn't know how to make anything but nets, she says it so that they can be two-together, only divisible by one and itself, so it's not really lying. His mum arrives and he gets swallowed good-bye by the soft closing of the car door. Ellie waves. No one sees her in the unlit shadow of her own door; only when her bum gets too cold does she get up and go in.

★

Ellie wasn't certain if she was sleeping. She was opening and closing her eyes in the dark room and trying to tell the difference when her dad's voice cut through the quiet.

- Kate.

She could feel his need in the broken bark of her mother's name.

- Kate, stop it now.
- Where is she? Where's my mother? Wake her up, get that child down here.

Now his voice crackled up the stairs and under Ellie's half-open door.

- Ellie, you up? Whatever you hear, you stay upstairs, right?

But Ellie was out of bed, already shuffling down the stairs on her bottom, muffling each movement. It is her fault.

There is her mum in her nightie, pacing the length of the too-small room calling, keening a word that sounds like mother. Ellie's dad sits in the kitchen, alone. Ellie can see his head resting in his hands and the rough prickles of his cigarette smoke catch at her throat as the bright tip burns itself out. He looks heavy, like a storm day.

Sluffslapsluff – Ellie hears her mother's bare feet on the cold tiles where the carpet runs out. She turns quickly and back onto the ghosts of roses, fast with the stickled jerks of someone caught or with something caught inside them, trying to get out. Kate stops watching her feet to turn to Ellie –

- Where's my mother? You said you'd bring her back for me?
- I tried.
- Ellie!

But her dad doesn't send her back to bed, he waits in the doorway behind his smoke. His blue coat is on ready.

- Tell me what you did?
- I did like you said Mum. I put out food, I lit the candle.
- Did you open the window?
- Yes.
- Then where is she?

Ellie tastes the spilt cream soda and smells the fire. It went wrong, she didn't know why. The wolf had come.

- Did anyone come?

- No.

- Liar. Who came for you?

The keening again and loud.

- I heard Granny. She wanted to come back.

- Liar.

- She said she wanted to come back but you weren't here. She didn't know me. I tried to show her the blue blanket but she was gone. We could catch her. Look, she was here.

Ellie shows her mum the folded blue blanket. Kate doesn't stop walking.

- She was here?

- Yes. We could catch her.

Ellie tracks her pacing mother, trying to find a break in the rhythm to enter, like a skipping rope turning. She leaps in, falling in step, sla-sla-p-p-sla-p-sla-p, bare feet padding. Ellie takes her mother's hand and she sings the song her dad taught her for getting home quick.

- Left, left.

And faster to outrun the ragged mother who wants to come in even though no feast is laid out and no candle is lit for her.

- Left left.

Ellie runs now, her mum following and the earth under them and two coal-warm eyes growing bigger and burning through the window watching.

Creak-crack. Ellie's little feet break pace first, sla-. She rolls onto her ankle and down. Kate stops, creak-crack, she settles then on the couch.

- We nearly caught her that time? Did we?

But Ellie's gone. Peter takes off his coat and wraps Ellie up in it as he carries her to bed. He brings up a hot-water bottle. She rouses at the comfort.

- Your feet are icicles pet.

He rolls his creamy sea-boot socks onto her small feet, rubbing the colour back into them.

- Deep breaths now.

He tugs at the thin curtains, not able to keep out the red eye of morning.

- No school today.

★

She plays dead saints by herself in the garden. The new fallen snow looks like the missing feeling, the ache in her stomach. Ellie misses Fletch. She had promised him she would make the things they needed for today, she had promised him they would die better. But she is to stay home and wait and keep her eyes open – her dad doesn't say what for. Outside in the garden, in her red wellies, Ellie stomps on the deepest clumps of crunch-snow, takes a handful to watch it melt on her palm, prickling into little streams of silver. Solid returning to water. The opposite of the wolf.

Douglas sits bad-tempered beneath the privet bush, drops plopping on her head and dripping off her whiskers. One for every bird she took this summer. Ellie's nose, fingertips and cheeks are so cold, she is so alive and awake after hardly any sleep: her eyes see through things. They see the crisp clicking of the snow, the blackbird – chookchookchook – bright black against the crackling white. Last year's Christmas tree, black strokes on white paper, smeared with lard. A blue tit scrapes its feet across the bark to loosen the fat. Yellow feathers noisy in the grey-white world. She turns to get her dad, he likes to see the blue tits. He used to wake her up with the teaspoon tapping his cup, 'Get up,' to see the first bird of winter and she'd kneel on her bed, staring past sleep at the cocky blue-and-yellow dip of it. A real visitor invited by gifts of crumbs and lard. He tries to teach her to be slowslowand-still but she is not her father, still as a tree, so the blue tit cracks open the cold air. It's crooked in its flight, it falls heavy like a bad dream, towards the blackcurrant bush then snap.

Yellow feathers spoof to the ground at Ellie's feet, blood-berries burst and sink into the snow, turning it pink. Ellie picks up a tiny breast feather. The wolf stands lightly, feathers stuck in its teeth and curling from its bottom lip. It scratches at a bull's nose of earth sticking up through the snow, kicking up the dirt with its forepaws, flicking it into the air, muddying the white feathers of its feet.

- You ate it?

The wolf half barks, half hiccups, then chews wetly. Ellie holds out her hand but it trots towards Ellie's mother pacing behind the glass door, left left. Its broad head, held low, follows her movements. Kate tutters behind the window. The wolf tilts its ears towards the sound and ruby beads drip-drop from its whiskers onto the snow. It yips, a slow growl curling out in white breaths, misting the glass where Ellie's mother is standing. The wolf scratches the boards trying to get in.

- She's sick.

The wolf yips in agreement digging harder, but Ellie shoves her shoulder under its chin, pressing its breastbone to keep it back.

- Are you my granny?

But her dad is rattling the pots in the kitchen.

- Go and tell Mrs Forster to ring the school.

And the wolf is gone. Ellie keeps the yellow feather for her box of broken things. Mrs Forster is watching from her kitchen window. Starling eyes. Mrs Forster is frightened, Ellie knows, of her mother, and so she does not bring the paper any more.

- Go on Ellie.

Ellie hates this, when Mrs Forster gets to know her business because they have to ask for help. She knocks on the back door; Mrs Forster doesn't like her to knock at the front, she has told her this many times.

- Don't come to the front.

The old lady keeps her waiting but Ellie doesn't mind because she got to walk across Mrs Forster's untouched lawn, crunchcrunchcrunch leaving her own trail. Ellie could only just make out the tiny little Ys of birds' feet on the surface of the snow. Finally the door unbolts behind the heavy drawn curtains.

- No school today?

There is no answer to a question like this, Ellie knows. Her dad has not given her any answers and she is not sure even he could shape one to stop up the tight wrinkled ring of Mrs Forster's mouth. 'I'm going to the moon today.' Ha.

- My mum is home.

Ellie knows Mrs Forster knows this already. She's been home for nearly a week.

- Dad asked if you could ring the school.
- Oh?
- Please.
- Oh?
- To tell them I won't be in today.
- Oh?
- Because my mum . . . please.

This is an adult game, making questions out of quiet 'oh's so you have to fill them up with things that are private. Dirty-beaky-trick. If Ellie had a tail right now it would be twitching, if she had pointy ears she would flatten them back to her head and growl.

- Rightio.

Mrs Forster says eventually, not smiling, even though it is a sound which makes you smile – the eeeyo at the end turning up the corners of your lips – so she must be trying hard not to. Ellie goes to step inside but the old woman looks down at her red wellies shiny with old and new snow and she closes the door, leaving only a little chink. The little gap is confusing – should she wait or go? She stands on the outside step watching Mrs Forster moving slowly as if the air were heavier on the inside. Douglas circles Ellie's legs, then forces the door wide with her paw and wriggles through. Mrs Forster takes out her fat Yellow Pages, letting the corners flick fast along her thumbnail, flopping open the heavy book. She licks her index finger and slides the tip along each column, making an eye out of her finger. Ellie shuffles from one foot to the other. Phone calls must be made before nine o'clock.

Ellie can hear her now, muttering the numbers to herself.

- How is your mother?
- Very well thank you.

Ellie answers too quickly.

- Settling in?

Was this another game? Ellie's not sure what settling in means when it is your own home, not a new school, and not when you have come back wrong from the pyjama place eating blue pills like beetles.

- Yesthankyou.
- Is she settling in then?

- Yes Thank You.
- Don't shout child.

Her hooked finger prodded at her new-fangled button phone. Booopbooopbooop.

- It's Mrs Forster, calling on behalf of Mr Fleck . . . yes . . . no . . . Ellie won't be in today . . . again.

Ellie could feel the eye of the school on her, disapproving, thinking things about her. Disobedient. Ellie does not make things this way but they twist all the same. All of this – the booop and the door and the wellies – was breaking the spell of this feathered winter morning.

- No it's the mother . . . not right . . . I said . . . people like that, they do it to themselves. Poor little thing . . .

'Poor,' said without tenderness, said like she was rubbing Ellie out.

- Ta ta now.

Mrs Forster shuffles over to Ellie.

- You shouldn't be missing school. Your dad has enough to worry about. Poor thing.

Well what could Ellie do about that? She blazes at these deep invasions, she knows Mrs Forster is not being an adult, she is being dirty tricks, spiky little pokes of an old sticky beak.

- When are you coming to visit Mum?

Silence at last.

18.

Peter tips more coal on the fire. It's dark, too early to be up, and the fire smokes coldly but will soon take with that wind rollicking down the chimney. It's turning cruel, getting in all the cracks; the boards on the door have dried out as he knew they would. He needs to fix it up properly – he doesn't ask with what.

Peter can't right himself here in this house. He needs to get out. All he wants is a bit of peace, to be over the dunes to the Prom just to look out to sea, take a look at the boats. To look at the sea, that'll still him. Ellie's sleeping. They'll be all right by themselves for just ten minutes if he goes by himself.

They have a pull on each other – he can see it now, he was right to bring Kate home to Ellie, her daughter, he was right. It was the same pull he felt to the sea. All he wanted was the winter tide ragged and foamy, high and running through the shingle – cracktshhh. If he could just hear it. Let his mind go back. Out on the water, with his father, the oars and sinking the long-lines. His hands now were scarred from the hooks, but he dreamed only of his whole boy's hands and the lines running through them. That was what he dreamed in the sound of his sleep – not Kate better, not Ellie grown.

The long-lines were best, they didn't rip up the flesh of the fish like nets, they just drifted a half-mile deep, baited and waiting, and you pulled the fish up whole, they didn't even struggle. Hands fast on the smooth oars, pulling out with his father, the dark bursting with the piping waders. You needed to concentrate on the hooks running through your hands because when first light broke, it shook your heart free. You were part of it – the drifting – it was every colour that made blue and every muscle felt alive and there was no way home or back. You were right in yourself. Was it a trick? Fishing was all tricks, the sweet-smelling bait hiding the hook. The nets you didn't see at all. They were safe at sea, the Fleck men, like the light, they knew how to move on the water.

Peter's father had told him the story as a boy one winter when they'd left the spitting fire behind to go to the pier-head and watch the storm. The north-east wind sent a surge that roiled everything right to the seabed. All they could do was watch, knowing that under the foaming water their gear was getting chewed to pieces by stones. It was something to see a storm like this and know that's where you had to live and make a living. Peter's father told him then how his grandfather had once pulled up the drift nets and wrapped up and tearing itself apart – it looked like a porpoise, purple like a newborn – was the sea-god.

- Cut me out.

They said together. And his father grinned his tooth-peg smile and leaned back laughing and Peter had tried to copy that laugh that was scoured hoarse with years of salt. And now Peter told the story to Ellie. So yes, he understood love, of course he did, and the first time Peter saw Kate he wanted to cut her free. When she left her shoes on the sand bell and dove into the water he wondered if she had come from the sea. When she did not come back to the surface he followed her with only his story to keep him afloat. He struggled. But there was peace inside the water too, not the cruel tick tock of a breath and then another and another; not the careless weight of years on him, just a pull. Then two small hands grabbed him under the shoulders and threw him on the shore, and in the end it was she who caught him.

When Ellie was coming Kate stopped breathing. He covered Kate's lips with his own and pushed his breath into her but she would not take it. He hoped his breath would reach inside her to the child, that she would take her first breath of air from him. But Kate was cold, like the winter-heavy water that falls and churns in on itself, builds and surges and shatters everything inside it. He had to cut the child out. Ellie was just like a porpoise but Kate wouldn't touch her. She kept saying, 'I don't know who she's like.' He held the child up to the light and named her after the boat because no two boats were alike – *Eleanor*, he said, because she was like herself.

Now he wasn't sure; he felt the current of the woman in Ellie pushing him out. She was like the dawn coming in quick now. If he didn't stare hard enough she would change, and he couldn't keep his eyes open, he was missing it. He had missed it. She had run ahead of him that day she ran away from school, drawing herself into circles, the tide ready to pull her under. Was that it? The last time she wanted him and he had come running – too late. She knows he can't fix Kate or this mess with the school.

- Kate.

She's still wide awake, them useless pills. He's still in the kitchen, his coat on. Always ready. She's turning something in her hands.

- What've you got there Kate? Is that Ellie's blanket?
- She wouldn't wake up.

Peter was up the stairs, two steps at a time, but Ellie's bed was empty.

- Ellie?

He pulled the wardrobe doors open, his old suitcase tumbling down on him.

- Ellie?

The house was too small for hiding places. There was nothing in the airing cupboard but the pressed sheets and warm wood smell. That bloody cat came tearing out from under the bed. Under-the-bed. The bed, Ellie's ship, where she would sail and walk the plank to under-the-bed sea. There she was, curled up like a cat herself and wrapped in his white storm mac.

- Ellie? What you doing under there?
- She took Granny's blanket.
- The blanket?
- She said I wasn't to sleep, she said I didn't belong. But I was tired. So I hid.
- Good lass.
- I'm a bit stuck.
- Too big for under-the-bed now aren't you.

He tries to lift the bed, feels for the strength in his hand but it twists in cramp. He lifts anyway.

- Out you come.

He won't go to the shore alone, he'll take Ellie with him. She can stay off school another day, no harm in that. She crawls out from under the bed, he thumbs the dust off her head. He had the same love for them both as he had for the sea. It did not belong to you but you lived off it and in the end you let it take you and you did not struggle.

- You tired?
- Nope.

- What about a walk?
- I want to go salvaging.

★

The things in Ellie's house don't come from shops. They come from salvage – treasures wrecked, found and mended.

- Salvage it is then. What's the wind today?
- Three knots.
- Perfect.

Winds were tied up in knots by witches, Ellie knew; the first knot was a gentle south-westerly, the second a northerly, the third was a wrecking wind. Today was a wrecking-wind day – all the old wreckage hidden under sand and rocks would be churned up to the surface. Ellie puts her foot in her father's boot print, head down to keep the measly sand from gritting her eyes. Her whole foot fits into the delve of his heel. What would they find today? The big brass clock in Ellie's front room was salvage. Ellie wound it carefully the same number of turns every time but it had been underwater and had struck silent ticks that had nothing to do with the sun going round the sky. It clocked the quiet blue time, slow in winter, fast in summer; only her dad could tell the right time from it. Her dad's hollows are now little pools that she sloshes and splashes in after him.

- Salvage. Sal-vage. Salllvaaage.

Ellie said out loud over and over – it was a funny word.

- Dad, what's salvage mean?
- Treasure.
- No I know that – what's it mean mean, like spellings?
- It's a sea promise, it means you have to bargain something to get something back.
- What like?
- Something precious, something you love, mebbe even your life, chick. The sea won't take less.

She could hear him wading out into the deeper water.

- Did you do it Dad? Did you bargain your life for something the sea took?
- I did.
- What was it?
- Can't tell you that chick. Now then, there's summat out there by the lip of the scaur, you see it?
- It's too far.

Ellie waded forwards, the scaur slippery beneath her feet, dulse and seersucker pulling at her ankles.

- Dad.

She took his hand and he let her.

- Brave lass, eh? A real Fleck.

Ellie felt it through his hand, a current pulling them out and her dad pulling her with it. She was a real Fleck.

- It's silver, you see it?

She can't but he wades in deeper, and with every step something flickers and seems further off.

- If we could just get out a little further.

Ellie could see something now, like a light.

- I can get it Dad. I'll bargain.

And she let go of his hand just for a moment but without him the pull dragged her under. Her dad tugged her up by her hood.

- You take it back. The promise, take it back.
- But you promised.
- For summat that was worth it pet, that – that's nothing. We'll go back.

Ellie couldn't see what it was but it was enough that he wanted it.

- Dad.
- You spit out that promise now.

He shouts this in his 'That's enough now' voice and she spits into the wind. As soon as he's out of the water he stumbles forward; he puts his hands out to stop himself falling but can't. His knees hit the hard shingle with a sickening crack and he can't right himself. He tilts his head, trying to fix his eyes on something still.

- What's up Dad?
- Nowt, just that vertigo pet.

His breathing is ragged and tiny drips of sweat run out from under his cap. But it's a chill sweat because the freezing wind is knotting itself up and haggering the sky to pieces. He shudders again and Ellie knows she can't let the cold take hold of them or that'll be it.

- What's it like?

He closes his eyes to tip out the dizziness.

- You see the sky there, the sea under it?

Ellie nods.

- Now tip them upside down.

Ellie sees the sea resting on top of the sky, heavy, waiting to fall in, birds flying too high and wetting their wings.

– It's like that, so sea is sky and sky is sea and I'm falling up into the water.

Ellie takes his hand, walking backwards towards the
beach. She goes slow and steady for him but now she can
feel all the teeth in the wind biting through her wet gear,
her heavy smock, right down to her skin. Her chest judders
like in Best Man Dead. She's never died from freezing
before but now she knows how it would go. She can see her
dad's shoulders stiffen and round, pushing the heat to his
heart, the rest of him slack. She needs to get him home.
She knows the way, past the hollowed rock that was Wolf
Rock, up onto the Prom and pulling him forwards whilst
he keeps his eyes half closed to hold himself steady. She
tugs him too fast because she can't feel her feet only the
white sting of the water sloshing in her boots.

– Easy now pet.

She helps him to lean up against a small boat on the Prom,
all the cobles lined up like shoes outside the school hall for
PE. He closes his eyes, bracing the wood.

– They used to be made of skin. The boats.
– What?

Ellie thinks he means that they were alive. They could
be alive, they have names and are all soft swelling wood
and waving oars, like whelk crabs in their borrowed shells.

- A long time ago, they were just cured skin wrapped up round wooden ribs. The Irish made them out of hide, light to chase the salmon.

In her head Ellie sees the other coble's skin, like herring scales, all silver darts of light. Inside the hollow bit delicate white ribs curve up from the backbone and fins fan out instead of oars.

- Where's *Eleanor*?

Her dad doesn't mean her, she's Ellie. He means his boat the *Eleanor*. She was the Flecks' boat before the vertigo and her granddad's boat before that and the sea-god boat before that. She's the Hoods' boat now and her dad always looks for her like she's a living lady who might walk by with wide blue hips and good to touch like a granny who hugs you tight against the wind. But the *Eleanor* isn't lined up with the shoe boats.

- She's still not here Dad.

Ellie tells him because he hasn't opened his eyes.

- They shouldn't keep her out o' the water this long.
- She'll dry out and they may as well sink her.

Ellie says because that's what her dad always says when the boat isn't there.

- Cheek.

He says and hauls himself up, smiling a closed-eye smile. Ellie tows him over the dunes and the road, his hand on her shoulder. The tatty wind tugs at him, trying to shear him off balance, but Ellie makes herself heavy and keeps the pace slow. She tries to breathe the cold out of herself in long breaths so she can keep a tight hold of him. He stops again at Mr Glover's garden – all hush with frost – and leans into the sturdy wall and finally opens his eyes.

- Ellie look at that holly, them berries, eh, like red stars.
- Keep your eyes closed Dad.
- You take my penknife and cut us a sprig o' that holly and we'll put it round the clock.

Her dad's pretending he's fine but his hands grip Mr Glover's wall too tight. Ellie quickly, carefully pulls out the blade, Mr Glover won't mind. Her dad will leave him a mackerel wrapped in newspaper and he won't even know why. No one else is awake to shout or bang on windows. Ellie cuts the juicy berries down. She tries to close the knife, but her fingers are frost-struck and won't bend. She pushes the knife closed between the fat parts of her thumbs.

- Watch your fingers, put it in my pocket now. Right then. We'll get you dry and you'll sleep tonight.

Ellie's teeth clickclack instead of saying yes, he thumbs her chin trying to rub some warmth back in but she can only feel a deeper cold under his rough skin.

- Back to school tomorrow eh?
- W–what ab–bout Mum?
- You leave her to me.

Ellie doesn't think she can.

As soon as they're home she goes up to the airing cupboard for fresh warm ganseys. She won't light the fire yet, you have to let the cold go out slow or it's too much of a shock. She gets her dad sorted: his boots are two inches deep inside with seawater. As soon as he's wrapped up and sitting still he starts to tremble just a little. He'd been too dizzy to shiver till now, she thinks. Her wet clothes sucker to her the more she pulls them, chafing. She gets her clean gansey on over her raw shoulders. Her feet hurt too much for socks yet. She'll have to walk the heat back in but first she settles her dad in the kitchen and guides a cigarette to his mouth.

- Don't fret, it'll pass, go on, get something from the shelf, you read to me for a bit. And put some socks on.

Her dad likes books on animals, boats and stars. She is allowed to read them but not if she is eating Highland Toffee, because she stuck the pages on Saturn and Jupiter together and now he can't ever see the dust rings. Her hands are clean so she takes down a book.

- What book is it?
- *Animals of North America.*

He likes this one because the pictures are like the cow-
boy films he used to watch, all red cliffs but no sea. He
can't look though because his eyes are closed again.

- There's a picture of a wolf, it's beautiful. Its eyes are
gold and it's got black rings around them.

Just like her wolf, but she doesn't tell him that bit. She
reads to her dad all about play and yipping and family and
nuzzling and howling, her finger running after the words.
Then her finger stops.

- What's next?

She reads the next bit only in her head – wolves come for
the old, the young, the sick.

19.

Ellie has to walk to school by herself, left left, because her dad is too frightened to leave her mum alone again. Ellie agrees. Her dad cut his pencil sharp with his penknife and drew the corners she should turn on the lid of their tea box. She turns and turns but still she's late and everything in school is wrong. No one is in uniform. They are in costume because 'the Christmas play is only around the corner' and Ellie is in her grey jumper and long socks and wrong. There are no books on the desks, only boxes. Prop boxes. Each box has a list of names on the side, carefully written by the best writer in each group. Fletch's name has been added to Stephen's box. Ellie doesn't have a box. Now they have to go to the hall. Where's maths? Where's spellings? Each group spreads out their wares from their prop box. Ellie whispers to Fletch.

- What's a prop?
- Shush Ellie.

At first each item bares its origins in the harsh glare of the hall – wire coat hangers; tea towels; mothers' old dresses. Then click and dim and each object is transformed by kinder light and the longing of its wearer to be something else. The hall fills with wise men, shepherds, angels. The huge Christmas tree spreads its soft starlight. Two haloed shadows fuse behind the branches of the tree. Ellie hears slurping. Rachel and Stephen. Kissing. Again. Yuck. Mr Lockwood sits in the corner playing the piano by himself, not looking. Ellie looks.

- She'll eat you up.
- Bog off Ellie.

But Stephen pulls back; he must have felt Rachel's hunger behind her teeth. Amanda's holding Steven-the-donkey's hand. Hatty's holding Wiggy's hand. Yuck.

School-time has ticked its fierce tick a hundred times faster than the underwater tock of home-time and left Ellie behind. She holds her breath to stop it until she's sick and a little dizzy. She tries to lead Fletch into a quiet corner as she needs him to explain props and time.

- Oi. Fletch is in our group. You haven't got a box.
- I've got a pen.

She picks up one of the thick felt-tip pens and puts a wriggly black line right through Fletch's name.

- She's mental.

Fletch follows Ellie to the dark corner.

- Props are the stuff for the play. You said you'd make them. Did you Ellie?

But he could see Ellie standing there in her grey socks with only the wrong books.

- Please don't do something mental, it's been bad enough without you.

She shrugs, pushing down the wings inside her lungs. She must not cry. Fletch smells different. Like ointment and boy and sulk. This isn't two-together or enemies it's both at the same time. She doesn't know what to do.

- Let's practise How Saints Die?

He lies down on the floor but when she raises the hammer to drive in the first nail, Ellie hears Stephen whispering.

- MadPaddy, madPaddy, madPaddy.

Fletch rolls out of the way.

- No, it's weird. It's not going to work. We need to do Mary and Joseph.

And she decides to say yes because he is as weird as she is and they will get eaten alive for it.

- OK.
- Really, OK?
- Yes. You lead, what do I do?
- You need to do your hair like this.

He pulls out the blue bobble that holds her plait in place – sting and tug – and he begins to unravel the rope of her hair with his fingers.

- Yours is longer than Rachel's.

Her hair falls in heavy waves, dark, shot through with gold. Her head feels light and tingly.

- The saints weren't going to work anyway. How could we do stones, nails and fire?
- We could have . . .
- No, we couldn't. They were killed and didn't die, that's a lie. You shouldn't lie Ellie.

He does not believe in the saints any more. Traitor.

- Like Catherine, she would've died on that wheel thing for definite.
- No – they put her on the wheel and she reached out to touch it and it shivered into splinters. It was supposed to break her. It was her miracle. She didn't die until after.
- How?
- He cut off her head.
- Who?

- The Emperor, she wouldn't marry him and he cut off her head. That's what made her a saint. We can do that. That's not a lie.

Ellie kneels on the ground, holding her head in her hands, her hair flowing down around her.

- Ellie stop it.
- No, Fletch, this is how she died.
- It's weird.
- It's not. It's true. It's what makes a saint. Cut off my head.

Still kneeling she pushes his hands together into a prayer shape.

- This is your axe.
- No Ellie, I don't want to.
- Why not? It's true.

She pulls his axe hands down upon her neck.

- Like this.

He's shivering, his hands slippery trying to pull away.

- Cut off my head.

Even if he kills her now he is still a traitor. He brings his hands down across her neck and the shock knocks her

214

forwards. She buckles and catches herself, resting her fore-head on the cool wooden floor, her upside-down eyes taking in the kings, the shepherds, the angels – standing around her watching and whispering their whispers. They all fit with one another. How did they learn to do that? They were there at the beginning with the baby and Ellie is rushing in at the end – to the people who wanted to die for him, blood and love and proof. Why is hers the wrong part of the story? It needs something more. Stones, nails and fire. That's what they need.

- I can make them – stones, nails and fire and a . . .

Rachel and Stephen stand right above her, Rachel's beautiful dark hair against a bright blue sky, night and day together in the hall. Rachel holds a perfect Tiny Tears doll in her arms and even it snaps its clear glass eyes shut at Ellie. *Hail Mary full of grace.* Ellie used to speak to her every night in the Before. The words flood into her head, pushing out this world and the pain growing in her stomach.

- Hail Mary.

Rachel hears Ellie say it; she closes her eyes, impressed at her new power over a true believer.

- Weirdo.

Ellie's head grows cold and dizzy and Fletch tries to help her up. He is white and golden and traitor because he had wanted to be Joseph who didn't even die. She must get up and get to the toilets, she doesn't belong, she's woken up wrong. She leaves Fletch behind, pale in a circle of hungry shadows. She pushes open the heavy double doors, their swinging hurts her eyes.

- Come back here Ellie Fleck, you are not excused.

In the girls' toilets her stomach wrenches her to kneel down. This isn't just the sea inside her like her dad. Does she have it too? Like her mother? Something caught inside her wanting to get out? She is sick into the bowl, tries to steady herself and leans her head against the cool cistern, tucking her sweat-soaked hair behind her ears. She is wet between her legs. Her fingers come back red.

- Are you all right?

The voice comes from deep under the water. Then everything goes black. Ellie comes to with her head sinking into the canary-nylon breast of the dinner lady who has found her – she smells of cigarettes and Daz washing powder. Ellie's bare legs are dry and clean. The lady must have cleaned her up, not frightened of the blood.

- You're all right pet, a bit young but you'll be all right.

Ellie retches again, she's very cold now and grateful for the sturdy warmth holding her still.

- Sometimes it makes you sick. I used to have a right do.

Ellie wonders if this lady had to kill her saints too.

- You'll get used to it. Best to get you straight home to your mum.

★

Mr Lockwood said Fletch could sit with her until she went home.

- Ellie do you have to go?
- If it gets too bad run away, out-of-bounds where I showed you.

But she knows he won't do that. There were a lot of voices then.

- Telephone the neighbour, get her father.
- He doesn't have a car.
- She can't be expected to walk home like this.
- I'll take her.

It's worse in the back of Mr Lockwood's car, the pressure not to be sick is overwhelming. The dinner lady had given her a thick cotton pad to put in her pants and a washing-up bowl to hold. A small round blue one, the kind they used in art to mix paint. It was stained with swirling marble patterns. Ellie stares hard into the rainbow smudges trying to hold herself still.

- Ellie, keep breathing, nearly there.

It is a new game, Woodsy's kindness.

- Are you ill like this often Ellie? Is it nerves? Is this why you miss school?
- Are you taking me away?
- No, I'm taking you home. Don't you like school?

Ellie shook her head, making herself retch again.

- OK, OK. Head over the bowl Ellie, head over the bowl.

Her dad opens the car door and lifts her out. Her head feels so heavy, she wants to warn him about Woodsy's tricks but she can't speak. She washes up into his out-stretched hands, his sleeves rolled up ready.

- Thank you Mr Lockwood.
- She misses a lot of school Mr Fleck, is this why? Is she often ill?

It's a trick she thinks, don't answer, but her dad does not know the rules.

- No.
- Then why is she away from school? What do you keep her at home for?

Ellie's mother stands in the doorway, more translucent in the weak daylight, but her lips are fierce red against her bone-white face. Mr Lockwood looks as though he has been struck. He is taking something in, making a sum in his head, and Ellie can hear the clackclackclack of his abacus mind as her father stands holding her, breaking down whatever it was that held Ellie, her dad and her mum all together and getting it wrong.

*

Her dad puts her down on the couch, already made up with blankets; the fire is lit, burning steady as though he was waiting vigil just as the lifeboat wives did for rescued souls. But Ellie wasn't rescued. He takes off her shoes and socks, and she knows that he mustn't know about the blood. She takes his shirt and climbs the stairs to the bathroom.

Ellie stands in the bath, filling the jug from the tap and pouring it over her head. There is only cold water to clean herself with. She shivers at first but soon her body stills to a cool numb ache. She scrubs with the pale soap to warm her skin, and pink water trickles away between her toes. She prods her tender stomach which has bowled out a little from her hips like rising bread. There between her legs is a stray wolf hair, two, she tries to brush them off but they are stuck like needles growing from her smooth white skin. Has the wolf done this? She is sick and now it will come for her. She tucks herself into her dad's checked shirt, it's full of clean-after-rain smell that she wears over her red-blood smell.

Downstairs Ellie burrows into the warmed blankets,

tucking herself in deep enough around the pain. Her dad brings water, lukewarm, and she takes little sips.

- Now then what's up wi' you?

He lays his warm hand on her head and she's frightened that just touching her he will know that she's bad and wrong, that her skin doesn't belong buttoned under his clean shirt any more. She feels it like a current running between them. She doesn't know how she knows this, only that the pushing pain in her belly is wrong and not Dad. So she pulls away from his hand and digs under the blanket with her bare legs until the wool scratches them. She hears him go, the door clicking behind him and then only the popping of the fire.

The world turns red through her closed eyes as she drifts in the first worst dream. The iron-flecked belly of the sea, swelling and churning up over the sand dunes, crawling over the dune grass and swallowing up the streets all the way to her house.

Ellie jolts awake.

Rain outside fizzing on snow, the room forgetting its shape in the darkness. Something presses cold at her head, moving her sticky hair away.

- Are you awake?

Her mother. Ellie can't speak. Her mother gives her a glass of cool water and she drinks a little sip.

- Better?

- I have to get back to Fletch. The play is only just around the corner.

But she can't sit up, the ache in her belly has woken up with her, it is hot and roaring as the fire. The dinner lady said tell your mum. Could she make it stop? Could her mum see, that she'd woken up wrong like she said? There is Ellie's rope by the fireplace, frayed and blackened a little by the years of soot and heat. Her story – come from the sea, cut out, for luck. Then the wolf came and now she was changing from inside out.

- What happened at school today?
- I got a tummy ache.
- What were you doing?
- I was being St Catherine.
- I'm Katherine. Kate.
- I know Mum, but the one on the wheel? She didn't die on the wheel did she?
- No. She didn't. Do you know Ellie? How to kill a saint?
- Sort of but I need stones that don't really bruise.
- Is that what hurt you? Killing St Catherine?
- I don't know.
- Where's the ache now?

Ellie lifts her father's shirt and points to her swollen belly.

- That's not your tummy. Are you bleeding? Down there?

Ellie nods with just her eyes.

- Is it because I went to sleep? Is it because I killed the saints? Will I die?
- Let's see.

Kate takes Ellie's head in her hands, turns her face to the fire, and Ellie's cheek glows hot, red.

- Is that my mammy I can see in your face?

Kate pushes Ellie's hair back, catching tiny strands, stinging Ellie's scalp.

- Who's this now?

She presses her face to Ellie's, so close Ellie can see the skin drawn tightly over the tender bones.

- Do you hear voices? That's what he kept asking me. Dr Milligan. You know? Do you hear voices? I wouldn't tell him. And then he put that rubber stopper in my mouth, like a bath plug. Tasted like gin. He said I could go home. I did. And I saw her. My mother, you know. Saw the kitchen light flickering on, the daylight was going but, and the wind was shaking everything, and she shone, the last of the summer light on her. She went fth, like snow, snow there in August, you know how you can feel it sometimes – all the seasons at dusk. And I saw her, just her outline, pass the window once. The white tiles and the kettle boiling. Just once, this is love, I said. Looking in from the outside. This is love before opening the door.

There it was, the flickering thing, like a bright bird burning in her mother's eye, burning out the way the bulb burns, hot and white and snap. Ellie knows this game. Stop she says inside her head, her own voice and shush and shush and out.

- Stop it Mum.
- Who's that? I don't know what you are.
- Mum, it's me.
- I don't know you.
- Mummy.

Kate lets go of her head, letting it fall. She's the one who woke up wrong. Not Ellie. Ellie stretches out and takes her rope down from the fireplace, holds it out to Kate.

- You don't even know my story. I came from the sea. Not your Green Hill. Look.
- Then go back. Go back and let me go home.

Why should she, when her father pulled her out of the sea and she was his?

- No, you go.

And she goes and Ellie is sorry, it was bad to say it out loud. Not a wish. Just a want. She is hurting and bleeding and wants a mother, not a dead one or a ragged one or a wolf one, not even a Before one – just Mum.

She wants Fletch as well, she wants to be two-together. If she could make stones, nails and fire she could go back and be normal but still kill her saints. Ellie takes a lump of coal from the bucket and tests its hardness. She drops it onto her foot. This stone would definitely bruise.

*

Ellie's father carries her to bed. He leaves the curtains open so that she can see the full moon. It is not a cat's-eye, cold sharp moon, no, tonight it is full and pale gold fire. It pulses with a moon-bow around it. Even though her dad stays with her past goodnight, there is only Ellie and the light – she curls up, safe in its cradle. It starts to snow again. Her dad tries once more to break through and reach her.

- How's that bellyache?

Ellie had seen him turn away when he gutted his pale silver mackerel. He wrapped up the red guts in newspaper. Secrets to be thrown away and she did the same now with her white cotton pads.

- Make a wish pet.

Ellie shakes her head.
He doesn't wake her in the morning and her school clothes

aren't laid out. Today is an old bent-backed man of a day, grey within grey within grey. Ellie pictures the heavy surface of the sea like herring iron, waves turning slowly against themselves. She's getting better, the blood ebbing, brownish red and thickening now like dulse, less like a wound. She needs to catch up. Ellie still needs her props or she can never go back.

Her dad calls her downstairs and puts on the Christmas tree lights for her in the front room, they flash and spill different colours across her exercise book. Ellie likes the blue bauble best, a shiny pale blue, like no shell, like nothing she has ever seen before – *untarnished*, she writes in her sentence. He's 'off out', he doesn't say where, he just pulls his cap low over his brow.

The fire burns down to well-sucked lozenges of coal and her dad is still not home. On the floor by her shoes is a stone, grey and white. Ellie picks it up, it's so light. A stone that will not bruise. Next to the stone is a small brown bag, inside are more cotton pads. Her mother is awake with her tea and her pills and her red mouth, chuffing out pale drifts of smoke.

- Don't go back.
- What?
- Nothing. How did you make it Mum – the stone?
- Come with me.

The back door is locked so Kate kneels before the damp boards, tugs and Ellie hears the thin wood splitting. The draught wakes the fire, startling sparks up the chimney.

- Come on Ellie?

The wings inside Ellie's chest are beating too fast. And her mother is out and down the back garden path. Ellie follows her to –

– No, we're not to go in, we're not to touch without him.

But her mother opens the door to the Baithouse. She reaches up to the ceiling and plucks orange floats from the nets like plums.

– No, they're his.

Kate drops the mallet and split – the floats are broken into pieces. Ellie sees now how she had made the stone light.

– Pass me the brushes.

Ellie reaches for the back of the shelf, careful to let her fingers glance over hooks to reach the paintbrushes. Kate mixes up black and white paint in one of the empty jam jars until it is brittle rock grey.

– Do you want to have a go?

Ellie did. She paints all of the foam floats until they are a little nest of rocks huddled like raided eggs. Ellie gathers them up, wanting Fletch to know that she had fixed it. Even though he was a traitor.

- What's next?

- Nails that don't pierce.

Ellie scratches at her palm with a short grey screw, testing the hurt. It pierces. She slides it between her fingers and still its rough helix grips and tears her webbing. She tries a smooth long nail. She pricks her finger on the nail tip. How could she change its nature? It's going to be much harder to get back to school than she thought.

Had Fletch survived the morning? If only she could tell him – she had made the stones.

Kate lights a cigarette and Ellie quickly moves the jars of turpentine away. Her mother lets the ash fall between the cracks on the work table and picks up a nail, twizzling it in her fingers. Ellie tries to twizzle one too but it falls. She blows the ash away, like little gusts of dirty snow.

- That Milligan, he said I tried to kill myself you know? That's a mortal sin.

- I know.

- It wasn't that. You saw didn't you? You saw the rain and the window and it was easy to put my hands through it. I just wanted to get home. Did you see the lightning? It was beautiful, no? Like sheets snapping. I could get through it nearly – did you see – the lightning, the rain. I was nearly there. The rain. It smelled like home. Made me thirsty. I used to be like that – imagine – like rain holding its own shape. Before they cut me.

The words crackle out – a new current passing between them. Ellie wriggles down off the stool to turn on the light in the dark morning.

– Turn that off.

She flicks it off, she doesn't want to hurt her mother.

– I only wanted to get out. To get home.

Ellie doesn't want to know this story. But Kate digs her fists into her sore eyes.

– And you saw, Ellie? You saw too? Tell me what you saw through the window?

Ellie saw her mother's hands go through the glass. And for a moment it was all right. She had done it. She had gone through the window. And then her mother's arms, pale as eggshells, broke into red cracks. Then blood, heavier than the rain.

– He pulled me out too soon.
– Dad?
– No, don't you call for him.

Kate puts her hand across Ellie's mouth.

– He's the one who cut you out.

Ellie can't breathe, she knocks her hand against the wall to call her father, that's what she does when the first worst dream comes. Taptaptap. Her mother pins her hands to the wall.

– Stop. My head is splitting.

Kate lifts her cigarette above Ellie's face.

– Mum.
– So you do have a bit of your granny in you. Now what else was it you said you needed to kill your saints?
– Nails.
– Do you remember when I'd make the bread?

Ellie remembers her mum pounding the dough with the heel of her hand – spuff – a puff of flour rising up. Ellie would let go of the breath held tight inside her – spuff. This was not like the thudtickticktick of gutting. Her mother would stop to pat the swollen belly of dough then knock on its hollow dome and wait to hear if something knocked back.

– Listen.

Ellie listened. Then it was all stop, no more touching, no more fingers sinking.

– I remember.

The letter that came saying dead.

- Now then, we'll need some twine, some eggs from the house and the silver paint. And get my sewing tin while you're there.

The balls of twine were bright orange. Kate cut off lengths a few inches long. Then she cracked the eggs into jam jars, separating the white from the golden yolks. She used an old brush to beat the whites.

- Here pet, you paint the twine with this and it will make them nice and stiff.

Then they put the lengths on the stove to set.

- Now then. We'll paint them.

They painted each one silver.

- Nails that do not pierce.

Ellie was astonished.

- And what's the last thing?
- Fire that doesn't burn.

Kate took down a tin Ellie did not recognise. It was covered with painted birds: song thrush, blackbird and magpie, and others that were too bright and that she had not seen before. The tin was blotched with rust but the birds were still beautiful. Kate pulled the lid off, pop, and inside were hundreds, thousands of wrappers from chocolates and sweets, all crinkling and crackling oranges and reds, foils and cellophanes. The tin smelled of metal and chocolate and all the Christmases it held inside.

Kate licked the end of a red thread but her hands shook – worse than Mrs Forster's – and she could not get it through the eye of her needle. Ellie took it from her and threaded it. Then her mother tied a knot at the end with just one hand by rubbing her fingers together and she pushed the point of the needle through the foil, over and over. Ellie threaded her own needle and copied until all the wrappers had gone.

It was deep dark outside the Baithouse, like the deepest parts of the sea. There was the tinny thrum of a car engine, headlamps coming home, scattering light across the ceiling, jackdaws rawking. Ellie's mother lifts her arm, blood no, blood is red, this is orange, gold – flames leap out from her hands. The breeze from under the door picks up the fire trails, rattling and sparking. Ellie sees the trick. Her mother lifts her hand once again and the flames flick and tut back to life but do not burn. She slowly winds the flames back up and then gives them to Ellie.

They crawl back through the hole in the door. Together they pull the boards back in place so her dad will not guess they got out.

Ellie lies by the fire, still holding Catherine's flames but secretly, all balled up, and she starts her homework.

There was once a mother who could make stones that will not bruise, nails that will not pierce and fire that will not burn.

20.

When Peter gets back he can see that they've been in his Baithouse. There are flecks of silver where they shouldn't be. He can't see what they have made, just the mess. He douses a rag in turps but stops himself; the marks are too much like the stars on the still surface of the sea. They make him feel sound, quietening the spin inside him. Back in the house he clinks the spoon loudly in the cups and smacks the bacon in the hot pan to see if they'll show him what they've made. Ellie's on her belly by the fire, her legs crooked up swinging. Kate is on the rocking chair, her eyes half closed, like when she prays. Mouths tight shut, only the wind sneaking in through the broken door. What was it between them – whispering like burning paper?

- What've the pair of you been up to?
- Nothing.

Peter's own joke, thrown back at him to keep him out. That's it now – enough – Ellie will be ready for school on

Monday. He saw the eggs were gone and the lid half off Kate's sewing tin. Kate was always good at making things; she could make something out of nothing, what a trick. At the Swan Hotel she'd put on these big buffets for Race Days and the food set out was always somehow more than food. Once, a boxing match with lobster boxers, red claw gloves. Once, a blue gelatine sea and the Yellow Submarine, with them Beatles and a real Octopus's garden. It was a shame to eat it. But they stuck their fat fingers in, drunk from winning and losing. They couldn't see the magic of it. He thought he knew some tricks but he couldn't do what she did. He missed it, he missed her. What was it they couldn't show him?

Long before Ellie started school, Kate had the idea they'd go to the beach for Easter Sunday. Kate had fallen out with God again. She'd wrapped up the brass Jesus in a tea towel and put him under the stairs with the old shoes. Peter was pleased. It made him sick to see Kate kiss its feet. That morning the bairn watched out the window at the other kiddies sitting on their walls, faces mucked up with chocolate and gold foil blowing down the hot street. Ellie wanted to know what Easter was. So Kate packed a bag with goose eggs and bread and all sorts of little treats she'd stowed away in the pantry. She'd even made fatty cakes, thick with butter and golden syrup – Peter licked his lips. She put a towel in the bag and dressed the bairn up in a little blue dress and got her wellies on.

- We'll go to the beach.

And that meant Peter too, even though Sunday was a good day to go out on the boat. She had that look, the look that said she was going to pull off a trick and he couldn't miss it. When Peter went to take the bag she wouldn't let him, so he held Ellie's hand. They walked along the Prom until they reached the groynes for a bit of shelter. There weren't many folk on the beach, they didn't come the way they used to. Instead they had sand-less patios made from broken paving slabs, 'crazy paving' they called it, mugs, and tiny paddling pools from Argos you could barely get one foot and your arse in. When they could have the whole sea? They'd buy anything wrapped in plastic, even water.

Kate put the blanket down on the sands but couldn't sit still. She went picking driftwood, all bleached white and split on the stones. Peter showed Ellie what was growing on the groynes, the clicking mussels, limpets, barnacles. He slid his penknife under a limpet and lifted it from the salt-stewed wood to show Ellie its living orange sun. 'Ooh,' she said and went to touch. 'No, bad luck.' 'Bad luck,' she said. 'That's it pet.' He held the limpet on the groyne until it could sucker itself back on. Ellie got lost in all the layers of living weed and crusty shells that suckled on the sea wood. A new world for the lass. Her fingertips gentle now that she knew how soft the bellies were beneath their shells.

Kate came back and started to scoop a deep hole in the sand with just her hands. Ellie watched and helped with her orange spade – good little lass. All the time Kate smoked her cigarette with no hands, rolling it from one side of her mouth to the other in concentration, puffing up smoke like a welcome home. She was small but she never seemed little to Peter; her total concentration on a task took up all the room around her so she was like a little pip in the body of

one of them giants she was descended from. Kate dug too
deep for someone with her tiny hands, through the dry sand
to the shingle layer. She made a nest with old paper and then
the driftwood. Peter knew what she was up to then.

- There's no fires on the beach.
- Says who?
- Says the lifeguards.
- And where are they?
- They'll be along.
- They're not here now.

And she tossed her half-smoked cigarette onto the bone-
dry wood. Whoosh. The breeze caught the air in the
scooped-out hollow and Peter had to pull Ellie back before
her eyebrows got scorched. Kate lugged about in her bag and
pulled out a huge copper pan and cradled its heavy bottom in
the flames. How'd she hidden that in there? She took Ellie
and the bucket down to the sea for water and soon the pan was
bubbling away. Now Kate was pulling the seaweed from the
groynes with hair-tearing sounds. Bad luck, Peter thought,
but there was no stopping her and the bare patches grew.
Dulse, bladderwrack, sea lettuce. Red, orange, green. She
threw them in her pot and stirred with a driftwood wand, like
the Irish witch his mates warned him she was. Then she took
out the white goose eggs and nestled them on their bubbling
bed of weeds. Ellie watched them sink one by one.

- Leave them, wait.

And they waited while the fire burned, the smoke disappearing into the blue sky, the eggs knocking the side of the pan all hullos and let-me-outs. Ellie waited, stirring the sand in the rock pools, letting pea crabs tickle-leg round the world of her palm. Peter waited digging a trench around a sandcastle like a right tourist. Kate waited by taking off her good red dress, her bathing cossie beneath. She dropped the dress on the sand next to Peter, who pulled it safe away from the fire.

- I'm going for a quick dip. Don't worry, I won't swim all the way home.

She said, disappearing into a slick wave. Peter wasn't so sure.

By the time Kate came back the tide was lapping in. She put her dress back on and it stuck like a second skin.

- Ready?

She spooned out the eggs but they weren't eggs any more, not that something wide-footed and land-scratching could make. Kate cooled them in a hollow of damp sand. Ellie wanted to touch but Peter held her little fingers back. He wanted to touch too. The shells were all colours, marbled like the pictures of the planets – Saturn, Jupiter, Neptune – in Peter's books.

- They're mermaids' eggs.

Kate told him, as true as the promises and the quietnesses between them. Yes they could be, yes they were – mermaid's eggs – like she said, it was her best trick yet. Kate picked one up and cracked it. Split it and gave half to Peter; it tasted beautiful of salt and air. But Ellie wouldn't eat. She kept her egg in her little pocket to wait for her mermaid to hatch. Better than any tinfoil-wrapped chocolate shit from the supermarket. It had been a good day.

Peter carried Ellie home, her head on his shoulder – her sleep-heavy head smelling of beach fire, sand in her ear shells and her bare feet kicking. 'Shush,' he said like the sea running with them over the dunes and into her dreaming head. Once back they trailed sand through the house over the wooden boards. No carpet – 'Just the bare essentials,' Kate said. The golden sand looked pretty on the wood, picking up the light in scattered sparks. What if it was the done thing to carpet a house in sand? How quiet and shush the mornings would be, Peter thought.

The next morning came loud and scraping; Peter had slept in so Kate and Ellie had his bait packed ready to go out on the boat. They walked him to the Prom but kept out of sight of the lads. Goodbyes are bad luck. Women are bad luck. Red-headed women are double bad luck. But as far as Peter could see Kate was something that belonged to the sea, the way she moved in the water, the way she'd fished him out with her little-big hands. She was best luck, wet and salt and love luck. Two kisses for luck – Ellie and Kate and no out-loud goodbyes.

He caught up with the lads on the slipway.

– Where've you been?

Peter just smiled and jumped in the coble before the tractor backed her into the water. It was a grand morning to be out. The *Eleanor*, his little boat, shook and dipped as its steep bow cut through the surf. They were all glad to be out. They said little between the three of them, keeping the quiet so as not to spoil the morning. They each knew the drill, let the net out steady. Then – thunk – something rolled onto the deck.

– What in God's name is that?

Tink was always jumpy, didn't like anything out of the ordinary. And this was out of the ordinary. It was the egg Ellie had kept, she must have sneaked it into Peter's pocket. Without thinking, Peter stood to look back at the Prom where he'd left them.

– What the hell are you playing at Fleck?

Too late. Peter's look rooted him to the shore. You mustn't ever look back, not once you were in the water; the sea would know then that your heart was for the land and what it held, that your heart wasn't hers. It was enough to wreck you there and then.

– Sorry Tink, it will be all right.
– Will it?
– My great-grandfather James . . .
– Oh Christ not that story again. Sit down man.

Peter sat; it didn't matter what Tink thought, he knew

what Ellie wanted and he hadn't needed to look back. She wanted him to give her mermaid's egg back to the sea. He dropped the egg over the side. You couldn't hear the splash for the waves slapping the boat.

The water calmed Tink and soon he wanted to share his worries.

- Them councillors have said they'll stop us selling fish off the sands. Said they'll ban the boats off the Prom. What d'you reckon Peter, will they get away with it?

- Course not. The cobles are as old as this place. They're just blow-ins. They won't dare.

It wasn't a bad catch. They came in on a steady tide. But as soon as Peter's feet struck land he lost his footing, as though he needed the weight of water under him still.

- Lost yer sea legs?

Tink laughed but then swallowed it back down when he saw Peter couldn't right himself.

- Davy get yer arse over here and help me wi' him.

They got Peter home, carried him like a drunk between them. They knocked on Peter's door for him and lifted him onto the couch. They were even polite to Kate though they hadn't come to their wedding.

- What's wrong with him?
- Looks like a touch o' the sea legs. He'll be right as rain in no time and back on the boat.

Davy said, smiling at the kiddie.

- He looked back.

Tink told Kate.

- Looked back at what?
- You.

Tink knew and might as well say it – Peter'd had it.

Before the summer was out the boat was sold. The *Eleanor,* his father's boat, named for his daughter, gone. It was a cheap sale, the fishing was going downhill. The councillors, flat-footed thugs, had indeed stopped the fishermen selling fish off the sands and forced most of the cobles off the Prom. No one wanted the worry of a boat. That made it worse, the pitiful amount of money he got that wouldn't last them to Christmas. The cramps in his hands started the second he let her go. Peter had to make money baiting the lines or mending nets and creels, but they all liked their new-fangled nylon nets now. Peter didn't understand them, they tore up the fish. So he went out every morning, with only his own bait, just to beg a spot on someone else's boat. As much as they had their new-fangled sonar beeps and radios, they were wary of him. Course they were. Peter had looked back and it was only a matter of time. The fishermen knew what was wrong with him – vertigo the doc said, but the fishermen could see – it was only when he was on the water that he was still.

*

Kate was making things again, beautiful tricks that could make you love her even while you lost everything. What had she made for Ellie? It would be beautiful. Peter knew what it was like to feel full of the magic she gave to you, as though you were flying just before the ground came up to meet you. Enough now.

21.

Ellie gives her mum her first pill early, to give it time to work before they leave her on her own. Ellie does want to go to school today, wants to see Fletch's face when she shows him what she's made for their Christmas play. She gets herself ready and combs her own hair. She paces at the door waiting for her dad to get his bike. Her stomach churns. She checks the front door again.

- Is it locked pet?
- I can go on my own. I'm much better.
- We'll be quick.

Her dad pedals faster than normal, the bike ticking quick like her heart. When they get to the lollipop lady they have to stop. It already feels like too long.

- Go home Dad, I'm fine from here.

He tries to give her a quick bristled kiss on the top of her head but she's pulled up her hood against the wind that cuts right through her, so she crosses the road unkissed. She feels him waiting at the kerb, watching her up the road. Go, she says out loud in her head. Go. He does. It will take him only seven minutes to cycle home, he'll be there before she reaches the playground. It will be all right.

She walks through the playground protective of her bag so that the darting wind-whipped children will not bump her precious things. Mrs Hill's whistle blows; Ellie's forgotten this bit where they freeze on the playground and snake into position. She braces, ready not to be wound into that rope of shining heads, ready to be cut out.

- Ellie, get in front of me.

Fletch. And here they all are, small and still and smiling their Monday smiles, all neat white teeth. They are wedged into thick coats and smelling of milk and cough syrup. They try to hush themselves but the Christmas lights behind the steamed-up windows spark their faces with colours. They're beautiful. Ellie holds tight on to her bag, fitting badly but fitting still into the shuffling, muttering line of Christmas wishes for Tiny Tears and Transformers, bright plastic things that click and light and beep and cry in the right place.

They march all together into the dim classroom. The Christmas lights glow rainbows.

- Where's Woodsy?
- Is he off?
- Is he sick?
- Is he gone?
- I like your hair Ellie.

Rachel said from underneath her permed mop, her eyes a little less tame. Fletch sits at his side of the desk. In the absence of Woodsy the room tickles with chat. Amanda gets up and puts the lights on hushing them with her folded arms. Then they hear the sturdy clip-clop of Mrs Hill's winter boots coming up the corridor.

- Mr Lockwood will not be in today so I will be taking your lessons.

Her brow arches around the room for silence.

- I understand that you are preparing for the school play. Who can tell me what you did last lesson?

Hands shoot up.

- Amanda?
- We were making props miss, they're in the boxes over there.
- Very good. Newspaper on tables then and aprons on.

Ellie lays her gifts on the newspaper – stones, nails and fire. Fletch picks them up turning them in his hands – *astonished*.

- Ellie, these are ace. I'm sorry about, you know.
- Yup it's OK. So do you want to do the play with me?

She did not need to ask, he was already unravelling the fire. They busy themselves with their new treasures as Mrs Hill clops over.

- Welcome back Ellie, what's this? What will you be doing in the play?
- I don't know if I can because I have been off miss.

Her red-painted nails clickclack over Ellie's props.

- I see you've prepared something. What is it?
- It's about saints miss.
- Very good. But you're not on the programme? I suppose Mr Lockwood didn't realise that you would be back in school in time. Will your father be coming to see you?
- Yes miss. He will come, if I'm in the play.
- Good, good. Not to worry then, I'll rectify the programme whilst Mr Lockwood is away. Remember now Ellie, tell your father to come on the 16th, I'll have Mrs Clarkson get the tickets ready. Carry on you two . . . Who needs scissors? Line up here!

Ellie lines up for the scissors, fastening her apron in a tight bow at the small of her back.

- What are you doing Ellie, we've got all our props?
- I need to make one more thing.

22.

- I can't go.

- You don't have to go. Just have a bath and then we'll see.

The day of the play begins at sunset and the world is tilting, Ellie can feel it, a pressure behind her eyes. She has been to school already and come home and is to go back again. It is all rush rush rush – have you got your whatsits and everything?

Her dad runs her a bath even though it's only Wednesday not Saturday and the smell of Avon Skin So Soft fills up the house. Ellie watches the oil glazing the surface, she waves her hand to mix in the hot water, the resistance reassuring. Her stomach goes round and round.

Ellie's belly is flat and white again, but she has seen the tight dome of her mother's belly threaded with a red-stitch door and wondered. There was a story she told – her mother was the greedy wolf who ate all the goats, she said, and had rocks sewn into her tummy by Mama Goat. Her mum used to bark and howl at Ellie on her hands and knees and Ellie would let herself be caught and eaten up with kisses. That was the Before, the best Before.

Ellie thinks about the lines she has to say tonight. What Catherine has to say. She mouths them. If she says them out loud the bathroom shudders. Why did she think this was a good plan? It isn't anything like real Best Man Dead. Just her and Fletch and death.

A moth swoops drowsily towards the wrong moon of the round bathroom light; it must have been hibernating in here. It's soft and drifting at first, then all flit-flutting feathered drumming like the thing in her mother's eye. Ellie scrubs her hands in the water, checking for sea-coal under her nails. Stones, nails and fire. That's all she has to remember. She feels the fear under her skin and scrubs and scrubs to scour the feeling back to nothing. Is it right? Killing her saints at Christmas? She smells different even to herself, lathering her head over and over until she feels every root tingle.

- Ellie out now. Time.

She stands, too quickly, steadying herself on the sink, water slooshing over the side of the bath. The cold air rushes in around her and she clicks off the light to let the moth know it should go back to sleep. The flit-flit-flit stops.

She hears her dad outside her bedroom door, hears his crackle breath, he's smoking.

- I'm putting your suit out Kate. Ellie, come and help your mum.

Kate sits by the dressing table. She used to have a rhythm for getting ready, Ellie remembers, there was a way to do it, a place to start. Ellie opens Kate's make-up bag – tubes, pencils, brushes. The smell is forbidden – 'Don't touch mummy's things.' *Pancake* – the colour of pale puddings – swirling puffs of powder. Ellie patpatpats her mother's cheeks on, puffs of sweet snow smoothing out the sharp hollows.

- Come on Mum.
- Not like that. Would you like a go?

Kate takes the soft sponge to Ellie's face; it is damp, delicious and grown up. Her mother's face is fixed in concentration, tilting Ellie's head up in the shallow light of the bedroom. Patpatpat. In the mirror Ellie's dark-moon circles disappear behind pancake cloud. Kate takes a slender pencil and rubs a patch of grey onto the back of her hand, then holds it up to Ellie's cheek.

- That's how they do it in the shops to work out your colour. Grey to bring out the green in your eyes, like mine. Look up for me Ellie.

Kate warms the nib on her hand till it's soft and then works it round and round each of Ellie's eyes, soft stippled dabs then more confident strokes. Kate's eyes flicker over her work.

- You've got all the colours in your eyes look – grey, blue, green. I don't know whose eyes you have. Look.

In the mirror Ellie sees the wolf's black-ringed eyes staring back at her.

- Stop.

Ellie stands, knocking over her mother's tea, pale as the pancake before it sinks into the carpet. The blue pill spins for a moment and starts to dissolve. Ellie stares, startled by the new edges of herself her mother has found with her patpatpat.

- She's not old enough for that.
- Dad, I said she could do it.
- Clean her face.
- There's not enough time.

The paraffin heater sputters out, and Kate slips on her long narrow tweed skirt, the colour of burned heather, it slides easily over her hips. Tights? There are no tights. Dad has forgotten to buy tights. Ellie gives Kate her best white socks with diamonds, and Kate puts them on and tiptoes down the stairs. Her Derry boots are warming by the fire. The boots, still warm, crunch through the new crust of snow. Ellie walks ahead, keeping pace. They are late now as they trail towards the school.

★

The hall is dim, bigger with its blurred edges. Ellie tugs down the sleeves of her mum's blouse, down over the gill-white marks from the broken window, and she gives her the pink stubs of rough paper – PARENT. The tree at the back of the hall winks and Kate is sucked into all the 'hiya'ing and 'hello'ing, puffy arms of ski jackets reaching out pulling the crowd together, the warmth of hot cars rolling off them. The bitten-off murmurs start low, louder – 'LockedupmadPaddy.' But her mum is elegant in her good suit and best Derry boots – a different creature from them altogether with their slash of electric-pink lips. They are technicolour, all mod cons, Ellie's mum is stone and earth and fire that does not burn.

The darkness off stage is like being out-of-bounds, like floating in her own water that day in the pool. She could be all Ellies at once and not have to cut and choose but when the lights go on she will have to be one thing only. She doesn't know what yet. Ellie-who-says-yes, Ellie-out-of-bounds, Catherine?

On.

The lights flush out across the crowd. She sees dark heads tilting, like stints running. Mr Lockwood says blah-de-blah. Ellie tries to find her mum's head but the tinfoil stars dazzle everything.

- Blah-de-blah Ellie Fleck and Robin Fletcher.
- *How Saints Die.*

Ellie said but it was both of them saying it, she and Catherine, a shush under her tongue, two-together.

First the stones for St Stephen.

- Ow. Ayaz.

Fletch-St Stephen said. Once you opened your mouth to speak they knocked you to the ground; the stones knew what to do. The light made them real. The crowd said ooh and ayaz too, as though the stones did bruise – their mouths opening into nothings.

Nails for St Andrew now, through the wrists. Fletch is brilliant, wriggling and shouting as she bangs in the nails through the place that was true. Some of the parents stand up but do not clap. Clapping's for later – the end. It's not the end.

Now it's Ellie-Catherine's turn to die. Catherine does not want to get married, she just wants to stay alive and keep her visions. The man who wants to marry her really wants to kill her instead.

- I will not marry you, I only want Jesus, I would rather die.
- Jesus isn't here and you will die on this wheel.
- Good.

Now comes the wheel for breaking, spinning you, so up is down and down is up. Whoosh, turn turn turn. Ellie steps forward and spins with all the fervour of a God herself. Fzzzzt, the fire, the world tilts, upside down, fzzzzt. Ellie *is* showing them. Fire in her hands, setting alight to it all. The world righting itself on the spinning wheel, all faces all colours turning, everyone's head turning up the right way except – there is her mother. Ellie-Catherine they are the light, lit for the dead and gone. Lit to bring them home. Ellie burns across the jagged darkness to her mother. Kate stands. A low inarticulate hum thrums from the open mouths around her.

- KidmadPaddyskidmadPaddyskidmadPaddyskid.

Kate can't win, they won't let her and Ellie win. Ellie had rushed to the end and they didn't recognise their cruel God in this story and his favourite deaths. Kate claps hard, defiant, as though she was slapping the slack open mouths, slapslapslapslap.

Mrs Hill claps too, scooping thwacks that pull them back into the now, the normal, the 'just children' of it all. She seals over the strangeness with airtight applause, trying to right all that Ellie has upturned. Then what can they do but follow? Only Fletch's mum at the front keeps her hands still. Ellie had run to the end, past the sleeping baby and the wandering star to the other side of the story. She found her way there, found her feet, and she could run and run and run. But this is not her end, and she stops, mid cartwheel, collapses down, winding into herself. They are clapping but no, this is not the end. Ellie kneels before them all, her head tilting back, her mouth wide, her arms opening like angel wings, so slowly. Craaaaaaaaaaaak. Fletch chops off her head, and it rolls off the edge of the stage into the lap of a mother holding a child. The child screams in delight.

Ellie had made the head from papier mâché and a balloon, she had tucked it up under her dad's old fishing smock. Thud, it's a surprise. They are *astonished*. Kate stands because Ellie knows, they both know – how saints die the best dead and then . . . they come back. Ellie had won, they had both won. Fletch went off left, Ellie went off right.

★

Behind the blackout curtain in the corridor behind the stage Mr Lockwood waits for Ellie. The turning and the clapping and the laughing have made her dizzy. The fire trails are still streaming from her hands and feet. She keeps walking into the dark, she keeps pushing to get through the curtain and then . . .

- Don't step on that.

She walks across one of the gym mats by mistake, big blue and spongy under her feet.

- Sorry sir.

Then he has her shoulders cupped in his hands – he squeezes.

- Look at me.

Ellie looks, but she knows he hates it when she looks right at him.

- You are sick, a sick sick child.

She is shaking, no, he is shaking her.

- Look at me.

His spit wets her face and she does not want to look, she knows it's a game and a rule at the same time, she should not look.

- Look.

His teeth are yuck with coffee stains, his lips pare right back from his teeth.

- What was that performance? Who said you could do that?

She opens her mouth and her teeth chatter in the too-hot corridor.

- Don't speak to me.

His fingers dig in as he pulls her closer. Will he bite her?

- You arrogant little . . .

The ends of her fire rustle on the floor, the fire her mother had made for her. Mr Lockwood treads on it, paddling it. Making it just paper. Ellie lifts her hands to keep the fire safe.

- Don't you dare raise your hand to me.

He grabs her wrists, the fire damp and darkening from his sweat.

- What's this rubbish? What is this?

Now she looks at him, her eyes burning, she is already dead, she is Best Man Dead. Ha.

- Don't you look at me like that.

She wanted to burn him up. He had a hold of her shoulders again, his fingertips digging for the soft bird-bones under her skin, lifting her onto her tiptoes. She is paddling the air. Ellie opens her mouth to let out the winged thing inside to scratch out his eyes.

- Don't cry.

He says. She can hear crying, but it isn't her, she has no breath, it is Rachel, her beautiful dark hair and her face all red. Stephen is there too, he is the best runner – he ran.

Ellie makes everything go quiet inside her head. On-off. Through the broken-toothed door and into the . . .

- Mr Lockwood.

Mrs Hill. Woodsy drops Ellie. She crumples onto the floor. She was flying but now there is just pain where her wings had been. She can't pull a breath in. She needs her dad, he cut her out. He gave her her first breath.

\- I liked the fire Ellie, Ellie are you OK?

Stephen is trying to pick up the fire from the floor but it's all torn.

\- Whoa Ellie, Woodsy totally spazzed out.

Stephen, who held her face in the dirt because she pushed him down, Stephen who could run the fastest, had run for Ellie, because she had won. He held her tattered fire out to her.

\- Ellie your dad's here.
\- Ellie.

And she took the first breath he gave to her.

\- Where's Mum?

He'd left her. That wasn't the rule. Hold on to Mum. That was all he had to do. They are walking very quickly now, Ellie's stompy run-walk right into the crowd of mothers, the good mothers who huddle in gaggles at gates with fags for mouths blowing Ellie's mother up in smoke. What do they see when they see Kate? Ellie knows. They pull and push and pluck. They dig their stumpy fingers into Kate's soft-as-moss suit. They throw words like stones – madPaddybitch – that bruise. They tear, they scratch, they cluck. They snag their nails in her hair. The nails pierce.

Ellie lets go of her father's hand, she can squeeze in

between the cracks of the crowd to her mother. She pushes
their hands back, spits and shows her teeth. She knows how
she looks to them. She's died once already tonight.

- That child is damaged.

Ellie knew damaged. That was Mrs-Fletcher-Call-Me-
May. Fletch was crying and Ellie felt the shame for him.
She reaches out to him, they are two-together.

- Don't you touch him.

They said, like she was on fire.

- *Au revoir.*

Ellie mouthed to him.

★

There was once a mother, they said, who was mad, mad-
dymadmad mental. They had heard she would open up and
swallow them all, like the earth, like the big bad wolf. All
laughing teeth and clapping claws. They said she'd burn
their children up. So they put her out. Good riddance.
That wasn't the way it was, but that was the story they told
themselves and they got full marks, well done.

23.

The next day is Present Day. They'd had a letter saying, 'Please bring a present suitable for school for 17th December, preferably stationery. Yours sincerely Mrs Hill.' All the children in Ellie's class queue up next to the big red plastic bin filled with sparkling parcels while Mr Lockwood plays them Christmas pop songs. Tinny wishes, warm heads nodding together, Mr Lockwood on the outside. They each grab their parcels and go back to their desks, crackling paper.

Mr Lockwood writes the last word for their topic of *Family* on the board – 'GRANDMOTHER' – and he circles it. Hands shoot up – hands holding new pencils, hands that have unwrapped shiny paper and pulled forth plastic wonders, hands that held the living answers and each other.

- Child.
- Protect.
- Love.

Ellie spins her own new plastic pencil, shining the light through it onto her paper and holding her word in her head. Ellie does not have a grandmother who has her round for iced buns and takes her to see *ET*. Their words for grandmother keep coming:

- Old.
- Smile.
- Cuddly.
- Cosy.

Her grandmother, Granny Lil, had sent her the big red *Children's Book of Saints for Every Day* when she was very small. In St Francis's story everyone was afraid of the wolf because he walked their hilltop on his four legs, through streets only made for people and their two-legs. There was a picture in her head of a hungry grey shadow, wandering under white washing strung between houses, his back warmed by the Italian sun, looking for people to eat. St Francis, he went out to see the wolf and the wolf put his soft head in the saint's hands just the way her wolf had done. The wolf did not eat St Francis as he was not that kind of saint.

- Hereditary.

That was Fletch.

- And Ellie, do you have a word?
- Wolf.

The children giggle.

Then the twitching hands go still because her father is wheeling his old green bike through the blue gates, wrong-wrongwrong. He leans his bike up against the porch of the entrance hall. 'Not allowed,' they all think. 'No bikes – no bikes in the playground.' They put down their pencils and their empty hands all fill now with the rules. Mr Lockwood stops writing on the board. He won't look at Ellie.

– It's cos Woodsy grabbed her, isn't it?

Fletch knows because they all know. Even though it was private. Rachel had seen – had told – she was crying – but Stephen had run to get Mrs Hill – had told on Woodsy. Then Rachel told everyone. They all knew her dad would have to come.

– Back to work in silence.

A dense hush and the faint animal scratching sound of thirty-two pencils writing 'wolf'. Mrs Clarkson came in; she did not knock.

– Ellie, come with me, there's a good girl.

Mrs Mole Hill has a special office for visitors where Ellie has to go now, and she's shivering, tssstssstsss. Her dad is there. It's all wrong – all wrongwrongwrong – his leg and his socks, here. She sees him and bangs her knee, not looking. Something tickles her breath, like when you want to cry.

There is a low coffee table and square, green prickly chairs that smell strongly of Mrs Hill's expensive cigarettes. The room is choked and too warm for the winter's day outside, condensation bubbling down the window. Ellie-who-said-yes and her father are here together in Mrs Mole Hill's special office; no one is where they are supposed to be. Her dad looks ridiculous, like a giant, his long legs bent so high his knees almost touch his ears. He's wearing his good trousers, the colour of dry sand, the hiss and crease of the iron still fresh on them. He has on his checked shirt, blue on white like squared paper, and his tie. But also his blue coat and cap, as though he is sitting in the kitchen not here in the special office. Ellie sees his pale skin above his sock, blue-white-white-blue. She remembers when he was bitten by the horsefly and the blue-black map of the bite tracking up his leg. Wrongwrongwrong – her stuttering heart. He does not understand the rules of this place, he knows nets and sea-coal and thudtickticktick but not this.

- Now Peter.

Soft, Mrs Hill was brown and soft today, standing at her window with her back to them. Mrs Hill had known her dad from before, when they were both young. Her dad had told her. Mrs Hill, then Miss Marsh – Marsh-Hill, Hill-Marsh, high-low-Miss Marsh had gone in the speedboat with her dad – *Sea Lover*. Maybe Miss Marsh was green, as Ellie could not imagine the brown solidity of Mrs Hill flying along in the water in *Sea Lover*, her solid legs swaying and pitching with the sea beneath them.

- Sit still.

Mrs Hill's cheeks are a high colour. She lifts the pot and pours tea for her dad, pulling the old thread which held them two-together. Ellie can see it now. Her dad all angles and she all soft, sort of fitting. The words float above and around Ellie and Mrs Hill's puddle eyes blink at her dad and she wonders if she should be here. But Mrs Clarkson had come to get her, so Mrs Hill had sent for her. She wonders, if Mrs Hill had been her mum, whether she would have been Mary and good and normal and not a saint killer, and she pushes the thought away. Traitor.

- Remember Lifeboat Day?

Stitch –

- . . . that boat . . . my hair . . . whatastate?

Stitch –

- . . . hahaha . . .
- Absences.

Snip.

Mrs Hill spills her tea into the saucer, onto her knee. She brushes it down her brown skirt, trying to brush away the words she does not want to say but she has to come out with them and break that old thread.

- . . . absences . . . knockedaboydown . . . runaway . . . nowthis . . . stonesnailsfire . . . headoff . . . erratic . . . MrsFletcher . . . concerned . . . report . . . socialservices . . . damaged.

Ellie was waiting for the thick clods of truth that Mrs Hill, well practised, threw down before you. 'Do not run,' splat. 'Stop that chewing,' slop. But today it is all light words which dance around, not knowing themselves where they will land.

- . . . nevertheless . . .

That was Mrs Hill's word. Her brow would arch on the 'the' and you waited for the strike of the 'less', like the school clock chiming – ting – when she would smooth over the creases and brush it all down and make it all right. It would come out now, Christmas and Mr Lockwood and the wrong of it all and Stephen running. Yes, it was her word entirely. The brow arched and took aim.

- manage this with social services . . . a sensible solution . . . to help everyone . . . not to punish . . .

But she doesn't say anything about Mr Lockwood and the Christmas play. Ellie's stomach pitches. It is not all right. It is Ellie who is all wrong. She has made her dad come here where he does not belong, where he is too big and his skin is too thin, and it is her fault. The brow arches and looses and strikes – Ellie.

 - I must look after the interests of all the children in my school.

Adults knew all the things children weren't supposed to know and wanted children to keep pretending they didn't know them. Her father puts down his teacup to rub his head, he's shrinking, the fight rushing out of him. Mrs Hill pats the air above his shoulder. She places a blue letter down in front of him, with a dark blue rectangle and a cross next to it. Her dad takes off his coat finally, his arm flinging out so the tea-cup goes flying off the little table, but it does not break, it just spins on the coarse wool carpet. Ellie sees him write his name in long looping strokes; she bites down hard on the cry inside her, she bites away the part of her that wants to push his hand away. He has learned the rule. Mrs Hill had had to talk to her father because Ellie had won at the Christmas Play, and when children win the adults have to make it look as though it was wrong and their fault. Mrs Hill picks up the blue paper.

 - I think this is the best way to deal with it for every-one concerned.

Tssstssstssss. In class they are waiting for it, for Ellie to come back and win, because that's what had happened. They knew it.

- Miss Fleck has an announcement don't you Miss Fleck?

- I'm leaving.

They look *astonished*. And inside her head she thinks of a new sentence, 'I will *vanish*.'

Who had won?

Ellie walks with her dad as he wheels his bike through the yard out-of-bounds. All of the children watch the wheel clicking round and round. Tickticktick. This is not winning. They feel it. Then Fletch waves, then Stephen. Then tickticktick and gone.

Win . . . Victory . . . Conquest . . . Conflict.

The words make no sense, they are no good, they can't possibly tell her what winning is like. They're words for simple conflict where people only died so they did not have to come back to school or start a new one. Ellie has no idea if anyone has ever won at all.

24.

When the snow froze over last year on her birthday Ellie's dad showed her how to walk on the slippery crust. Feet wide, slowslow-slipslip-slow, the trick is not to put your mind in your feet but in your belly button – where you cup your balance. The crisp snow had cracked and crunched like the icing of her birthday cake between her teeth. It's her birthday again today. 18th December, one eight, the tall straight lighthouse of one next to the wave of the eight curling in on itself. Ellie-who-said-yes would be at school for the last day and birthday cards and birthday bumps, but this Ellie is expelled here in the in-between, in the leftleft nights.

A white feather cradle-rocks down as though the air isn't fall-through at all, as though a breath were enough to hold you up. There are more – a spuff of them, almost invisible on the snow. Like breadcrumbs they trail under the empty blackcurrant bush. It was a pigeon, Ellie can tell by the feet. One foot is curled up and boneless like a red rubber band: it was sick then. There is no head left. The ribcage is open and its secret contents gone. The wolf has plucked and eaten it neatly; there is only one smear of blood on a breast feather. Ellie picks up this one as evidence for her box of broken things – a present for her birthday, maybe even luck.

She thinks of Ellie-at-school who says yes and Fletch and the time ticking past, leaving him behind and her cracking like snow between teeth.

Mrs Forster is outside, pecking in the cold ground. She's pulling out skull stones with Douglas lapping round her legs. Ellie grins as Mrs Forster sees the dead pigeon and gives the cat a clumsy pat, her fingers curling under the proud chin.

- Good puss, good . . . What are you looking at girl, you should be in school.
- I've been expelled.
- What for?
- Killing saints.
- At Christmas? Still, you've a right to your education and you can't be at home under your father's feet, not with your mother and all. Get to school.

Mrs Forster is right. Ellie will go to school; she was there only yesterday and today is the last day – why not? She will go and see Fletch and she will tell him it is her birthday and she will tell him what she should have told him straight away – that there is a wolf. And he will listen and frown and she will tell him everything slowly and he will add it all up inside his warm blond head. He will work it out. He

269

will tell her she is prime. And who the wolf has come to kill. She will take the feather as evidence.

- Leftleft.

Ellie marches. Leftleft. She knows the way. At the lollipop lady's crossing there is no lollipop lady but Ellie can hear the fastasyoucan-tig-youre-it-catch-fall-cry of it all up the black road long before she sees the gates. She looks left and right to cross. The roads are empty, just slush and footprints and old leaves and still cars. From the gate she can see his white hair; he is a small sun trembling and holding a gun. He is killing them and they are dying fast and slow. She is still alive at the gates.

- Traitortraitortraitor.

Fletch makes the noise. 'Ackackackackackack,' and the line of boys judders and falls twitching to the floor. One of the spiky kids, Ed, gurgles splurting blood sounds which impress Ellie despite herself. The bodies pile up on top of one another, finally still.

- I think Ed was the Best Dead.
- Aw.
- Me now.
- So this is what you play with that weird lass?
- Yes.
- Is she any good?

Now he sees her, Fletch looks right at her by the gate. He had never thought before that she did not belong in his world. But now Ellie is standing on the other side behind the blue bars, her hands wrapped around the metal, her long dark hair blowing across her white face, her red hood haloing her hair. Her colours make their world thin and grey, her strangeness demands something from them, a kind of beauty. It terrifies him. The red-rose flowers of her dress shout across the playground from beneath the hem of her father's blue smock.

Her lips move silently – a prayer or a curse, she knows both – traitor. She watches and she knows he belongs on their side of the gate, their side of dead where it is a game of falling and littlecuts-laugh-spit-shove-aw-me-now.

– Is she Fletch, is she any good at being dead?

Stephen answers for him.

– Yeah. She's totally mental. Look at her, she's a shitting witch.

Fletch stares at her just the way they stare at her.

– Traitortraitortraitor.

Then he comes. She must test him – are they still two-together? – and she pushes the gate open, rust flaking on her hands. Which side is he on?

- Ellie? Are you allowed back to school? You've not got your uniform on.
- What were you playing? With them? Just now?
- Are you coming in?
- Did you play Best Man Dead with them?

He will not lie to her face but rolls up his sleeve to show her the red speckled marks on his pale arm. She touches it; his skin is smooth but she can make out the fingerprints from the Chinese burn. Fletch tries to swallow a cry but it sputs out of his nose and Ellie gently tugs his grey jumper down. They hurt him, so he isn't a traitor.

- It doesn't matter if you played with them, that's just playing. Do you want to stay here and play or do you want to come with me on a mission?

He slips through the gate to her.

- Fletch is out-of-bounds.
- I'm tellin'.
- Tell then. Wazzocks.

She takes his hand and they bolt, two-together.
Their breath blooms out in front of them like the thickening fret rolling in off the sea. Black road, green dunes, then splashsink into rockpools. Wet socks let in the cold. Their faces burn with sand and salt.

- We're out-of-bounds.

Ellie laughs close to Fletch's ear. Here she could take his hands, here she could spin him on the wide sands and open him up to the peeppeeppeep.

– Fletch.

She says, which means let's run with the little birds, the piper and plover, around the spill of the tide into the deeper mist.

– Fletch.

She says, which means you came to me – you are Fletch-out-of-bounds. But he is not running with her, he is slow, his breath shortening, the mist making him paler, his hair sticking in wet slicks to his forehead. She has made him split.

– I'm cold.

She takes off her scarf, letting the wind wrap its arms round her, and she tangles her scarf around him to bind him all together.

– You'll feel better soon.

He is shaking.

– What's our mission then?
– It's my birthday today.
– Happy birthday. Is that our mission?

- No.
- Ellie is there really a mission?
- Yes.
- So?
- So I need to show you something.
- Come back to school with me.

He wants to sound big and all knows best, but Ellie can see he is frightened. He doesn't have much time here, the cold is hurting him and his words come out in judders, as though he's doing Best Man Dead. She sees it but she can't stop.

- I can't go back, not until I've shown you.
- OK, OK.

It is difficult to see in the fret but Ellie can just make out the jagged black outline of the rock at the shore tip of Jenny Leigh's Scaur, where she had first seen the wolf's eye. She needs someone else to look, she needs Fletch. He follows her to the edge of the pool.

- Look. This is where I found it.
- What?
- I was going to cut a limpet and it opened its eye and it was a wolf.
- You are saying the rock became a wolf?
- Yes. No. Not the rock. Out of the pool. Water to solid. You know like snow?
- Wolves don't even live in this country.
- Wolves of water do.

- Ellie you're making it up.
- I'm not, it was there in York. It nearly went for you.
- This is mental.
- But now my mum's home, I think it's after her.
- You think a wolf made of water is after your mum?
- Yes. Sort of. I think it came because wolves kill sick things and my mum is sick.
- But she's home. She's better. Isn't she?
- I think there's something wrong – inside her.
- Ellie, we need to move. The tide is coming in.
- I've got evidence.

Ellie took the pigeon feather from her pocket.

- See it's got blood on it. The wolf ate it because it was sick.
- That's evidence that something killed a bird, not that a wolf killed a bird.

He took the feather, looking at it closely.

- Maybe a cat?
- It was a wolf.
- Ellie do you know how to get back?
- Of course I do.
- I can't just run away from school.
- This isn't run away, that's bad.
- This is bad Ellie, we're going to get in big trouble.
- Why did you come then?
- Because we're friends.

- Friends don't play Best Man Dead with wazzocks.
- Friends don't lie.

He stepped off the rock, his foot slipping on the wet seersucker, and he yelped and slid into the pool. The barnacle teeth nipped through his school trousers. Ellie tugged him back up but his foot would not come loose.

- I'm stuck Ellie, something's got my foot.

Ellie pulls but he's right. Mussels click for the incoming tide, hungry and exposed. She stirs the pool, trying to clear aside the red hair of dulse and the sand murk, and feels the rope snaring Fletch's foot. The rope is sodden and swollen and she can't loose it.

- Stop it you're making it worse.
- Keep still.

Two jackdaws circle above them, raking at the air. The tide is coming in quickly now. Ellie squeezes her fingers in between the coils of the rope, burning them – too tight. She can't get him out.

- We'll be all right Fletch, I can't drown at sea. I'm protected. It will be all right.

She tells him, slicing her knuckles on the barnacles trying to find a sharp rock to cut the rope. The salt is stinging her cuts.

- It will be all right.

- We're going to drown Ellie!

- I was pulled up from the sea.

- Liar.

- I never lie.

- What about your dead mum?

- I didn't mean dead-dead, I said it to scare them away and it worked, they went away.

- Liar.

The sea gurgles up, circling around them.

- Ellie you need to go and get help.

- I won't leave you by yourself.

- Ellie, please go and find an adult.

- Adults don't help. Besides, the sea can't hurt us because this is my story. Listen, my great-grandfather, he cut a sea-god free from his nets for luck – we can't drown. My dad told me.

- Then your dad's a liar.

- My dad is not a liar.

- Hough.

The wave strikes him like a fist, knocking him off and down into the water. With his leg trapped he can't right himself and the sand-water clogs his duffel coat and holds him down. Ellie drags him back onto the rock.

- Ellie go and get help.

- If I go you aren't protected.

- Go.
- No, we can't drown.

A wave punches through her pulling her out and away. It holds and hushes her, like the sound of her own blood rushing. She opens her mouth into the salt sting to say it out loud – 'Take it, whatever you want' – and the sea smacks her lips and swallows her promise. Ellie reaches through the grey iron water to Fletch and then . . . She can feel it paddling, dragging her by the scruff of her neck to the shore and away from him. It drops her on the shingle, the stones crunch. She tries to get up but it hip-slams her to the ground, pushing down on her chest. It kisses her head, bristly warm.

25.

Dark at two-thirty, though not dark enough for the lights on so Mrs Forster hung close to the window. Her fake tree, pristine, unlit. Who would see it? Who would come? The house is so cold, but she does not want to put the heating on. Silly really, she spent most of her married life thinking about how to save a penny here and a penny there but she doesn't need to watch money, not now, not after he died. It was just who she was, her knack for money – watching, wanting, holding back. 'Penny-pinching,' Maisie said. That's the way she proved her worth; she was never pretty, plain at best. Invisible mostly. She dressed appropriately, not well. Even her silks were practical, but she loved the feel of them. She couldn't cook, hated food, the way pastry got under her fingernails and her woollens would hold the smell of gravy. Arthur didn't realise that until it was too late. But then he didn't like anything fancy. Wouldn't have appreciated it if she could cook. Good solid food he liked, thick pastry crusts with weak chicken gravy and pale meat. He didn't want too much stimulus. And Mrs Forster was happy to oblige – so that was that. He ate so unnaturally, hunching over the table, taking not just his mouth but his whole body to the food. Like one of those snakes off the nature programmes. He'd heave great sodden clumps on the fork, opening his elastic mouth, enveloping, barely chewing. Getting it all over and done with as quickly as he could. Sucking it up and bellowing 'ahhh', not out of satisfaction, but relief that it was over. She never suggested going out. Maisie was always out with Stan to the Swan Hotel for the carvery. She could never stomach being out with Arthur, seeing other people's faces as he winced bodily around his food. She couldn't do that to the appetite of innocent paying customers. No, food was not her thing. But she could account for every penny in and every penny out.

Not like them now – they didn't even look in their purse, just pulled out plastic. Plastic! She knew what was in her purse – to the penny – by the jingle. How long could she last today without the heating on? Maybe till 4 p.m. She tripped then trying to get right to the window. The council had pulled up her emerald-green carpet to fit the radiators and never put it back down right. She is unable to lift her swollen right knee today, and more days. It will kill her, that carpet. She should get Peter to come and trim it down. But she won't ask, not now. Not after he sent her out last month, the cheek of it, to send her out like that when that flash woman came, with her red boots and camel coat 'to talk about the children'. She'd show him. He got no paper now for that.

She had broken her favourite cup again, an accident this

time, and it stood on the kitchen windowsill, carrying its own broken handle. She took messages round of course, just the bare essentials. She had been trying to protect him, why couldn't he see that? He didn't know this woman from Eve. What woman wears her hair like that? Who did she think she was, Lady Di?

She got herself pulled round eventually and rocked her way slowly to the shop and there was Maisie on the corner. They heaved in, Maisie hooked in Alice's arm. Roasting it was, inside the shop, money to burn, Mrs Forster thought. But she loved the smell, always had, the boozy gassy smell of fruit going off, and dust and sweets and ink – all mixed together – tasty and foul at the same time. Tinsel hung limply from every shelf, the Sellotape unpeeling itself in the heat.

Still, Mary was behind the counter bursting out of her elasticated trousers with gossip. This May Fletcher apparently had sailed out of the shop just yesterday, nearly knocking Maisie off the step. 'Just milk and bananas,' she got. 'What can you do with just milk and bananas?'

- She nearly had me over.
- Eeh.

Mary mouthed single parent, her mouth working its gummy way around the shape of her disapproval. Maisie translated.

- Single – parent!
- Oh.

Mrs Forster took it like a blow, she couldn't speak. Oh – she thought. Well – to treat her like that, a single mother? Mrs Forster teetered on the edge of her anger and then let herself fall head first, enjoying its release. She unburdened herself then and there, the visit and the banishment and those red boots, that hair, those heels – she knew it, had read her like a book.

And the ohs and wells and eeeehs as Mary and Maisie lapped up all the old sour milk. Mrs Forster felt the warmth fill her up her bones for the first in a long time. Maisie and Mary, warm and fat and shocked, had just the right amount of seething disapproval to make her feel she almost loved them. Here in this toasty shop, all glowing and puffing up. They pushed out the cold shock of rejection Mrs Forster had felt. The room swelled with their mutual judgement. They each took their turn to have a good go at this May.

- Single, oh.
- Parent, eeh.
- Well.
- Eeh I know.
- Oh.
- Slut.
- Eeh.

They were quite dizzy when the collective flurry of half-gasped insults finally wound its way to a close. Mary stuffed a marshmallow in her sunken mouth, offering the jar to Maisie and Mrs Forster, who shouldn't – blood sugar – but go on then. Because it was free.

The fluffiness, dry and dissolving into a sweet stickiness –
beautiful, and Mary and Maisie – beautiful. Mrs Forster
took her paper and made her way home. It was only later,
her tea stewed and the heating still off and the dense cold
seeping into her bones that she felt it – shame. Cold and
shame. The things that she had said and that had kept her
warm had only been the flash of a match – a short brittle
light. She remembered how hard it was when she first had
her little boy. He didn't feel like hers, he looked like his
father with his arsehole of a mouth closing around her
breast. Her hard body gone soft and doughy and everything seemed to pass through her as though she wasn't
really there.

Arthur would come home and she would be in the kitchen staring out at the washing line, nappies and nappies
and nappies.

– What are you looking at? He's crying?

She hadn't realised, it was part of the sound of her life
now – water running and crying. She picked him up in
her hands but in her head – marshmallow. The other mothers sat in tweed-tight circles and wouldn't open their
mouths about anything to do with mothering. Waking up
at six, if they slept at all, to get to the church hall for ten
sharp. Hair perfect – that's what you did, you went to be
seen.

– Eeeh, it's as if she never had him.

And it was, the edges of herself were worn away. Arthur was no help, treated the baby like every other mess, he just pointed her to it.

- He's crying.
- He's wet.
- He's this . . .
- He's that . . .

He's bloody well yours now. Arthur, the father-commentator – his only duty was to describe the event from behind the newspaper.

- He's wet.

Snap. If she did not react quickly enough, he would give the broadsheet a quick snap.

- He's gone, Alice, he's gone now.

Snap.

Always single, mothers, except – extraordinarily, not single, joined to something so acutely you dissolved. So she couldn't cope with just herself, after. Her husband could not know this, being so wholly solid and himself.

Mrs Forster wished, she wished she had said hello to May Fletcher, a mother still, despite the red boots, said that she understood, she knew something, a little of the secret. The delicate hot head rising and falling beneath your palm, so delicate and tyrannous, you would catch your breath.

She was so sorry, she made the shape of the 'sor' in her cold kitchen silently – she knew she would never say it, not out loud, but she would not make her phone call to Maisie at seven-thirty to go over the day, not tonight.

Peeep.

Bloody phone.

- Four-double-eight-zero-three-nine . . .
- Mrs Fleck. Ellie's run away and taken my son with her. Whatever happened to you, I don't give a shit, you've damaged her, your own child. I can take her away from you. Do you understand? If anything happens to my son I will take your child . . .
- I'm not Mrs Fleck.
- Sorry who? This is the number I have for the Flecks, four-double-eight-zero-three-nine.
- Yes that's right. That's my number.
- Who the hell are you then?
- Me? . . . We've met before . . . I'm the neighbour.
- Shitshitshitshit.
- I'll tell Peter right away shall I?

Alice felt all warm again. There he was, she could see him through the kitchen window. Head in hands and well he bloody might. Red boots. She knew it. You don't need to knock with news like this. She was in.

- Pete, your Ellie's kidnapped a social worker's kid-die. It's that May, the one with the red boots, she's a social worker. I said there was something not right with her didn't I? And I said Ellie was wild and now they'll take her off you.

Alice stopped to let him take it in. She knew she shouldn't, but it tasted so soft and sweet.

26.

Peter's feet make thick splashes on the wet belly of sand as he puts Ellie down safe on the stones.

- Ellie you stay there. Where's the lad?
- Out there, at Wolf Rock.
- What the hell's he doing there?
- He slipped on the rock . . . there's a rope around his foot . . . cut him free.

Peter wades out, plunges and pulls Fletch up, balancing the pale boy over his knee. He takes out his knife, the one from Ellie's story, and cuts through the matted vein of the rope. Peter hopes Ellie is watching, hopes that she sees past the stories now, that this is what it is to cut someone free. It's fear and salt and shush and blood. Thud – Peter gives Fletch a hard slap between the shoulder blades and then another to be on the safe side and clear his lungs. He throws him over his shoulder, like a sea-coal sack, but this boy is much lighter, there's nothing to him.

Peter lurches up and down, over the high sand bells, stepping up to his knees and sinking down to his hips. Drifts of fret rub him out and back again; he rolls as though he's part of the current. Peter looks straight at Ellie. What was she playing at? But he knows it's his own fault. He knows what he put in her head. And he can't keep his eyes on her because if he looks away from the swell to the land he will tip and he and the boy will go under together. The sea's tilt rights him, pitching him back to his father and his father and his father.

- Dad.

She said as though she knew to haul him back.

- Dad.

And he comes with his knife and the boy over his shoulder.

- You cut him free, just like you did with me. I told him, I told him the sea-god wouldn't let him drown, I told him.
- By God.

The rag of the boy flaps there. He grabs Ellie with his other hand.

- Is that what you think? The sea-god saved you?
- It was luck Dad.

- It was that old bitch next door.
- No, because we're Flecks.
- You're no Fleck. You're no fisherman's daughter dragging this poor laddie out here to drown him and yourself too. You don't know the sea.
- I do. My story? My rope?
- There's no stories Ellie.
- Traitor.

Peter sits Fletch on his bike and holds him up by his hood. The winter dusk curls down.

- We've got to take him back to the school now Ellie.
- School's finished.
- To his mother then, where's he come from?
- I don't know, I haven't been to his house. Look at his leg Dad, we have to make him better first.

The boy's trouser is torn, and beneath the tear, the barnacle lashes bloom red, they're bitter cuts that'll scar.

- We'll take him home with us.

Peter sets the pace and walks home quickly, as the dark drops and the yellow lights of the Prom flick on like fizz-bombs. Ellie trails after him.

- Stop Dad. There's something else. It's not just his leg.
- What is it?

- He doesn't have a shadow any more.
- Enough Ellie.

★

Mrs Forster's curtains twitch as her dad wheels the bike up the yard, Fletch all droopy on the croggy-bar. Home safe. Sort of. Her dad's not talking to her and no one knows where Fletch is but them. Is that kidnapping? Her dad puts Fletch down on the couch and Ellie feeds the fire with sea-coal packets without being asked to.

- Get me the fix-up tin and some dry clothes.
- My clothes? But he's a boy.
- Now.

She comes back with a smock. Her dad wears smocks all the time and he's a boy. It'll do.

Fletch is all white and fire licks of orange in the dark; he looks strange and buttery, but not yuck. Her dad pulls the blanket up around the boy.

- Eh? What you looking at. Get me that tin and some hot water and a flannel.

It's like gutting a fish – washing the blood away so you can see what you're doing. Her dad drizzles salt into the water. Fletch's forehead crinkles in pain. Just the marks left – flecked rope burns and feather flaps of skin where the barnacles have torn and torn. Her dad wraps him all up like a present. Happy birthday. Blow that damn candle out.

27.

- Come on son, that's it, you're all right now. Your mam's come for you.

He is sad and sorry and her dad and not her dad and she is not a Fleck. A Fleck would have been safe at sea. A Fleck would have been good luck. It wasn't the sea-god or her promise that saved Fletch, it was her dad, just her dad.

Mrs-Fletcher-Call-Me-May follows behind him not knocking, not a visitor.

- Ellie, I want to see your mum.

May Fletcher looks like the wolf, like her teeth are itching.

- Where's your mum Ellie?

Ellie knows it's a trick question and waits for her dad to answer.

- Go get her pet, it's all right.

It's not, her mum is too raw and slow for Mrs Fletcher. Ellie isn't allowed in her parents' room, she isn't allowed to wake her mum. So she waits at the door and listens for Kate's breathing but there is only the shush of her own head.

- Dad?
- Won't she come?
- Dad. She's gone.
- Put your big coat on.
- You can't take that child out tonight, not after what she's been through.
- I can't leave her here. Your son is fine. Take him home.
- I'll take her too. You look for your wife.

Ellie takes her rope from the fireplace, for luck – good or bad she doesn't know now. Her dad locks the door behind them and takes off on his bike around the corner and away. And then it happens with no goodbye ta ta wave wave – she is taken away too. Traitor.

★

Cars swish past Fletch's house, spattering light around the strange room – the grey and red and black stripes of wallpaper, curtains crammed with smiling trains. Fletch's room smells of washing powder and biscuity dog and boy, even though he's next door in his mum's room. She is wearing boys' pyjamas with Transformers on them, ready for bed.

Fletch's mum comes in, no knock. She is a traitor too. She is not just Fletch's mum, she is like the grey man. She's going to take Ellie away, not just here away but further maybe even to the in-between place. Ellie tries to stand, but her head is splitting.

- I've got you some paracetamol, you've got a bit of a temperature.

Two white-and-blue beetle bars to keep Ellie in, next to the orange juice.

- I can't stay. I have to find my mum. Thank you.
- I can't let you go Ellie, you're only ten.
- Eleven.
- Sorry.

There is a bowl on the tray.

- Are those real Frosties, like the ones with the tiger?
- Yes. Robin's favourite.

But he wasn't her little Christmas Robin any more. Poor Mrs Fletcher.

- I've never had them before.

May puts the tray down on the bedside table as a black Labrador pushes his way through the bedroom door, wet nose first.

- No Flint. He's friendly, you don't have to be afraid.
- I'm not.

She isn't but when the dog puts his head under her hand and rubs hello she thinks of her wolf. Where is it now? She needs it to come for her or it will find her mum instead and her wolf isn't safe like this loved dog. This dog sits patiently looking from Ellie to May and back at the bowl brimming with milk and the impossibly yellow flakes. He's not stray. Ellie gives him the bowl and he slurps happily.

- I thought you wanted those.
- He wants them more.
- Get some sleep, I'll wake you in the morning.

The bed is crumply soft, no dead-granny blankets, and sleep picks at the edges of her. This is what it would be like to be just Ellie, just girl, just eleven years old and learning five new words a day; knowing that she wanted Hawaiian Barbie for Christmas and what a bidet was; not knowing how saints died and how to make nets. Her face just her face, and no one hiding in it. It would be lights-out and tucked-in and sweet-dreams and night-nights.

Thumpthumpthump.

Flint bumps her legs with his tail. The dog thurrrs a soft thur into Ellie's sleepiness.

Crickcrickcrickcrack.

It was coming from the landing.

Crickcrickcrickcrack.

Crickcrickcrickcrack.

May tramps downstairs and the kettle sputters on. Ellie gets up to find the thing that made the noise in May's room – a big typewriter with blue paper shivering inside it where May's fingers had triptrapped over the keys. A new story.

```
At risk     crick
erratic behaviour     crack
intervention    ping
```

Hearing May on the stairs, Ellie goes back to her room; kneeling up on the bed she can see all the houses in between Fletch's house and her own, all the chimney stacks – like blowholes in the black sky – and all the TV aerials. If she wanted to draw them all she would only need a pencil, a ruler and a brown crayon. In her head she opens the doors in these in-between houses and sees all of the families doing bedtime things – making tea, washing faces, feeding babies, reading books, watching telly – ping-slosh-whine-suck-swish-bzzzt next channel bzzzt next channel bzzzt. It would be good to keep these pyjamas on and for it to be bedtime and up-time and Frosties-time and to sleep long enough; it would be good and wrong and traitor. Her dad will never find her mum on his own.

Ellie dresses in the dark. Her rose dress is torn and the smock is crusted with salt and Fletch's blood rust. Her wellies are good. Wellies are always good but she steals a pair of Fletch's grey boy's socks as hers are wet. Fletch's mirror is big and watery in the dark. She's never seen herself whole in a big mirror before. At home she could only see a little bit at a time and all the pieces seemed to fit. But now the frayed blue smock drapes over her like a pelt and her torn dress droops a red tail from beneath the smock's hem. Her face is a long pale oval with a pointed chin and her dark grey eyes are ringed with black wolf shadows. Ellie smiles, running her tongue along the sharp edges of her teeth – and a not-girl, not-Fleck smiles back.

- You really gonna wear that?
- Fletch? I'm sorry about . . .
- I know.
- You OK?
- I'll live. You going?
- I need to find my mum.
- Let me come?

She kicks his leg, just a light little tap, almost nice and he crumples.

- Ow, you wazzock.
- See? You can't come.
- Let me help then. You'll freeze like that, you can borrow my stuff.

He scrambles in his wardrobe and grabs a black jumper and grey trousers covered in pockets. They smell fresh, of gardens. He doesn't have a box of broken things in the bottom of his wardrobe. His clothes feel soft as she slips them on. There she is in his mirror, not little pieces.

- Do I look like a boy?
- Nope.

He untucks her hair from the collar of the jumper, hooking out the cotters with his fingers, tugging gently.

- Who am I like?
- You stupid.

Ellie shuffles to the stairs.

- The third step creaks, step over it.
- OK.

She stops at the solid white front door of May's house – it's made up of eight panels bolted together; you could not break through this door even if you wanted to.

- It's locked.
- You'll have to go out of the dog flap. It's in the kitchen.

The deep carpet muffles their footsteps. This house isn't old enough to talk, not like Ellie's. The kitchen door opens without a squeak. Flint follows Ellie and Fletch, his nails clickclack on the lino. He butts his dog-sized door and paces, whining for his night-time wee.

- Shut up Flint.
- It's OK Mum, I'll let him out.

- Shush, you'll wake Ellie. You should be in bed. Wait there I'm coming.

Fletch quickly unhooks the dog flap, letting in a blast of cold night-time.

- Ellie wait.
- What?
- What if the wolf has come for your mum?
- You believe me?
- Sort of.
- Robin.
- I have to go.
- But the wolf?
- I dunno. I'll just have to stop it.
- How?
- I have a rope.

And a knife. But she doesn't say that out loud. She leans into Fletch, sort of butting his shoulder with her head and he wraps his arm around her, solid and warm and not yuck.

- I'm sorry.
- Go.

Ellie follows Flint through the dog flap. From outside she can hear Fletch's mum talking to him. Her voice is soft, like a car engine. Flint's peeing goes fizz and then he crashes round the garden in delight at being out in the cold. He barks, wanting her to play too.

   – Flint. Shush.

The security light plinks on, lacing the whole garden in blue frost, a complicated arrangement of bushes with crystal fingers. Flint rounds back to her, his bum high in the air, tail all wag, running to her and away and wanting to be chased.

   – What is it Flint?

Ellie throws a slobbery ball for him.

   – No, that's it now.

Ruckruck he shouts after it. She edges along the fence shadow to the garden gate. Flint follows and she bends down to him, nose to nose.

   – Goodbye.

Wet and licking and leaving, not taken away.

28.

The North Star, clear and low, Jupiter side by side with Venus. The Dog Star the brightest. Her dad taught her the stars, how to follow them out to sea and back home. But she is not going home. She keeps close to the walls, away from the shadows of the bare trees, careful not to get caught in their criss-cross patterns on the pavement. She moves out into the deeper cold, the one winter has been holding back until now. Chookchookchook – blackbirds – their song certain and straight, singing out to babies that will come, singing out to the worms that will feed them, singing out the song-shape of their home – a halo place still curled in frost-fisted buds, waiting for the song to open. 'Fastened to the Rock which cannot move,' Ellie hums, quiet as the dark as she hunts her wolf. She knows what it is hunting, the way she knows seven and four are eleven. She checks in her pocket to make sure the rope is still there, for luck.

The houses light her way. Ellie stops. She shouldn't, but look at that friendly blue door, what a blue, the kind of blue you would paint a boat full of hope. Inside children are jumping from chair to chair. It is bursting with light. Is that a family, is that what holds a family together – blue?

Ellie can feel its low thurrr first through the soles of her feet, then its smell – its salt and spray and must – and she's after it, her feet pit-padding over slush and ice. Together they swerve away from headlamps and into the cobbled streams of the alleyways. They chase the wire-tail of a rat, until it scurries under a Baithouse door. They glide onto the promenade where the sleeping cradles of boats rock in their A-frames. Past the lookout at number eight Fisherman's Square, where a squat light beams out to let those who are lost know someone is watching. The wolf catches the scent, it angles its shoulders low and turns sharp. Fthhh, straight as an arrow now. It slinks through the park gates, Ellie wriggles through too, slower, her breath coming in and out in punches. The roundabout, an upturned moon of spinning white, dazzles her. Where did the wolf go? There is only one place from here – church.

Ellie picks up its prints in the churchyard and two-together again they blaze through the gravestones, sheer with frost. The wolf skitters on the gravel path towards a shadow at the church door. Ellie skids and she's down, her knee scraping, and it's gone again.

- Mum. We need to go.

- No.
- Please Mum.

Ellie tries to take her mother's hand.

- I wanted the world to open up and swallow me Ellie.

Now Ellie sees the wolf. It's quiet, circling. Its eyes light up. Lit for the dead and gone, lit to bring her home.

- And it did, you know, it did. I feel like I've been under for so long I can taste the grit in my mouth.

Kate's fingers taptaptap at the church door. But Father Doorley's in his big house over the road. Ellie can see him, his face washed-out in the light from the television. He's laughing without his collar on.

- He's not there Mum.
- It doesn't matter. I don't need him.
- Come home then, with me.
- I don't know where home is pet.

The wolf chitters, it knows. It wants to take her there, to take her where she wants to go.

- I know Mum, it's there – past school and the lolli-pop crossing and the post office.

Not under the Green Hill, Ellie thinks, not there.

Kate walks round the church, one hand trailing, tracing the stone. She stops at the statue of the Virgin, worn out by salt and rain.

- You know Ellie, my own mother was a shit.

Ellie did not know. Did not know mothers could be 'shit', it was not a word she could put into a sentence. It was a Stephen schoolyard word. Bad, wrong, red pen. Not a word for mother.

- I needed her, needed to go home just to get pulled right. But she wouldn't let me through the door. For wickedness. And I wished the world would open up and swallow me. And after – I felt nothing. Nothing. Like I was under the earth and there was black dirt above me and between me and everything. Between me and your dad, between me and you. And you were so small and the whole time I thought I would lose you so I couldn't even touch you. And I was under and nothing could pull me out. Then she was dead and she'd never even looked at you. Just sent you that piece-of-shit blanket.
- I love my granny blanket.
- And there was all that rain. Beautiful. You know, that day with the window. And I thought each drop was like something new. I just thought if I could get out into it, if I could get my hands up to the water, it would get me out of that dirt and I might be able to touch you.

Without the weight of her on me. Without the need for her shit love. D'you understand Ellie love?

Ellie did not. Kate reaches out her arms to Ellie.

- He had to cut you out.

That was a lie. She was not Fleck.

- I know, he said he cut me out of his net. But it's a lie.
- That's right pet, it wasn't a net.

Kate opens up her dress – her belly rising, round and neat.

There was once a mother . . .

He cut her out. He asked her to love him there and then still holding the knife. He rocked her in the ocean of his hands. Ellie could see his knife slippery along the black belly seam of a fish. Along the white moon of her mother's belly. He cut her out?

- I'm sorry. Jesus. I'm as bad as her. Forget it. He cut you out of the net, like he said. It's true. You come here to your mummy now?

Kate closes her eyes, afraid of the answer, and the wolf lunges snipsnap out of the dark at her outstretched fingers.

Ellie snares its neck with her rope and it pulls, it yips, confused, dragging her feet through the winter muck.

- Go now, Mum.

Kate has already turned away and she thinks Ellie will follow the way she did on leftleft nights. And then the wolf arooarools.

- Shushshush.

Ellie says, and pulls down hard on the rope, bringing its head down. Blood flecks and foams in the soft black creases of its gums. It pulls, it pulls to get to her mother —snip snap. Ellie can't let it go. Her heart says thudtickticktick with the pull. Shush. And the wolf's heart thudtickticktick with her own. Shush.

Ellie is eleven, she learns five new words a day. She knows how to make a net, how to gut a fish, how to kill a saint and she knows who her own people are.

- Arooarool.

Its eye clear, reflecting Ellie back to herself, does not even see the knife. Its eyes – warm amber fire – light Ellie home. Thudticktick. Thudtick. Thud.

- You're back.

Peter says as though they had just popped out to the shops. And he stays sitting down in the kitchen, as though Ellie's allowed to the shops by herself and it's all right to stay sitting down when someone lost comes home. It's not. You're supposed to get up and put your hand on their head and say, 'Well done pet, where did you find your mum?' and, 'Do you want a bacon sandwich?' and, 'I'm sorry you had to kill your wolf.' But he can't because he's a traitor and he let her mum get taken away and he let Ellie get taken away. Ellie doesn't ask him why. She doesn't ask what her mum meant when she said, 'He cut her out.' She watches him, her eyes warm fire as he boils the kettle like a traitor and fills the bowl like a traitor. And lifts her mum's still-bare feet – left and right – into the water and says –

- Is it cold out?

The water goes first black then red, Ellie doesn't know what that means.

- Yes, a bit.
- Did you see anyone?
- No.

Her dad rubs the feeling back into her mother's feet with his hands like it's an any-old-day-day, and Ellie takes the bowl away, all her questions hidden in the dirty water.

29.

- We'll go to Midnight Mass.

Just as they did in the Before. But it is not the Before. Ellie is not to touch the squishy tubes of ringlets that sting her head, she is not to dirty her red velvet dress. She is to put her coat on and say goodbye to her dad who won't come because the bad-luck priest is not his God. Instead her dad is going to get the house ready for Christmas Day, he says, but he stays sitting in the kitchen with his blue coat on and the Christmas lights off. 'Just nice and still here,' he says, holding his head as though it isn't still at all. He doesn't even give them a going-away wave.

Ellie's mum is trying to be good and not shit. They walk – leftleft – and stop finally under the tree shadows of the church. The church is full of lambs and doves and donkeys and keening saints wrapped in stone. Ellie watches them. She knows how cruel God can be – he chose stones, nails and fire for Best Man Dead, they were slow and mean deads. There they are, all lined up, shushshush they say – all the dead and the living lined up wanting to mix their story up with yours.

Father Doorley caroos on – ofthefatherandoftheson – and his hands flap like a fat bird, arse up in the water. Blah-de-holy-blah. The Jesus-biscuit sticks to Ellie's tongue. After eating God she is supposed to sit quietly and think. She knows the Mass – every sin and mercy and salvation. But she hates this bit, after the 'Lamb of God' and before the End because there is nothing in her marble Mass book to tell her what to say now in this little gap of holy quiet. Her head thrums in the space between the Lamb and the Amen. Maybe there is just enough room here for the pieces of her story – **There was once a Fleck. There was once a mother. There was once a wolf.** Then it comes before they can all stand, it rushes under the church door – the first worst dream, the sea coming up and over the dunes. Choughchoughstoosh. But only just inside her head.

- Ellie say Amen.

Says her mum as though that's it, the End.

- Amen.
- Home then?

30.

Today is Christmas Day, but Ellie does not have that Christmas Day feeling, the snow-falling-outside, snow-melting-in-your-belly feeling. Not like the Christmas Tree night with her dad – all orange and tingle and stars. She rolls her blanket down and hauls up her dad's long sea-boot sock from the end of the bed. Never a stocking above the fire, no, that's for townies, fishermen always give something that has been over water, rough to the touch and bulging with presents round enough to fit. She empties it – green Granny apples all shiny and then . . . oranges. She splits the skin with her thumbnail and peels one. Sweet spray fills the room with its wake-up smell. The orange is the world and love. The red burst of juice in her unwashed mouth is sun and sweet.

Downstairs the radio hums on, the pip pips for very early and no Wogan – just hymns her dad rumbles along to. The kitchen is filled with thudding and ticking and bubbling and stirring. Her mum's hair is in rollers, her apron on, her fingers floured. Her mum is 'getting the dinner ready' which means all the pans are out and there's steam and smoke and 'don't touch'. Ellie steals a crust of cooling stuffing, licks a sage-and-butter finger.

- In here Ellie.

Her dad is sitting by a big square box wrapped in red wrapping paper, too much Sellotape.

- Help me open this.
- Who's it for?
- All of us.

Ellie tears the paper carefully; it's not a box, it's glass and knobs and all mod cons. Her dad plugs the TV in. It flickers on.

- How d'you like that then?

Ellie doesn't know. It looks wrong now. There's the fire talking with its mouthful of coal. There's her dad, hands cut with baiting scars. There's her mum in the kitchen turning the bowl around. There's the broken door looking back in the front room, held together with driftwood. And there's the TV – all dark glass and dials and who knows whose stories trapped inside it. The picture fizzes like snow as her dad jiggles with a cable. Sound bursts out and then a goblin king takes a baby away to under his castle on a hill with big-eyed goblin people singing. Ellie knows taken away. She is caught, she can't move forward or back, she kneels down in front of the screen letting that other world flicker around her, split her, eat her up like a juicy orange.

- Ellie, how d'you like it?

Ellie likes it very much.

★

A family sits around the table, red crackers, silver knives, paper hats and white teeth – smiles in all the right places. 'Put the TV off,' her dad says. Ellie turns the button and says goodbye to the goblin people. There's snow falling with the dark falling. Lights off and the tree flickers. Lights off and the pudding comes in burning blue fire. Ellie's dad's glass is filled with golden beer. Clink. Ellie's mum's glass is filled with red sherry, red as her hair. Clink. Ellie's glass is filled with the nose-tickle of Babycham better than American cream soda. Clink – 'better by Christmas' and Ellie's mouth swells with bubbles. All the food is just for them, just for Christmas. Prawn cocktail and stuffing and fire pudding and brandy sauce and Viennetta. The candles are lit. But not for the dead as the window is fixed and closed and quiet and no one else is invited.

The record player goes on. Click, crackle. Kate kicks off her good shoes and her feet move, not just left left, but left right and round and round with Ellie's dad following her feet and holding her up by her arms and she holding him up by his arms. As though Ellie's mum is the sea and she is holding him still and steady. Ellie sips her bubbles and watches, teaching her feet to dance, left right left – she'll show Fletch this she thinks – swinging her legs in practice. This is a game where no one falls down dead. This is blue Ellie thinks. This is family. And the Before is behind them like the tide going out, and in front of them is blue-blue-blue. She takes another sip of bubbles and is certain that if it wasn't for the left right left of her own legs holding her here she could fall for ever up into the open eye of the sky.

31.

Boxing Day, St Stephen's Day. For boxing up everything that you don't want and sending it away. But Ellie's done. Today she will let them all out, all of the broken things, and she's tall enough now to reach the top of the wardrobe without standing on the bed. Snip snap. Open the case. Here they are. Here's the half razor shells. Here's Headless Barbie, with her melted face and bald head – still hot and angry from the day her dad pulled her head off. Ellie's little china cups. The black stub of her Communion candle. Here's the yellow feather from the sick blue tit and the white feather from the pigeon. They're not evidence any more. There is no wolf, it is dead, Ellie killed it, eye blistered back to limpet shell, soft fur slicked back to cold rock. Ellie opens the window and lets the feathers go into the wind. If they are lucky they might be salvage and they will get to be something else and not broken.

The green striped lining of the case is torn; something else wants to get out. Beneath the silky paper Ellie sees something stuck – it's dark blue and hard like a Christmas card. She can see the long curls of her dad's writing and below it, loud writing in gold.

Mr P. M. Fleck
BRITISH PASSPORT

On the card there is a lion with his tongue sticking out, not lapping milk out, but bog-off out. And a unicorn on its hind legs, kicking. They are gold too. Ellie opens the PASS-PORT and there's her dad's name. Next to profession it says FISHERMAN in blue and where it says ***Wife** / *Femme* there is a long blue line, nothing. This is from his Before, before Ellie, before her mum. **Colour of hair /** *Couleur des cheveux* it says FAIR. Fair. Not nearly white as it is now. In the picture his face has no lines worn in it, none of the famil-iar creases of hellos and night-nights. She looks but she cannot see her face in his. She thinks again of her mother's criss-cross tummy. She doesn't know what these things mean, only that they make his and her story a lie.

Ellie shakes the case to make sure all of the broken things are out and finds the coin, from her tooth, the one she used to wish to get back to the Before. It was stupid to wish that, that's why it hadn't worked – she knows now that there are other Befores. She takes the coin and turns it once, twice, three times for luck –

– I wish . . .

Downstairs there is bang ba bang bang. Ellie runs down to the front room, to the broken-toothed door. Not fixed.

Not broken. The same. Nothing coming in or out except the wind. But her dad is laid on the floor, his arms flailing out as though he is swimming. Her mother tries to reach for his hands.

- He fell.

Ellie heaves with her, pulling him onto his chair. His eyes look left, right, but can't find a hold.

- Close your eyes Dad.

And he does.

- Where am I pet?

Ellie knows how to bring him in.

- Stokesley, Jenny Leigh, Pardon Bank, East Flashes.

She says so he can see the sea lights marking the Scaurs. She says it as though it's a prayer. As though it's good luck. He tries to right himself but he can't pull himself level. Ellie's seen it before, the panic. The live fish flapping on the big wooden board, slapping their tails just for the hope of water; to them the sky had looked so clean and cool and kind – letting birds ride the arc of its belly. At night, it would close its vast blue eye and rest and the fish would come to the surface to kiss the stars. That was her dad now. He needed the weight of water to hold him still, like the upside-down of her story.

- Tell me my story.

Her dad's hands close gently on her shoulders and there it is between them, the current.

- Where do I come from?
- Hush pet, let me keep still.
- Tell me my story.
- All right. You come from the sea.
- How?
- I pulled you up in my nets. And I cut you out. I cut through the net holding you. You were blue like a porpoise. I held you. I gave you your first breath. That's your rope there by the fire.

Ellie takes her rope down from the fireplace. It smells of salt and home and wolf. Ellie drops it into the fire, sparks hissing out around her feet. Peter grabs for it, stumbling, burning the soft hairs on his hands. Bad smell. He holds the rope out to her, singed, lights dancing along the threads.

- Take it.

She can't, it's not her story.

- Who am I like?
- You're like me.

She can't see it, she can't see him in her face. And she cuts the rope.

316

32.

Kate had put him to bed and he was dreaming of his father again. He woke once with Ellie's hand in his, his hand fast around hers. She was half under his bed. He didn't know who held who steady. She said she'd had that dream, the one with the tide coming in up over the dunes, right up to the house, so she slipped into his room and took his hand. She asked him what he was like when he was little. He said he was like her, he meant he was fearless the way she was at the tideline. 'But what if it comes right to the door?' she said. 'Aren't you afraid the sea will come and take you?' He was back on the boat with his father. 'No,' he said to her and to himself, 'you're my anchor.' She smiled and sang back at him, 'Fastened to the Rock which cannot move.'

He wakes with his hands clenched around oars, the strength swelling back into them. The thud thud thud of the wind on that broken door makes him get up too quick, and he tilts. Enough now. He can't keep the wind out. He pulls off a board that was only held on by the nub of a nail. He cradles it, imagining the long curve of the plank fitting into a whole boat. When he stretches out the memory it's like tearing a muscle. He knows the wood now, the wide-hipped curve, the blue paint. He spent enough summers pasting it on, there is a tub of it still in the Baithouse, Royal Blue. Cobles weren't built by spec, they were built by eye and no two were alike; there was no doubt now, he was stupid not to see it before, it was her, *Eleanor*. She'd been here all this time, split and holding his house together. He could see, he could feel in the rough of the wood what had happened. The Hoods had left her out of the water too long over the summer, the sun sucking her dry, opening gaps between her timbers. There's no caulking in cobles, they come to life when they hit the water for the first time, the wood swells watertight. Peter always thought it was funny how it was water in the wood that stopped you sinking. He knew the Hoods had gone part-time, no money in it they said, still, that's no excuse to ruin a boat. They must have left her up on the top Prom, idiots. Then they would have fancied a row out. They wouldn't have thought to check her over. She'd have launched easy enough, smooth into the water, then gone straight down under their feet. The Hoods would have walked right back to shore a bit heavy with water, watched as the tide came in and sank her and done nothing. Then all it would need would be a surge to crack her to pieces. It would have taken months of care and patience to get her ready to go back in the water. Peter would have done it for nothing. He would have eased her in every day, down the slipway, let the tide wash over her, just a bit, then pulled her back – like bathing a baby. She'd have been right by Christmas.

He thinks he might bury her in the sand, the soft dry stuff near the dunes. The Vikings buried their boats and people inside them. It was the Vikings who brought the coble over with them, warships that were strong and double-ended for beaching on the shingle or launching high into the foaming breakers. That would be right – burial. Kate would understand but she'd say burn it. No fires today pet. That's what he'll do, he'll take her back to the sea, and with this he feels the pull into the morning and eases off the rest of the boards not letting the nails split them.

Peter slips through the alleyway to get to the Baithouse, the boards safe under his arm. Once out of the door he can see the damage he's just slept through. The sea had come right up over the dunes, shifted cars from where they were parked and left them adrift on sandbanks. He was glad he was the first to see it, it was a rare sight. Just like the stories that the little tide book couldn't predict but warned about at the back – 'Times and tides must be treated with caution.' The street is still sleeping; there'll be hell on when they get up. There'll be talk of a sea wall again. As though you could hold her back? He lurches just a little and slows his pace; he's better in the Baithouse with all his tools around him. He gets his sea-boots on and his thick gansey and his storm mac on top. Then over the Prom and down to the dunes. He's like a space man running through the dune slacks, the sands blown grey with sea muck, as though he's really on the moon. The tide's about to turn, it's a gift, a morning coming on like this after a storm. The clouds stretch out like cats and he squints into the haze over the flat sea, a deep dense blue.

He starts to dig a delve big enough for the boards but the more he digs the more the hole fills with water. The stubs of his fingers numb with cold and grit and icy nips shoot up his arms and grab his shoulders. There's all junk here – green bottles, crisp packets, squashed pop tins – he can't bury the *Eleanor* here, what would his father say, leaving her in a rubbish tip? Their boat who had carried them at sea and found a sea-god, mucked in with all this? His father would say to bring her back to the sea where she belonged, where she could soak and swell with water. Put her back in. The closer he gets to the water's edge the steadier his feet, the stiller his head.

He sets her away in the water and he thinks the tide'll take her out, but the pieces of her roll right back to shore. Peter worries that some old lad will take her for firewood or kids'll pick her up and spark her at a beach party. No. He knows now that he can't leave the *Eleanor* here at the tide-line with all of this other broken shit and feathers. She's salvage that wants to get home; let the rough and gentle laps of the sea wear her down to sand.

He needs a boat for this, a real one, not one of them Tupperware glass-fibre jobs the storm has tossed onto the road, splitting their showy bellies into rainbows. The *Audrey Lass* is still there, sitting in her A-frame, small enough for him to put in the water by himself with the tractor. He walks down the slipway, clearing a path, kicking away wrecked gear, nets and split pots. The wind nantling at him, pulling him left and right, but he keeps steady as if that vertigo had shifted, as if he was already cupped in the bow of the boat.

33.

Ellie couldn't sleep for the shushshush voices; she tried to push her head into her pillow to shut them up, it didn't work. The voices were still there. She couldn't shout for her dad, not now, so she had to get up by herself and follow the sound coming from his room. The lamp post shining orange over the bed. Her dad was sleeping next to her mum but he wasn't tucked in, the covers were creased under his arms. He seemed thinner and his veins stuck out through his skin. His hair was white in the funny not-dark and there were new shadows under his cheekbones. His fingers were curled up but not gripping tight. She'd seen this before; he was dreaming of rowing far out with his father. The bed was pressed close to the wall so when his hand pushed down to raise the oar out of the water it made a gentle sound against the wall, a skin-on-paper sound, shushshush. That was it, his hand against the wall, not a voice from the other side of sleep. It had just got into her head, the way a crab gets in a creel and can't find a way out. Her own bed felt too small, then her feet too cold sticking out from under her granny blanket.

The paraffin lamp sputtered; the smell made her drowsy and she tipped headlong into the first worst dream. It's always the same, like looking out of the same window every day. Even before her mother was taken away it was like this.

She's on the beach and it's dark but she can see the waves close up as though she's flying over them. When you really look at waves they don't break, they curl like fingers and fold and split into white veins that lace the water like a net. She jumps then, out of the waves and back into herself and she's trying to climb up the dunes, cutting her hands on sea grass, digging her fingers into red clay, her feet sinking into the sand. The waves are reaching up and splitting behind her. She knows she mustn't let the water touch her, but she wants it to. She keeps trying to get away, pulls herself up onto the dunes and runs over the road with the sea following her in foamy black slicks. She bolts through her back door and pushes it closed behind her, pressing her palms against it to keep it shut. Tap tap tap says the sea on the door. The door is broken, it is always broken, shush and the sound of breaking glass and the sea comes right in and Ellie wakes not knowing how to take a breath in, her palms and fingertips white from the pressure of the door.

But that's not the worst bit, that's just the bit she would tell her dad and then he would tell her their story, 'I gave you your first breath,' and she'd take in a deep breath and be 'all right now pet'. There was the other bit she never said out loud, when she was still on the beach and she was so close to the waves that she was the sea, streaming up the slipway to the Prom. In this bit there's always someone else standing on the slipway, she doesn't see who, just that they are pale and tall and she is the sea running up under their feet wanting to pull them under. That's what it was — the bit that scared her, not the shushshush, not the sea, but the pull inside her.

She shakes her head now to stop the fear from sticking. The early-morning house has got that empty blown-out feeling. She kneels up on her bed to see herself in the window, looking for the wolf's dark rings around her eyes. Then it comes, even though she's awake, like a cat's-paw wave, right to the door. Taptaptap, it says, even though she has not put out a feast or lit a candle. Taptaptap. She tiptoes downstairs. First she checks the front window where her mother broke out. The putty is cold and all fixed. But on the other side of the room the broken-toothed door has lost all its teeth and now it's just a hole blowing right through the house. Ellie holds her hand out to the dark waiting for . . . the wet nub of a nose, the deep salt lick of a mouth, the wave to come.

- Hello?

But it's her dad, the tap of the pedal as he wheels his bike away, his white storm mac rattling, his shoulders squared like gull's wings, his back to her. The morning fret smudges him out as he goes. Ellie sits in the shock of the empty room, too small in the space her father is leaving behind. The wind gets in, lapping up all the pieces of him, everything he has touched and mended — dulling the shiny arms of the rocking chair, stopping the wind-up clock's slow tick.

Ellie pulls her smock on straight over her nightie, steps into her wellies and drags her red coat on over the top. She takes the charred rope from the fire and her knife. She pushes through the door on all fours and as soon as she's outside and round the front she can see it all, the split wood and feathers. The sea had been right to their door in the night, sucking away the snow. A three-knot witch wind, definitely. Salvage. That's where he's going.

Ellie runs after. The storm has left its swirling scars all over the Prom. She crosses swells of sand-dogs and weed-dogs slumped on the black road. Little bodies – white and red crabs all legs and half-moon shells. His green bike is tethered to a bench with twine, she knows his knots. The sun is pushing its head up. She runs through the dunes and down down down to the sea where she can see the white wing-flap of his storm mac as he stands on the slipway.

- Dad.

Her dad stands in the last huffs of the storm, part of the spray and the wind, white and shattering. He climbs into a strange boat and slips into the water. Ellie runs to the tide-line where she was told never to go.

The Redcar Rock Buoy and the Fairway Buoy blink to light the way along the Scaurs. She takes off her wellies and leaves them at the water's edge. In her bare feet she walks along the spine of the scaur out into the water. It is nothing like the dream. The cold water is a punch – hough – right through her body, pushing her breath out, rising over her knees. There is a rock and a sway to it like dancing, like

324

when her dad walks with his sea legs. When the water gets to her thighs, her skin burns.

She knows the way out on Jenny Leigh to the hollow tip where the wolf used to sleep in the rock. She tastes salt on her top lip. Now she can see him in the boat and she shouts his name into the chopping wind.

– Dad.

34.

Peter rows out until the land is a fading line of lights and then nothing but sea and fret rolling in towards the place where the land must be. The pieces of *Eleanor* are tucked up safely under his knees. He follows the scaurs out. His steady hands on the oars are ticking him back to his ten-year-old self, his father naming the grey shadows passing under the water.

- Stokesley, Jenny Leigh, Pardon Bank, East Flashes.

Beneath the boat is the hard ground. There'll be damage under him. Pots chaffed and smashed on the rocks by the storm. The surges can rip right to the bottom of the seabed, raking up a shower of stones that could smash through steel. He can't drop the *Eleanor* here. She'll be torn to pieces. He hauls further out, even closer to the scaurs. A Kittiwake trails after him, too delicate in the widening sky, working out whether he is worth following, working out if he is lucky. The lips of the water rise from a deep current. Peter hears it, a clear bark across the morning.

- Dad.

And he does the only thing he mustn't do now. Looking back, he can just make her out, on the tip of Jenny Leigh's Scaur, where Wolf Rock used to stick up above the water-line, a girl with ragged tufts of hair like ears, silver-flecked with foam, calling him home.

35.

- Dad.

She tries again, half cry, half growl, just so he knows it's her because she has heard it – the sea calling his name. As he said it would. It calls your name and you have to go and not struggle. But it can't have him. Ellie tries to keep her balance in deepening water, her feet hooked on the rocks below her.

A kittiwake swoops in low, screeching, almost knocking her under. She sees her dad pull too close to Jenny Leigh. The old scaur arches up, breaching the surface where her father's boat crosses the top of the high stones. Then the rock flexes, punching into the soft belly of the boat.

- Dad.

36.

The sea makes her own wake at the tideline. She leaves everything here, everything she has found, everything that has lost its place. It is never a straight line, it is never the same. Sometimes the tideline is just bodies. So many you can't imagine all of the creatures who once moved in them – all becoming sand. Crab shells that are no longer crabs. Starfish waiting to be thrown back in. The night of the storm, the sea had come in, up over the dunes onto the Prom and over the road, so that walking anywhere meant you could see them all. It was like watching the sea remembering everything she had lost.

Her dad had told her never to walk the tideline, mucky he said, don't touch, and then there were the sand fleas. Yuck. But sometimes the sea will leave something there for you to find. 'Look what you might need?' rolling at the water's edge. You can leave it, just more muck at the tideline, or you can take it . . .

Ellie knew as soon as she saw it, washed up and snagged on the little jut of stone where Wolf Rock once stood – just a bit of rope, the curve of what it used to be. She knew whose it was, knew who it belonged to. So she took it. Because the sea had taken something of hers and that is only fair.

37

Everything washes up at the wake except a body. But nor is he caught in the scattered line of people ebbing in and out of the house. The towering men from the lifeboat and the little people who crept out from under the Green Hill. They came in through the front door though because they weren't dead at all.

Ellie walks straight in off the sea with the fret, sand in her shoes, into the black crowd. Her rope is held tight in her fist. The crowd moves away even though it thinks it hasn't seen her. It's the smell – the salt and weed – it reminds them of the sea coming in right up to their doors.

She slips away into the garden, tripping over stray stones and crab shells. She wants the tideline to stay here where she can see it, she wants the sea to come in every night so that she can still hear the shushshush of him in the next room. But her-next-door-who-doesn't-speak is already sweeping up the sand.

In the Baithouse Ellie takes her dad's knife from the shelf, wrapping her long hair once, twice, three times around her hand then she cuts. It is easier to plait now, like rope, and she will hang it on the hook by the fire. Her short hair is dark red and flecked with silver, like blood and snow, like her hair and his together. Ftsss.

Ellie will wait. Her hair will grow back. She will plait it herself. She will wait in her own story, she will get bigger and she will have children and they will grow and she will look for his face in the half-light, for his story in their faces. This is not a prayer or a wish.

- Bad luck for a girl to cut her hair.

Her mum stands at the top half of the Baithouse door, spuffing her cigarette.

- I'm not a girl.

Kate knows what Ellie is. She tried to make Ellie's dad's story a lie, but a story is like a net: you have to make your own; you have to throw the loops just right; you have to be careful what gets in and what gets out, what you catch and what you keep.

- Look, I've made it into something else.

Ellie hands her mother the rope of her hair. The ragged thing flitflitflits as she watches but it's all right, it's not getting out.

- It's beautiful pet. Do you have a story for it?
- Nearly.

38.

The boat creakcracked, then it was just Ellie and her dad in the water, bound together by their rope. She saw the quick silver of his knife just as his ten-year-old self washed over him and under a breaker, his hair salt-flecked and gold. And she wanted him to take her up in his giant's hands, but they were gone, too small for scars or for a whole life lived in and through them. His face was smooth too, his eyes clear, grey-blue-green, just like hers. She wanted him to call her name, but he could not, he did not know it yet. So she called for him – Dad – a word for love, making no sound in the water, only bursting all of the air out of her lungs. And she took a breath – not of air, of water, but she could not drown. She was strong enough to keep him up, and he asked her to love him, there and then, still holding the knife, so she cut him free of the rope and sent him back into his own story. For luck. For love.

39.

The hood of Ellie's red coat scratches her neck where her hair used to fall. May Fletcher has come for them in the car and Fletch gets out of the front seat to let Kate in. She is carrying a bunch of snowdrops. Ellie pinched them from Mrs Forster's garden. Everything is growing fast in the sea-weed soil after the storm. Ellie has birdseed too, so that the blue tits will come down for him, even though Ellie knows he is not there under the earth because the body did not come back. Even when she walks the tideline – especially when she walks the tideline, she knows no body will come.

40.

It's still cold but now the frost doesn't stay past morning. Ellie goes to the best place to be, along the alleyway and over the cobbles; she unlatches the door to the Baithouse. She twists up newspapers to light the stove. His tools are all still here. The net needle for making nothings, his knives; the things she's not to touch. But it's all right because she can see him in her hands. She unfolds the leather bundle: each knife has a bone handle. The skeining knife for the mussels, the littlest one and then bigger and bigger. Silver like fins. Which one did he use to cut her out? Ellie can hear the thudtickticktick. She remembers the gentle cut in the fish's white belly, along its seam. She hears the thudtick-ticktick along her mother's spine. Why the net and not the knife? Why did he choose that story for her and not the other? The knife would have made a very different Ellie, quick and silver and biting. Her father asking her to love him there and then, still holding the knife. Her father giving her that first breath of air. The knife hanging by the

fire instead of the rope. Yes, that would have been a different story. He knew.

There was once a mother . . .

Ellie began in pen blue as the sea.

When she had written as much as she could, she looked
at his old bike, just bike. Green. The paint was flaking,
rusted underneath in sore red bubbles. She took the wire
wool from his shelf and set to work.

41.

Alice had gone to bed early, nothing on the telly, and now she woke sluggish having slept too long. Brand new TV and still nothing but rubbish. She had given the old one to Peter after he'd fixed that bit of carpet, and he lit up just like a kiddie at Christmas; that's what she loved in him, his gratitude. She'd gone to the funeral to show her face. Kate had it at the fisherman's church, not the Catholic one. Thank God she had the good grace for that. But Alice hadn't truly felt it until now. His going. It was like a real pain under her ribs, as though she had lifted something too heavy and whatever it was that held her together at the middle had torn. She swigs down the strong painkillers the doctor gave her for her knee hoping they'll hit the spot; they're gritty and the water in her glass is so cold it hurts her teeth.

Creakcrack.

What is that? She struggles up the bed to look out of the window into the garden. Douglas? No, the cat is curled up on her bed, nose to tail, purring with defiance. Cheek.

Alice squeezes her eyes shut, then opens them and puts her glasses on. The garden strangely came to life in the pools of weed the storm left behind. Who would have thought? Pete always said it would happen – the sea would come in right up over the Prom. Nothing at all to stop it really, and now it had she was glad. She was glad something could pull free and flood those grooves that kept her in line – always the right money, skirt always the right length, 'don't cry' Alice. But the cheek of it – to come right to her front step – it was proof of something, wasn't it? The snowdrops there in the middle of the lawn, salt white, nowhere near where she planted them. Everything was budding but her roses – they were gone. She had hated those roses, such a mucky pink. 'Roses should be pink,' Arthur said, when she wanted peach, peach like a full-mouthed scream. That's what she wanted. To scream out loud, like the flaming petals on a June rose – at her little boy's funeral and every day since.

What the hell was that racket? Ellie mending her dad's old bike. Why wasn't she at school? She's wild, she'd told him enough times. He didn't listen. Not that he could do anything now. She pulls on her dressing gown, stretching out into it. It fits around her like a warm day, not like those stockings pinching up her thighs and those stiff skirts. She might wear it all day after all, but not today. Today she wants a word with that Hattie bloody Hill. Who did she think she was turning up at Pete's funeral wearing brown? Brown! And after what she did, expelling his poor kiddie from her school, even if Ellie is as wild as they come. The bare-faced cheek.

- Off the bed you.

Douglas opens one eye and stretches, not shifting. A little powder though first, she thinks, a bit of warpaint eh, she wasn't going to let herself go completely, was she?

42.

- Ba bang bang.

It is so early it's not even time for the radio pips or clinking cups to wake her mum yet.

- Ba bang bang.

Ellie tucks her head under the curtain, not turning on the light so she can spy who it is. A pale face presses up against the glass. The window is closed but the ghost talks loudly, his breath steaming up the window. His breath?

- Ellie it's me, open the door.
- Fletch?
- Ellie, you have to come back to school.
- I can't go back I was expelled.
- It was only a play, they'll calm down.
- I nearly drowned you.
- I'm fine.

- But your leg?
- I'm getting scars – they're cool.
- I can't I'm ill.
- Ellie!
- I am.
- Get dressed.
- My uniform's not ready.
- Do you have any normal clothes?
- Oi!

She lets him in and Fletch follows her upstairs and picks out her corduroy skirt and a jumper. Her church clothes. Ha. No church any more, no mean-eyed church ladies, no blah-de-holy-blahs.

- What will we say to Woodsy? I don't have a note.
- Don't say anything, just try to be you know – normal.
- I am normal.
- How's your wolf?
- Erm.
- Get dressed Ellie. Now.
- Wait outside my room then.

Fletch comes back with a wet hairbrush and sets to work on the wild thick tufts of Ellie's hair whilst she howls until it finally falls in smooth short curtains around her face – all silver and red flecks.

- Your hair's awesome now.
- Wait.

Ellie pours some water and push-clicks to open her mother's pills.

- Ellie are you allowed to open those? It says childproof?
- I'm eleven.

Ellie gently wakes her mum and gives her the little summer-holiday blue pills.

- Come on Mum.
- You off to school pet? You look smart.

★

Ellie takes her dad's bike: she has fixed it and painted it silver, not like nails that won't pierce, but like the sea. She lowers the seat right down; that way she can reach the pedals. She stands on one pedal and pushes herself off, floating out into the brightening morning. Fletch jumps awkwardly on the croggy-bar.

- Let's go take a look at the sea first.
- We don't have time.
- We do.

The streets are empty of people, just sharp green shadows, and high up blueblueblue. She changes the gear, thud, and the wheel turns, tickticktick. They ride over the cobbles and up over the dunes. Ellie ties up the bike on the Prom and runs down the slipway and onto the sands. She can feel it stretching – out-of-bounds.

- Look.
- At what?

But she can't explain.

- The sea.

But Fletch scrambles, he wants to inspect the old rock where he cut his leg.

Ellie stands at the water's edge looking out at the morning blue. A wave rolls in from the horizon and breaks gently at her feet, white fingers curving into foam and sinking into the sand. Shush and again, another wave and another, soft and roaring – the thousand hands of the ocean bringing stones and feathers for her. 'Hello,' she says taking the salt spray deep into her lungs: belly rising, she breathes him in and breathes him out, her father. She bends, dips her fingers in the wave, quick before it pulls back. There in the turning, the pulse of the water – his hands are the ocean.

A kittiwake circles high up. She listens for her name.

- Ellie.

Fletch looses an arrow.

- Missed.

She sends one flying back. It skims his left shoulder, taking him down but not killing him. He lies wounded, stretching out his arms like St Sebastian. Ellie can see the healing marks on his leg.

- Again.

But she won't kill him today; she curls next to him, in the place where his shadow should be, it's warm there.

- Ellie we'll be late.

★

Bikes are not allowed. No bikes in the playground. This is the rule. Ellie rides in wide arcs getting bigger and bigger in her figure-of-eight, then skids to a stop to watch them – their hot heads turning, their arms open like wings to lean into the wind – part of their own story and hers.

Mrs Clarkson sees Ellie first.

- Oh Ellie, you look smart today. Mrs Hill's expecting you.
- What?
- Don't say, 'What?' Follow me.

Mrs Clarkson is very busy with lots of brown folders – putting them in drawers slamslideslam. With her orange skirt and black jumper and black tights she looks like a busy lady bee.

- Sit down. Do you want some hot orange and a biscuit?

Ellie does. She dips her biscuit in, it tastes glorious, like Christmas and summer all at once. Mrs Clarkson brings her more biscuits – a custard cream and a pink wafer. Then Mrs Hill opens her office door and coils of sweet-smelling cigarillo smoke drift out.

- Come on in Ellie, you look smart.

Ellie slides off her adult chair and follows Mrs Hill in. She breathes the smoke deeply, and it makes her feel calm and prickly at the same time, like Mrs Hill.

- That nosy old woman has been here Ellie. To my office. To tell me all about you. Without an appointment. As though I didn't know already. And poor Peter. I went to the funeral you know. Of course you know.

And she stops to sniff and dab at her spidery black eyes. For a moment Ellie thinks Mrs Hill will cry: her crêpe-paper chest puffs once, as though she too has a bird inside that flutters and cuts. But her brow arches up and the bird folds its wings away neatly.

- Well I do know all about it and it's very sad but there's no need for all of this silly nonsense – unannounced meetings and phone calls and governors. It's harassment. And here you are at school today, just like I said you should be. 'Of course Ellie should come back to school,' that's what I said to her. And here you are. Well done.

And Mrs Hill pushes a plate of Bourbon creams across her shiny coffee table to Ellie. Ellie takes one without knowing what on earth Mrs Hill is talking about. Mrs Hill tightens her headscarf and lights another cigarillo, jabbing at the air with its little light as though she were poking someone in the eye.

\- So, Ellie – how is your mother? She'll be well on the mend by now won't she?

Ellie pauses. Pausing is wrong. There is a wrong and a right answer, like with maths. The wrong answer is blue pills. Fletch said be normal. The normal answer is yes.

\- Yes Mrs Hill.
\- Yes! Well there we are then. What a load of non-sense over nothing. Don't you worry Ellie. Now you go home – at home-time – and you tell that Mrs Forster what a nice day you had at school. Off you pop, give this to Mr Lockwood and do take another biscuit. Well done Ellie, there's a good girl.

Ellie takes the note written to Mr Lockwood in Mrs Hill's looping certain writing and a biscuit. Ellie would like to keep it so she can copy the l's into her own name.

*

\- Ellie Fleck, what are you doing in school? In those clothes?

Ellie hands him Mrs Hill's note in answer. Mr Lockwood's face crumples when he reads it, like screwed-up paper, but he says no more to her about her presence or her clothes, which Ellie now knows are smart. He begins the morning story. Ellie has never been at school in time for this before. The story drones on a bit. It's supposed to be *Little Red Riding Hood* but modern-day, so there's no magic in it. It is one of those stories to teach you not to go off by yourself – boring as brown crayons. Mr Lockwood puts on the lights and points to the questions on the board. Ellie starts with the last question – rewrite the ending – because it's the only one she can do. In Ellie's story the wolf is the granny.

- I don't suppose you're finished your 'Family' story for me?

Says Woodsy still playing his game.

- Yes.

Says Ellie – winning.

Fletch had helped her to draw the wolf picture on the front. She had used her velvety blue pen around the final curl of the kicking k of Fleck. Now it thumps in her bag – taptaptap, against her back. Taptaptap wanting to get out.

Mother Wolf
By Ellie Fleck
Aged 11

There was once a mother . . . a mother-less . . . a mother-less girl . . .

– Who are you like?

The people would ask her.

– Who are your people?

The girl told them stories to fill up their questions, stories that came tap tap tapping from all the dead lined up inside her mixing their stories up with hers. Stories to explain her pointy ears and sharp teeth and the dark rings around her eyes but they didn't believe her and in the end they would always ask –

– Where is your mother?

The girl did not have a story for that. Then the people would laugh at the motherless girl and the girl would put skull stones in their garden so the cats would know where to pee. So one day, when all the skull stones had gone a boy asked –

– Is your mother dead?

And a voice inside the girl's head said –

– Of course your mother's not dead you stupid girl.

So the girl set off in search of her mother, knocking the boy down on the way – cheek – for asking her an unasked-for question.

It wasn't long before the girl came upon a woman standing on a green hill by a white church. The woman was in her bare feet walking on soft green grass. She had on a long white dress that floated just above the sea of grass, like a bird. Swish went the grass. Swish went the dress. The woman was beautiful. There was something about her that was mothery to the girl. Perhaps it was her dark hair just like the girl's own, or her red lips, just like the girl's own or her pointy ears, just like the girl's own. The girl approached the woman, softly softly, sneaking up. Taptap the girl patted the woman on her back – when the woman turned around it was just like looking at herself in dark glass.

– Are you my mother?

The girl asked and just as she said it the woman shook and shivered and twisted and shifted into a white hare. The girl grabbed the woman, holding on tight as the mother-hare wriggled and jiggled and dug and dug and dug deep into the green hill and underground. When the mother-hare finally stopped the girl found herself under the green hill. Tap tap tap the mother-hare stomped with her big hare foot on the grave of the dead people under the earth. The people reached their hands out of the wet brown earth and wrapped their bony fingers around the girl's face and looked at her. They turned her head this way and that and her eyes flickered – grey-blue-green.

– Are you my people?

The girl asked.
One of the bony dead people gave the girl a green cloak to try on, made of the softest green moss you could hope to sleep under. The girl felt the worms wriggling and tick- ling inside it, felt them wishing for the rain.

– Close your eyes and we'll teach you all about death and bones and Best Man Dead.

And the girl learned well but she did not like the dark and the cold and the wriggle of worms.

– You don't like the worms.

The dead people said. The girl did not like the worms — all they cared about was rain.

– We are not your people.

At that the mother-hare appeared, a flash of white foot in the dark and the girl chased after her and caught hold of her tufty hare tail and held on for dear life as the hare scrambled up and up and up. Black mud turned to golden sand. Worm tittle-tattle turned to gull's keeaws and green grass became blue skies. The woman stomped her foot and once again she stood in her white dress, making foot-prints in the sand, five-toed lady footprints. Once again the girl saw her face in the woman's face. Didn't the girl know all about dead under the green hill now – weren't they the same?

– Are you my mother?

She demanded and off the woman leapt into the wet blue sea. The girl went after quickly, diving into the foamy breakers and reaching out to catch the woman's foot but this time she caught a silvery, slippery tail. The girl held on for dear life as the fish-woman dived down deep, down through the whitecaps, down through blue rush, deeper into salt-heavy blackness. And in the wet dark there were people – black pips in the watery hips of the sea, they looked like seals and porpoises, they had fins and flippers instead of fingers.

– Are you my people?

The people in the sea gathered round her, their grey-blue eyes huge. They held her face in their finny flippers – soft velvet fur and silky scales. They turned her head this way and that and her eyes flickered – grey-blue-green. They gave the girl a cloak of the most beautiful scales to try on. Oh it was wondrous. It looked like a thousand new moons sewn together into one shining wish of a cloak. It fitted well too, like a second skin. So the girl stayed with the people under the sea. She learned deep-water things – how to swim and how to breathe long lungfuls of air and dive deep. And she loved it there, swimming with the finned and flippered people. But the girl's fingers were not webbed and though she could dive deep, she always had to go back to the surface where her friends were told never to go, afraid that they would fall for ever into the sky.

– Why do you have to go back up there for air? Stay down here with us for ever.
– I can't.

Said the girl.

– We are sorry, but we cannot be your people.

With that the fish-mother appeared, silver and shiny, and the girl grabbed her by the gills, like a net, and the fish-mother swam all muscle and silver and certain to the surface of the sea. Here the light prickled and stung the girl, so used to the deep water, but she could breathe easily in and out and shush. On the sand dunes the fish-mother shed her fins and scales and walked in her bare feet away and into the woods. The girl followed – it was winter in the woods, the frost grass was sharp as knives. The woman's white dress trailed ahead like snow falling – fth. And the girl saw how the woman's face was long and pale like hers. And the girl had learned what it was to be a fish-girl, just as the woman was a fish-woman – weren't they the same now? The woman walked ahead, her feet growing feathery, furry into wide wolf feet. The girl wished for such feet that could run and run on the cold earth. The girl got ready to ask the question and reached out her hands to grab the wolf-mother's tail if she ran again.

– Are you my mother?

And the wolf-mother opened her anvil jaws wide and ate the girl all up. The wolf started with the girl's hands – its tongue was rough and velvety. Crunch crunch crunch. The wolf chomped until finally the girl floated inside the red sea of the wolf's belly. But the girl knew how to swim so she wasn't worried and she knew all about dead and this wasn't it. The girl tap tap tapped to be let out and the wolf-mother opened its throat, just enough to let the moonlight pour in and a song pour out. But not big enough for the girl to crawl out so she stayed like this – small – inside the belly of the wolf all through the moon's changes.

And the girl learned new things in her new home. Wolf things. Run. Earth. Smell. Eat. Blood. Teeth. Hunt. Hunger. They were good lessons to learn. The girl came to love the sound of the heart drum of the wolf as they ran. Thud, tickticktick it went, filling her up with wolf dreams. She loved the castle of the wolf. The curved hall of its ribs, the music of its heart, the song of its breath in and out. Red and soft and shush it said.

Then one spring day, the wolf said —

– Hey little girl, you've grown too big, you can't stay in there for ever.
– Please.

But the wolf took a long claw and cut its belly open. Criss-cross.

And there the girl stood in her own white dress and bare feet and around her ankles on the floor was a great wolfskin – red and grey and warm. There was nothing left of the wolf-mother but the wolf-coat for the girl to try on. The girl slipped her white arms into the front legs and stepped her long legs into the hind legs and pulled up the hood-head over her own. The skin licked and lapped and loped and bound itself to her and she was like herself and the wolf both together. She felt each hair wake up and open, and the coat became a thousand eyes wide. It replenished her. She stood on her four legs in her true skin and looked up at the moon. She had no wishes to make. In her wolfskin she could dig under the ground and see the people under the hill and she could swim in the sea with the fin people and she could run and be run and the earth under her and no one would see her running along their coast and she wouldn't have to hear their talk or their laughter. And if she needed to she could take off her wolf coat and walk on two legs and people would wonder – who were her people?

– 1 house-point. Weird!

ACKNOWLEDGEMENTS

This book would never have begun without Laura Degnan and Angela Carr. I would never have kept going without my husband Jez, Faye Simpson and the ongoing support from New Writing North. The two people who made Ellie's world real, Rachel Conway my incredible agent and Kate Harvey, my wise and intuitive editor.

Thank you to Kirsty Cox for always being willing to play make-believe with me from childhood to the present day. Thanks for reading the early draft and sharing school memories so I could get those details right.

Thank you to Saffron Mackay for wanting to read that rough early draft, that was brave.

A big thanks to Vic and your mum for talking to me about Social Work in the 1980s and present day so that I could show the response to Ellie's mum's breakdown and thanks for the work you do.

There are some moments in life when you stray and come back stronger and there are some moments when you are in danger of never coming back. That's when you need help to find your roots, so thank you Uncle Philip for taking me 'home' to Donegal to meet the ancestors.

I must also thank Allister Sudron for his baithouse memories; Fred Brunskill and Clive Picknett of The Zetland Lifeboat Museum for teaching me how to make a net and the Demon Beaters of Lumb for thrashing those demons. My eccentric English teacher, Dave Webster. Owen Gent for bringing the wolf to life with his perfect cover illustration and Bede, the wolfhound behind the wolf.

A special mention must go to the maternity team at James Cook University Hospital, because I promised I'd mention them in the book when they gave me lovely drugs and brought Magnus safely into the world.

Photographer extraordinaire Ian Forsyth who restored and delivered the picture of my dad at the last moment.

Thanks to my mum, Bridget, who told me 'you must never lose your imagination' and Mark, my dad, for believing in sea gods. They are why this book exists. And then ... finally thanks to the sea – where the stories come from.

It was the summer of 1984 and Lady Di was just about to marry my toy gorilla, Gogo. My mum was standing watching the rain and then she did something extraordinary. She put her hands through the glass of the back door. Then my dad grabbed Lady Di's (Barbie's) long wedding train (pillowcase) to bind my mum's wrists. Then the ambulance came and my mum was taken away and Di's broken head was left on the floor.

Children don't have a word for 'suicide attempt' or 'mental breakdown'. When an event like that detonates in your childhood there are so many aftershocks that ricochet throughout your life; so many choices that you can make, such as:

You can try to just keep growing up.
You can kiss the feet of brass-Jesus three times before you leave the house everyday to stop it from happening again.
You can get terrifying panic attacks at Mass and think it's because God blames you for your mother's illness.
You can become a school refuser because you're afraid to leave your mum at home, occasionally bunking off to the library for books and peace.
You can stop eating, like saints seeking redemption.
You can waste your love trying to redeem bad men.

You can go from a council estate to the University of St Andrews just to prove to them that you're not damaged. Look!

You can find yourself in the lovely Professor Douglas Dunn's office as he recommends you read Kay Redfield Jamison's *An Unquiet Mind: A Memoir of Moods and Madness* because he has noticed, the whole brilliant department have noticed, that you are burning this incredible opportunity and they don't want to punish you, they want to help.

Books had rescued me long before this moment but this was the first time I'd ever been prescribed one. So it was inevitable really that the way to finally understand that moment – that break where my childhood ended so abruptly – would involve a book.

My first novel *How Saints Die* takes the reality of adult mental breakdown but generates an imagined world where that reality can be contained and transformed. As a lapsed Catholic I'm drawn to supernatural interventions but as a survivor I know that true transfiguration involves a hard-won sacrifice of innocence. For Ellie, my ten-year-old protagonist, she must follow and fail a number of fairy-tale-like tasks to try to fix her mother.

Her first task is to carry out the Irish ritual of lighting the Halloween light to guide the dead and gone home for one night. But like all good fairytale tasks, it goes bad – and instead of Granny, a wolf breaks into Ellie's world from the sea. This sets in motion the tension between the good, obedient and holy child and the wild, untamed free child;

which will Ellie choose to become? Ellie knows holy, she knows that saints suffer and die but they can't explain how to suffer and survive.

Ellie's folk-religious rite doesn't deliver another adult, even a dead one, or a saint. Instead she summons a wolf. It has claws and teeth and is better able to protect her from all she fears, including her mother. The wolf runs wild in the human imagination because it has the power to save or devour, and Ellie's wolf remains true to that uncertainty.

By creating this liminal ground between real and imagined; between faith and folklore I make a place which can fully explore a child's experience of mental illness as a story she can rewrite and fix. In reality, a child is powerless to change anything; decisions are made without consent, questions are met with silence and yet none of this insulates the child from the trauma. As with my own childhood, and now as a writer, it's imagination that saves and compensates for Ellie's inability to understand or control the adult world. In the real world, Ellie is suffocated by diagnostic labels like 'damaged' or 'at risk' and trapped by the official story recommending 'intervention'. Imagination is Ellie's only form of resistance and so I've made a world out-of-bounds where she can run with her own story.